OPENLY STRAIGHT

openly
straight

BILL KONIGSBERG

SCHOLASTIC INC.

All rights reserved. Published by Scholastic Inc., *Publishers since 1920*. SCHOLASTIC, the LANTERN LOGO, and associated logos are trademarks and/or registered trademarks of Scholastic Inc.

Arthur A. Levine Books hardcover edition designed by Natalie Sousa, published by Arthur A. Levine Books, an imprint of Scholastic Inc., June 2013.

All rights reserved. Published by Scholastic Inc., *Publishers since 1920*. SCHOLASTIC, the LANTERN LOGO, and associated logos are trademarks and/or registered trademarks of Scholastic Inc.

This book is a work of fiction. Names, characters, places, and incidents are either the product of the author's imagination or are used fictitiously, and any resemblance to actual persons, living or dead, business establishments, events, or locales is entirely coincidental.

ISBN 978-0-545-79865-5

12 11 10 9 8 7   18 19 20/0

Printed in the U.S.A.   40

First paperback printing 2015

"The Hukilau Song" by Jack Owens is reprinted by permission of Owens Kemp Music Company. All rights reserved.

For Chuck Cahoy, always.

OPENLY STRAIGHT

If it were up to my dad, my entire life would be on video.

Anything I do, he grabs his phone. "Opal," he'll yell to my mother. "Rafe is eating corn flakes. We gotta get this on film."

He calls it film, like instead of an iPhone, he has an entire movie crew there, filming me.

So when he pulled his Saturn Vue hybrid up to a hulking building with a stone façade and I leapt out of the car to examine my new home for the first time, I wasn't shocked that he went straight for his cell.

"Act like you're arriving home after three years overseas in the army," he said, his left eye hidden behind the phone. "Do some cartwheels."

"I don't think soldiers do cartwheels," I said. "And no."

"It was worth a shot," he said.

The thing about it is nobody ever watches these videos. I have seen him record literally weeks' worth of video, and I've never, ever seen him watch any of it, or put any of it on "the Face Place," as he calls it, which he is always threatening to do.

"I'm going to throw that thing if you don't put it away," I said. "Seriously. Enough."

He removed the phone from in front of his eye and gave me a hurt look, as he stood there in his Birkenstocks, his knobby knees glistening in the sun. "You would not throw my child."

"Dad. I'm your child."

"Well, yeah," he said. "But you don't take videos."

He pocketed his other child, and we stood side by side, in awe of the stone fortress that was going to be my dorm, East Hall. All around us, families were unloading boxes and suitcases onto the sidewalk. Guys were shaking hands and thumping fists like old friends. It was a steamy day, and the huge oak tree near the front entrance was the only break from the hot sun. A few parents sat on the grass there, watching the car-to-dorm caravan. Cicadas buzzed and hissed, their invisible cacophony pressing into my inner ear.

"Well, they don't make 'em like this back in Boulder," Dad said. He was pointing to the old building, which was probably built before Boulder was even a city.

"That they don't," I said, the words nearly getting caught in my throat.

I felt as if every homework assignment I'd ever toiled over, every test I'd ever aced, it was all for a reason. Finally, here it was. My chance for a do-over. Here at Natick, I could be just Rafe. Not crazy Gavin and Opal's colorful son. Not the "different" guy on the soccer team. Not the openly gay kid who had it all figured out.

Maybe from the outside, that's what I looked like. I mean, yeah. I came out. First to my parents, in eighth grade, and then at Rangeview, freshman year. Because it's an *open and accepting* school. A *safe*

2

place. And then my soccer team sat down and we had a team meeting, and then they knew. Extended family, friends of friends. Rafe. Gay.

And no one's head exploded. And nobody got beat up, or threatened, or insulted. Not much, anyway. It all went pretty great.

Which is fine, but.

One day I woke up and I looked in the mirror, and this is what I saw:

GAY GAY GAY RAFE GAY GAY GAY GAY GAY GAY
GAY GAY GAY GAY GAY GAY GAY RAFE GAY GAY
GAY GAY GAY GAY GAY GAY GAY GAY GAY GAY
GAY GAY GAY GAY GAY GAY GAY GAY GAY GAY
GAY GAY GAY GAY GAY GAY GAY GAY RAFE GAY
GAY GAY GAY GAY GAY GAY GAY GAY GAY GAY
GAY GAY GAY GAY GAY GAY GAY GAY GAY GAY
GAY GAY GAY GAY GAY GAY GAY RAFE GAY GAY
GAY GAY GAY GAY GAY GAY GAY GAY GAY GAY
GAY GAY GAY GAY GAY GAY GAY GAY GAY GAY GAY
GAY GAY GAY GAY GAY GAY GAY GAY GAY GAY GAY
GAY RAFE GAY GAY GAY GAY GAY GAY GAY GAY

Where had Rafe gone? Where was I? The image I saw was so two-dimensional that I couldn't recognize myself in it. I was as invisible in the mirror as I was in the headline the Boulder *Daily Camera* had run a month earlier: Gay High School Student Speaks Out.

In truth, there were a lot of reasons I was moving across the country to attend Natick for my junior year. It was just that some of those reasons would have been hard to explain to, let's say, the president of Boulder's Parents, Families and Friends of Lesbians and Gays, because that person obviously wouldn't understand that while they had made life easier for a gay kid, the gay kid still wanted to leave.

Especially when said PFLAG Boulder president is your mom.

So maybe I buried the truth a little. I mean, it wasn't a lie to say that I wanted to go to a school like Harvard or Yale; I did. Mom was concerned an all-boys boarding school would be a homophobic environment, but I showed her that they not only had a Gay-Straight Alliance at Natick, but that the year before, they'd even had a former college football player who was gay come speak. There was this article in the *Boston Globe* about it, about how even a school like Natick was adjusting to the "new world order" where gay was okay. So she was satisfied. And unbeknownst to her, it was going to give me a chance to live a label-free life.

The night before, Dad and I had dinner at this Vietnamese restaurant in Harrisburg, Pennsylvania. What Dad didn't realize, as we sat there eating cellophane noodles and ground chicken wrapped in lettuce, was that I was silently saying good-bye to a part of myself: my label. That word that defined me as only one thing to everyone.

It was limiting me, big-time.

"Quarter for your thoughts?" Dad asked. Inflation, he explained.

"Just mulling," I replied. I was thinking about how snakes shed their skin every year, and how awesome it would be if people did that too. In lots of ways, that's what I was trying to do.

As of tomorrow, I was going to have new skin, and that skin could look like anything, would feel different than anything I knew yet. And that made me feel a little bit like I was about to be born. Again.

But hopefully not Born Again.

Dad opened the hatchback and began to put my duffel bags and boxes on the hot concrete. Sweat beaded up on my forehead and dripped onto my upper lip as I struggled to lift a box that had been underneath the duffels. It was a wet heat, something I'd first experienced when we hit the Midwest, maybe Iowa. I'd never even been east of Colorado before the trip, and now here I was, about to live in New England.

It took us four long, sweaty trips up the stairs to the fourth floor to get all my stuff to my room. My roommate, a guy named Albie Harris, at least according to the e-mail I'd gotten, wasn't around, but as we opened the door, we found that his stuff sure was.

Albie's side of the room was messy. Like earthquake messy. The furnishings were all pretty standard stuff: linoleum floors, two faux wood desks side by side, two white dressers at the feet of two metal-framed single beds on opposite sides of the room. But a box of Cap'n Crunch was open and spilled across the floor. A pillow, sans pillow-case, had traveled across the room and was under my bed, along with a black T-shirt, a science textbook, and what appeared to be a fake nose and mustache attached to a pair of eyeglasses. He'd gotten here maybe one day before me, since the dorms just opened yesterday, yet there were at least five crumpled Sunkist soda cans underneath and around his unmade bed. Two open suitcases lay in the center of the room, still full but with clothes overflowing in all directions. On his desk was a pair of two-way radios, as well as another radio with tons of buttons. Above his bed was a huge, menacing poster that depicted a car exploding. In big, bloodred letters at the bottom it read, Survival Planet.

I looked at my dad and opened my eyes wide, and he got this half grin he gets when he is savoring something that he can use for later. I'm the kind of kid who keeps spare Swiffers in his closet, and he knew me well enough to know how horrified I was at the sight of this disaster area.

I flopped down on the bed the roommate had left untouched. Dad stood in the doorway and took out his iPhone, and I groaned.

"A perfect match," he said, panning the room with his phone.

Nothing was more annoying than when my dad had an opinion, and it proved to be correct. For four months, and more vehemently for the 2,164 miles we'd just driven, he'd told me I was making a mistake. Normally, this would be my time to deny it, to insist he was wrong, but it seemed useless to argue. If my dad and mom could have paid my roommate to have my new room look like the worst possible home for me, this would have been it.

So I gave in. I put my head in my hands and shook it exaggeratedly, like I was really upset. "This does not bode well," I said.

Dad laughed and came and sat next to me, putting his arm on my shoulder.

"Hey. It is what it is," he said, always the great philosopher.

"I know, I know. I get to make my own choices and live with the consequences. I have free rein to make my own mistakes," I said.

"Hey," he said, shrugging. "The universe is infinite."

In my dad's language, that means, *I'm just a guy. What do I know?*

He stood up. "You want me to help you unpack?" he asked, his tone that of a man who had a 2,164-mile return journey ahead of him and really didn't want to place polo shirts in dresser drawers just now.

"I can do it," I said.

"You sure?"

"Yeah," I said.

Dad walked to the window, so I joined him. My room was on the back side of the dorm, which faced the huge, grassy quad. Outside, guys were throwing Frisbees, congregating in small groups. Guys, all guys. Mostly preppy. Very New England conservative. It didn't look that different from the pictures on the Internet, the photos that had gotten me interested in the first place. Very unlike what I could see of my roommate.

"You sure this is the right place for you?" he asked.

"I'll be fine, Dad. Don't worry about me."

He stared out the window as if the whole place made him sad.

"Seamus Rafael Goldberg. At the Natick School. Doesn't sound right, somehow," Dad said.

Yes, my name is Seamus — pronounced SHAY-mus — Rafael Goldberg. Try being five with that name. They called me Seamus as a young kid, then Rafael, which is almost worse, until I was like ten. I picked *Rafe* when I was in fifth grade, and I have insisted on it ever since.

He crossed the room, leaving me alone at the window, and I watched this kid loft a Frisbee a good fifty yards.

Dad pointed the camera at me, and I winced.

"C'mon. One video for your mom," he said, and I shrugged. I went to the middle of the room, next to the Cap'n Crunch spillage, and pointed down as if I were a tour guide at the Grand Canyon.

Dad laughed. Then I trotted over to my roommate's bed, put my two hands together, and leaned my head on them as if to say, *I'm in love!*

With the iPhone still recording, I walked back to the window, trying to come up with a funny pose. But then a strange thing happened. I felt this pang in my gut and I bit my lip. I'm not super big on emotional outbursts, which is what made it weird. I thought I might break down and start crying, starkly aware that as soon as Dad left, I'd have no one but strangers around me. Dad must have seen something in my body language, because he put his phone down, came back over to me, and gave me a sweat-soaked hug.

"Hey. You're gonna be a rock star here, Rafe," he whispered into my ear.

It was one of those things he always said, ever since I was five and going off to kindergarten. I was gonna be a rock star in the sandbox, I was gonna be a rock star in sixth-grade orchestra, and now I was gonna be a rock star at Natick.

"Love you, Dad," I said, a little choked up.

"I know you do. We love you too, buddy. Go kick some ass, take some names," he said, nearly tripping on the tipped-over cereal box as he let me go and stepped toward the door. "Find a boyfriend."

I tensed up. That wasn't exactly the thing I wanted broadcast in my first hour at Natick. Kids were walking by, but nobody stopped and looked.

"Give Mom a hug for me," I said, and I hugged him one more time.

"One last video for the road?" he asked, pointing his iPhone back in my direction.

I put my hand in front of my face, as if I were a celebrity who was tired of having pictures taken. And really I was. Not a celebrity, but truly tired of being on camera.

When you're Gavin and Opal's gay kid, you always feel like someone is looking at you. Not necessarily in a bad way. Just looking. Because something about you is interesting and different. But what you don't know is what they're seeing. And that's the kind of thing that could drive a guy crazy.

Dad took the hint and pocketed the phone for a final time. "Bye, son," he said, as a sweet, inimitable smile creased his face.

"Bye, Dad."

And he left me alone in my new world, staring at the semiblank slate that was my side of the room.

One thing I didn't realize when I created the idyllic world of Natick in my head was that the reality didn't include air-conditioning. Old building, I guess. My window and door were wide open as I tried to get some cross ventilation going, but it didn't do much to cool the oppressive room or my sweltering pits. So as I stuffed my second empty duffel bag into the dorm closet, I decided on a shower, since I smelled like my expiration date had come and gone weeks ago. A guy zoomed by the doorway, then I heard the footsteps slow and stop. He came back. Standing at my door in a royal blue tank top was a tall, built kid with black hair, blue eyes, and shoulders to die for.

"Hey, guy," he said. "We're gettin' a game going downstairs, do you . . . holy Jesus!"

"What?" I said, looking behind me.

"You look just like Schroeder."

"From *Peanuts*?"

"What? No. This kid. Graduated last year. Megapopular. You could be his brother."

"Oh," I said, my heart pulsing fast.

"I'm the first to tell you that?" the kid said, revealing a flawless set of pearly white teeth.

I smiled back, dazzled by him. I hoped I wasn't blushing. "You're the first to tell me anything. You're the first person I've met here."

"You're kidding. Well, come on downstairs. We're playing touch football, could use another player or two," he said. He stuck out his hand. "Name's Nickelson. Steve Nickelson."

"Rafe Goldberg," I said.

"You comin'?"

"Um, sure," I said. Showering could definitely wait.

We raced down the stairs, and when we got out to the quad behind the dorm, I saw a bunch of big, muscular guys standing around on the grass, tossing a football. Sort of an Abercrombie & Fitch ad come to life.

"So, okay," Steve said, racing toward them. "Who's this guy look like?"

"Your mama?" one kid said. Then the guys looked at me, and I saw a bunch of grins.

"Thought we were rid of the Schroedster already. Where's he at, Tufts?" This came from a guy with a deep voice and acne all over his face.

"Yup."

"What's your name?" The comments and questions were coming so fast that I had no time to notice anything beyond the fact that I was facing a group of, like, twelve guys, all built, most very good-looking. They were a huge mass, a giant blob of testosterone.

"Rafe Goldberg."

"Oh! You're the new junior, right? Where you from?" a kid with stringy blond hair and a skater T-shirt said.

"Yeah. Colorado."

"Right. Heard we had a new junior," a very tan kid wearing an inside-out Patriots jersey said. "You playing?"

"Sure," I said.

Introductions were barely made. It wasn't that kind of scene. Deep-voice Acne Guy stuck out his hand and said, "Robinson," so I said, "Rafe," back to him. No one else offered.

"Yo! Colorado," Steve said. "You fast?"

"Yeah," I said. Other than skiing, that is probably the best thing about me, athletics-wise. I'm an average soccer player, and the crowd I hung with back in Boulder wasn't much for pickup games of football. Here, though, maybe my crowd was?

They chose up sides. My team was Steve; the tan kid with the inside-out jersey, whose name turned out to be Zack; a quiet black guy named Bryce, who was wearing a T-shirt that read I WANT TO GO TO THERE; and a huge guy named Ben, who was twice as wide as me, with legs like fire hydrants.

"You get the ball first, 'cause you guys are gonna get your asses handed to you, anyway," Steve said, and we went back to do "the kickoff." I really wasn't that familiar with football, so I decided my strategy would be to hang back and watch.

Steve kicked off, throwing the ball really high and far toward the other team, which was facing us. Then we all ran toward one another, the strong sun blaring down on us, the air thick like honey.

It turned out to be pretty fun. The guys on the other team tried to block us as we ran toward the one who caught the ball. One guy put his forearms up in front of him while I ran at him, so I tried to run around him. He knocked me in the chest with his arms one time, which nearly knocked the wind out of me. Then I looked over and Steve was slapping two hands on the guy with the ball, and the play was over.

While the guys on the other team huddled up, Steve told us all what to do. I was supposed to cover Robinson. He came to the line, saw me, and smirked. He was taller and broader than me, with leg muscles way bigger than mine, and he wore a cross around his neck. I just figured that if they gave him the ball, I'd make sure to tag him before he got by me.

This tall kid with lily-white skin and a buzz cut stood in the middle, with two guys on either side of him, facing us. He yelled, "Hike!"

Robinson took horselike strides, and I backpedaled for a bit, staring at his face. His eyes got big, and he accelerated past me, so I turned and ran as fast as I could. I heard Steve's voice yelling my way, and I somehow knew to look up.

There was the ball, flying toward us. Robinson turned and was adjusting so that he could catch it. I was right next to him, and the split second before he jumped, I did.

I've played volleyball. I know how to jump high, and I know how to spike. I used my fists and smashed the ball down to the ground.

"Yo!" Steve screamed, running over to me like a crazy person. "He is Schroeder! Nobody brings that shit into my house!"

Zack was coming over too, and the two of them looked like I'd done something incredible. Blood coursed through my veins, and I felt the hairs on my neck stand on end.

"That's what Schroeder used to say," Steve said, high-fiving me.

I copied the voice Steve had used when imitating Schroeder. "Nobody brings that shit into my house!" I bellowed.

Steve looked over at Zack, and they bumped fists. "He even sounds like him!" Steve said.

I pointed at Robinson, who was jogging back to his teammates. "Nuh-uh," I said, wagging my finger at them. He ignored me and went back to his huddle.

Steve and Zack hugged in hysterics. "Now that one's pure Colorado. No finger wagging for the Schroedster! We gotta call you Schroedster Two!"

In my life there had been moments of great pleasure. I couldn't recall any, though, that felt anything like this one. It surprised me. I'd never thought of myself as the kind of guy who wanted to fit in with the jock crowd, but here I was, swelling with pride at being given a nickname.

Me, a jock? I thought about it, rolled it around on my tongue. It made me smile, and then laugh a little. I was elated. That was the feeling in my chest. Elation. I'd never experienced it before.

Bathing in it, I glanced over at Ben and Bryce in time to watch them share an eye roll. I stopped smiling, embarrassed. What was that for? What had I done to them? All I had done was enjoy myself. They reminded me of the jock versions of PIBs, back in Boulder — the People in Black, the kids who wore trench coats and sat on the sidelines and judged everyone. Who the hell were they to judge me?

Despite that, the football game was a good time. I was actually a bit relieved that the name *Schroedster Two* died a quick death when

I showed myself to be less adept at catching passes. Steve threw me two in a row, and the first one skidded off my hands, while the second hit me in the chest and bounced off. I thought I was close, especially on the second, but that didn't seem to count for anything, and the name fell away. Fine. Just another label to define me.

"Okay," Steve said in the huddle as we set up for our final drive, with the score tied. "Colorado, you do a ten-step buttonhook. Zack, go flat left. Benny, out and in. Bryce, flag deep. Okay?"

In previous huddles, he'd traced the routes on his hand with his finger, but suddenly we were getting names of plays. I had no idea what to do, so after we all yelled, "Break!" I tapped Ben the Jerk on his massive left shoulder.

"Um, what's a buttonhook?" I said.

He looked at me funny. Then he turned his palm up and drew the play for me, a quick run — ten steps, I guessed — and a turn.

"Thanks," I said, forcing a smile. "I owe you one."

He cocked his head slightly and went off to the other side of Steve. I lined up on the left, facing Robinson, and when Steve said hike, I ran the ten steps and spun around.

The ball was in my face immediately. It smacked me in the nose right as I put my hands up. Too late. The pain in my face knocked the wind out of me. The football glanced against my left hand as it ricocheted off my nose, and I adjusted, thrusting my hands out away from my body.

There was the ball, against my fingertips. I juggled it until it was cradled in my hands, and then I closed them in, brought my arms into my chest, and began running.

"He only got him with one hand!" I heard Steve yell, and I sped up, scurrying toward the other team's end zone. I knew once I got going, Robinson wasn't going to catch me.

"Touchdown!" Steve yelled. I spiked the ball, like I'd seen football players do on TV and like I'd seen some of the other guys do. Then I did a little dance, because you gotta dance when you get into the end zone. Everyone knows that. I shrugged from side to side, lifting my shoulders rhythmically as I moved back and forth.

"Kid's got moves!" said Steve, coming over to slap me on the back. I turned toward him to say something, and that's when I felt the blood.

"Oh, shit!" Steve said, and the other guys on the team ran over.

"Looks bad," Bryce said.

"I'm fine," I said. It didn't really feel fine, but I wasn't in the mood to have my celebration cut short, even for a medical emergency.

Ben grabbed my shoulder. "We should get you to the infirmary. Could be broken."

"Nah," I said, pulling away. "This thing bleeds if you look at it funny. I'm cool."

He looked me in the eye. His eyes were a translucent blue. He looked kind. I didn't want to look away. I realized that not being the gay kid here allowed me more access. I wasn't supposed to hold eye contact with jocks back in Boulder. It was understood: They accepted me, and I didn't freak them out with eye contact. Here, no such contract had been made. Ben blinked at me, I blinked back, and when it began to feel a bit too close, I averted my eyes.

That turned out to be the winning touchdown. I played the final set of downs with blood dripping from my nose, and when the game was over, Bryce came over and handed me some paper towels.

"Thanks," I said.

"No worries," he said, with a lack of inflection, and he and Ben walked off, all holier-than-thou, leaving me with Steve and Zack.

We walked back to the dorms together, and they asked if I wanted to have dinner with them later. "Hell, yeah," I said. And I went back up to the room with a bloodied nose and a euphoric feeling in my chest that was entirely new to me.

Wow, I thought, climbing two steps at a time up to my dorm room, keeping pressure on my nose with the paper towel. Here I was, two hours into my Natick adventure, and I was already in that entirely new skin I had fantasized about. Jock Rafe.

It felt freaking fantastic, to be honest.

Nothing could throw a wrench into this new plan, I thought, and then I cursed myself, because anyone who has ever watched a single Hollywood movie knows that thoughts like that lead to, well, big-ass wrenches.

Enter big-ass wrench number one.

The door to my room was open, and I peered in. Inside, a short, pudgy guy in a black T-shirt was unpacking the suitcases that had been in the middle of the room. Lying where they had been amidst the wreckage — cereal boxes, soda cans — was a skinny kid with spiky hair. He was facing away from me, and his hands were behind his head like he was doing sit-ups. I pressed the paper towel to my nose and then took a look at it. Still pretty bloody.

"So let me ask you," the spiky-haired guy said. "Let's say there was a gang of six-year-olds roaming the streets. And they attacked you. How many of them could you fight off?"

I stood in the doorway, as yet undetected. Aside from the disaster area that was the middle of the room, I was pleased to notice that at least things were being put away. A pile of what appeared to be nothing but black T-shirts on the short kid's bed was getting pretty high. He opened a drawer on the dresser next to his bed and started stuffing it with shirts.

"Do they have weapons?" he asked.

"No, just fists," Spiky Hair replied.

"Then probably four of them. Two of them could probably take out my legs, but I'd still have my arms. They could each grab hold of one limb, but then they wouldn't have anyone to go after my midsection. I'd be pretty much, like, incapacitated, I guess, but I'd be alive."

"Yeah," said Spiky Hair. "Probably four. I'd like to think I could take on four myself. I know if it was five, I'd be in some trouble."

"What if they had weapons?" Stocky Guy asked.

I crossed my arms and leaned against the doorway, which creaked when I put my weight against it. Both guys turned and looked at me.

"So why are these six-year-olds in a gang?" I asked, wiping blood from my nose.

Spiky Hair sized me up.

"Bad parenting," he said. "Their parents are like crystal meth addicts, and the kids don't have anywhere to go at night, so they roam the streets, looking for trouble."

Stocky Guy chimed in, "Also peer pressure. They have older brothers who are in eight- and nine-year-old gangs."

I nodded, folding the paper towel so that I could place a clean part of it under my nostrils. "Yeah, peer pressure is hard. Do they really want to do you harm, or are they just showboating?"

"Mostly showboating," Spiky Hair said. "It's like an initiation thing."

If these guys were at Rangeview, I thought, they'd be survivalists, kids who wore army fatigues and hung out at the shooting range and watched lots of shows about fishermen who got killed hunting crabs and stuff. Hence the exploding-car poster, I realized.

"I wonder what a six-year-old has to do to become a gang leader," I mused. "Knock over a 7-Eleven made from Legos?"

Stocky Guy squinted at me. "Don't be naive," he said. "It's a strength thing. Survival of the fittest. Toughest becomes leader. Like *Lord of the Flies*."

"Yeah, in *Lord of the Flies* there was a fight to the death for that role," Spiky Hair said, sitting up and facing me and rubbing a zit on his cheek.

"Right," I said. And then we were all silent.

"You're Rafe?" Stocky Guy said.

"Yep."

"I'm Albie. And this here is Toby."

"Hey," I said, coming in and sitting down on my bed. "You have a radio with lots of buttons."

"It's a police scanner. Knowledge is power," Albie said. "You have a bloody nose and lots of dirt on your legs."

"Football," I said.

Albie looked over at Toby, and they exchanged a look. "Great," he said, in a way that meant *not great*.

I glanced around the room. "So I'm guessing you're not studying to be a housekeeper?"

"Not so much," he said. "Are you seriously anal-retentive?"

"Nah," I said, realizing that I was, in fact, seriously anal-retentive, since just looking at our room was filling me with the strong urge to buy a vacuum cleaner. Or maybe a butler. "That's a lot of black T-shirts."

"Thanks," Albie said.

"Albie shops at the waiter's store," Toby said.

"Yeah, that's hilarious," Albie responded. "You shop at the 'I could never be hired as even a busboy because of my criminal record' store."

"Good one," said Toby.

"So what do I need to know about Natick?" I said.

Toby and Albie shared another look.

"Run for the hills!" Toby said.

"It can't be that bad. And I'm pretty sure I just came from the hills. I'm from Colorado."

"Well, then I guess it depends on what kind of guy you are," Albie said.

The old Rafe would have let it go. But I really felt like I had to call him on it. "Why do I have to be any particular type?"

He looked me up and down, in a very obvious way. "Well, you don't have to be, but you are."

I grabbed another paper towel from the roll on my desk and pressed it against my nose. "Okay, then," I said. "What's my type?" I crossed my arms and stuck out my chest a bit.

"I'm guessing preppy jock," Albie said.

"And that's . . . a bad thing?"

Albie shrugged. "Having a moth fly into your ear and lodge itself into your brain is a bad thing. Being a preppy jock is just . . . I don't know. It's a thing."

"You mean it's a bad thing."

"Well, it's not a moth burrowing into your brain, but, yeah, it's kinda lame."

"Geez, Albie!" Toby said.

"Well, he asked."

Maybe it was the adrenaline from the football game and getting the nosebleed. Maybe it was just the irony that I'd finally been labeled something mainstream and acceptable, and now here was my loser roommate giving me trouble. "And I see you're the type of guy who enjoys exploding cars and police scanners," I said. "Are you in a militia?"

"Yeah," he said. "You're a genius. I am in a militia. You should probably sleep with one eye open."

"Dork," I muttered.

"Republican" was his response.

Me? A Republican? I imagined my mother's head actually exploding. My face started to get red, and Albie turned toward me. His face had no expression, but I saw a flicker of something in his eyebrows. *Fear? Was he afraid of me?* No one had ever been afraid of me before, physically, at least. I felt like I had walked into a totally new dimension. Toby stood up and got in between us, which almost made me laugh, because it was like, *What? Are we going to rumble?*

"Is it horrified in here, or is it just me?" asked Toby. "Okay. Boys, here's what we're going to do." He walked over to Albie and put his hand on his shoulder. "You. Are going to stop being defensive to somebody who totally didn't deserve it."

Albie shrugged his shoulder away for a quick moment, and then relented. He nodded.

Then Toby walked over to me. He was extremely skinny, and his spiky hair was platinum in places. If this were Boulder, he'd definitely be a gay kid. But, then again, who was I to label?

"And you. You're going to take back your militia comment and never say anything negative again about that awesome poster, which happens to be for the coolest show in the history of television."

"*Survival Planet*? Never heard of it."

"Now that's something we can help you with," Toby said, squeezing my shoulder, and I blushed. Yes, possibly gay. And so, so not my type.

I took a deep breath before answering. "I'd watch," I said. "Always up for something new."

I looked over at Albie. He had paused in his unpacking and was just standing still, looking out the window. He looked sad. I thought about what I had said, calling him a dork. That was so not part of my plan when it came to the first conversation with my new roommate.

"Hey, Albie," I said, "I should not have called you a dork. I shouldn't have said any of that. I didn't mean it. I have Tourette's."

He looked over at me and rolled his eyes. "If you have Tourette's, then you did mean it. You just lacked the ability to filter your thoughts."

Now I had to laugh. "C'mon, dude. You're making it hard to take back the dork comment," I said. His face fell, so I walked over and tapped him on the shoulder with my fist. "I'm kidding, kidding. God, sensitive."

He seemed to ponder this for a moment. And then he shrugged. "Fine. Whatever. Start again?"

I grinned. "Sure."

He frowned, put his hands over his face, and then removed them to display a smile.

"Hi, you must be Rafe, my athletic new roommate."

I shook his hand. "And you must be Albie, my unorganized new roommate."

"Nice to meet you."

"I don't feel the urge to clean up this horrendous mess at all. And, by the way, great poster. I love that show," I said.

"Let's go play some sports," said he.

"Now that's much better" was Toby's response.

Albie went back to unpacking, and I lay down on my bed, a respite from the calamity that was the rest of our room. I wondered whether we'd work as roommates. On the plus side, they were both kinda funny. On the negative — well, why focus there, right?

"Shit, the lightbulb is dead," Albie said, switching his desk lamp on and off.

Toby put his head in his hands and pretended to sob lightly. "O bulb! We hardly knew ye," he said.

Ah, yes. The negative.

It's not exactly right to say I always wanted to sit at the jock lunch table back at Boulder. I mean, I'd enjoyed sitting with my best friend, Claire Olivia. We'd had a lot of laughs, and some of those laughs were at the expense of the jock kids. But I admit I had always wondered what it would be like to be at the top of the food chain.

On my first night at school, I got to experience the Natick version of exactly what I'd been missing.

"Your first day, huh? A hot one for ya," Steve said. I was sitting at a table with eight guys, all of them from the football game earlier. My nose had stopped bleeding, and now the only thing bothering me was a serious case of jitters. What if I said the wrong thing?

"Yeah," I said as I bit into an exceedingly adequate hamburger.

"Wicked hot," said another guy with a very round face.

"Was it hot in Boulder?" asked Mr. Patriots Jersey.

"In the summer."

"Bet you got a lot of snow." This was from Zack.

"Yeah, in the winter. Lots."

"It snows here too. But probably not like out there," said another guy.

This conversation has been brought to you by the good folks at the Weather Channel, I heard the Claire Olivia voice that lives in my brain say. I stifled the urge to ask if they were all studying to be meteorologists.

"Yeah," I said.

"I skied out there with my family a couple years ago. Vail," Steve said.

"Vail is excellent," I said. "I'm kind of an Eldora guy."

No one seemed to know what that was, because no one said anything.

"You traded up from the Rockies to the Red Sox," a guy said, and I laughed, because while I don't know a ton about baseball, I know enough to know that the Rockies are terrible, have always been terrible, and will always be terrible.

"You got that right," I said, smiling, and a couple of the guys chuckled. Then they started razzing me about the Red Sox beating the Rockies in the World Series back in 2007, and I was happy to take it. I had never been razzed about sports stuff before. I liked it.

"So what do y'all do for fun?" I said, to change the subject, and then I noticed I had said "y'all," which was weird, since I'd never said "y'all" before and Colorado isn't the South. I felt sure they'd razz me for that. *Strike one, Rafe.*

But Zack just said, "Homework. Flag football in the quad. In the fall, Sundays are all about the Pats. Saturday nights are all about hooking up with the girls from Joey Warren."

They explained that Joseph Warren High School was the local public school, right across Dug Pond from us, and I nodded and said, "That's cool." I tried to imagine myself part of a pack of guys who picked up local public school girls on weekends. It was hard to envision, but I was definitely willing to try. Not the pickup part. Just the being in a posse part.

"Who are you rooming with?" Steve asked.

"Albie. Albie Harris."

"Oh, man," said Zack. "Tough draw."

I nodded and took a sip of my soda. "Yeah, we already sort of clashed. But he seems okay. His friend Toby too."

"They're a little . . . different. All that survivalist stuff," Steve said. I could tell he was being polite because I was new here. I appreciated that.

"Yeah. I was trying to figure out if they were serious or kidding," I said.

The guys kept on eating; no one seemed to have much of an answer for that. They argued and joked around about someone named Jacoby Ellsbury, who was a Red Sock, apparently. I just listened, wondering if it was possible to be part of a posse when you don't ever contribute anything. At the same time, I was enjoying it. It was totally new to me, and I felt like an anthropologist studying another culture.

As I started digging into my brownie, Steve asked me if I was going to play soccer this year. Natick was too small to have a football team — that much I knew from my research.

"Yup," I said. "Midfielder."

"Right on," he said. "We could use your speed."

I nodded.

"You in shape for it?" he asked.

"I dunno," I said.

"Well, you better be. Soccer is a religion here," Steve said, looking directly at me. "You play well, you're set. You don't play, you don't matter. And losing, not an option. You gotta man up and give a hundred and twenty percent. Ten and three last year, lost in the playoffs to Belmont. Gotta do better this year."

He seemed to be waiting for me to chime in, so I answered in the affirmative, trying to sound like a chorus of boys doing the same thing. "Yep ah mmm uh-huh uh-huh," I said.

A little weird. I'd have to work on that. *Strike two.*

"Some of us," he said to the kid to my left, "need to step it up this year. Because, I gotta be honest . . ."

"Uh-oh," I said, without thinking.

The conversation ceased. So did my heart, momentarily.

"What do you mean, *uh-oh*?" Steve asked, his eyebrow raised. Everyone was looking at me. I realized Steve was the leader. Maybe he wasn't to be questioned?

I tried not to stammer. "Uh, back where I'm from, my, uh, best friend," I said, not specifying that this best friend was a girl, since I had a feeling that wouldn't play so well with this group, "we had this thing. It was like, anytime someone says, 'I gotta be honest,' it's like, get the hell out of there. Because nothing in the history of the world has ever been said after those words that was nice. It's never like, 'I gotta be honest, what you just said was really smart,' or 'I gotta be honest with you: Your breath smells like fresh mint.' It's like a polite way to say, 'Do you mind if I insult you now?'"

It was silent at our table. The guys looked at one another. This was the kind of stuff Claire Olivia and I riffed on all the time, and now I was realizing why we didn't sit at the jocks' table. Not that they were better than us, just that they didn't quite laugh at the same things. And I was like, *Strike three, you're out. I'll head off now and find the weird kids' table. Where are Toby and Albie?*

And then Zack cracked up. "I gotta be honest," he said to the kid on my left. "You probably shouldn't play soccer."

"I gotta be honest," the kid said back. "Your mother needs to stop calling me."

"I gotta be honest," said another guy. "Have you considered acne medication?"

"I gotta be honest. You might want to look into buying a blow-up girlfriend."

Soon we were all laughing, and even Steve was smiling as everyone got real honest with one another. A wave of relief passed through me, and I realized I truly liked these guys. I hadn't laughed this much with a group of guys since, well, ever.

My cell phone buzzed. I looked at it and saw it was Claire Olivia. We hadn't talked since I'd arrived on campus, and I knew I should pick up.

I quietly declined the call.

"Who's calling you?" Steve asked.

"No one important," I said, smiling. "I gotta be honest."

Big-ass wrench number two appeared that night after dinner, when I went down the hallway to pee. I ran into Ben, the big guy from football who had rolled his eyes to his friend Bryce about me. They hadn't sat with us at dinner.

I know about urinal etiquette. For one thing, you don't say anything beyond "What's up" to another guy while peeing. It's common courtesy. But I'd never had so much fun in one day, and here we were, two jocks, peeing next to each other. All I wanted to do was keep things going. So I broke the cardinal urinal rule.

"How's life?" I asked.

Through my peripheral vision I could see him look up at the ceiling. "Fine," he said.

Silence.

"That was a good game today," I said.

"Yup."

Again. Silence.

"You're not really supposed to talk at a urinal," I said, like a crazy person. "I actually know that. I'm breaking the rules."

He laughed. "You're a rebel."

I was so grateful that he'd said something back that I turned toward him. Maybe that wasn't the greatest idea.

"Dude," he said, recoiling slightly. "Really?"

I flinched back to the forward position as my entire face turned red. "Sorry."

He took a deep breath. "You missed, but should that even be an issue?"

"Really, really sorry," I said. "Very not cool. I can't believe I just did that."

We went back to peeing next to each other in silence. There's not a color for what I imagined my face looked like. Time for damage control. Major damage control.

"I have a peeing problem," I said. I meant it like a joke, like, "I have a drinking problem," but as soon as the words left my mouth, I could see how it might not make sense.

"Ah," he said.

"I meant it like a drinking problem. Not that I drink pee or anything, if that's what you're thinking."

"Of course," Ben said very quietly.

It was so awful that I couldn't help myself. I started laughing.

"This is the worst pee ever!" I said.

This cracked him up too, and that made me feel a bit better.

"I don't think I've ever said so many wrong things at one time. Wow." Tears were running down my cheeks now. I'd tucked myself away and was just standing there. Ben tucked himself in and flushed his urinal.

"Wow. Well, I guess I'd say it was really nice, but, maybe just it was really weird meeting you? I'd shake your hand, but . . ."

"Right," I said. We both went to the sink to wash our hands.

"I guess it's been a weird day," I said. "This is my first day ever at boarding school and —"

"You don't know how to pee in public. I get it," Ben said.

"You know what I mean."

"Yeah," he said as he punched down on the paper towel dispenser a few times and tore off some sheets.

"I feel a little out of place, I guess. It's hard."

"We're all out of place in our own way," he said.

I tore my own paper towel off the dispenser. "Deep," I said.

He smiled ruefully. "Yeah, real deep."

"No, I mean it," I said, continuing to wipe my hands even though they were now dry. "I like stuff like that."

He averted his eyes, and I averted mine. We were back to weird, and I'd taken us there.

"So, anyway," I said, well aware that our conversation was basically over, but somehow, not wanting it to be. "I also have the weirdest possible roommate. Albie?"

"Ah," Ben said.

"He has a police scanner and this apocalyptic poster thing. It's freaking me out. Is he, like, a survivalist?"

"I think he's an ironic survivalist."

I laughed. Ben looked pleased.

"Anyway, I'm not so thrilled about the whole 'My roommate is a dork' angle. Won't exactly help my standing here."

Ben half grimaced, baring his lower teeth like he'd just eaten something that didn't taste too good. "Well, good luck with that," he said, tossing his paper towel out. "Bye."

"I didn't mean . . ." I said, but he was already out the door.

And I was like, *Can I get a urinary do-over?*

"**Now,** I'm familiar with nearly all of you, and I've read some terrific essays on *Hamlet* and *A Separate Peace*," Mr. Scarborough said, prompting a few mutters from some of my classmates, who clearly didn't enjoy the flashback. "But in this elective writing seminar, we're going to embark on an entirely different journey. We're going to write about ourselves. I am well aware that some of you seniors think this is the English equivalent of Rocks for Jocks." Several of the kids laughed. "I assure you, that's not at all the case. You will be challenged in here, challenged in unforeseen ways. And I want you to know right now, if you're unwilling to be introspective, drop this class now. Today. No questions asked. I know there's still room in Mr. Stinson's Dramatic Literature class.

"Steve Nickelson. Can we know others if we don't know ourselves?"

"No?" Steve said, half question and half answer.

"Correct you are. Bryce Hixon. What do you think we gain by writing about ourselves?"

I looked around. In a room of white faces, Bryce was the only dark-skinned person. He was dressed better than most of the other kids; whereas most of us (myself included) were wearing jeans and a polo shirt, he wore black slacks and a blue blazer over a tan, pin-striped button-down shirt. He stood out.

"I guess we can learn about who we are," Bryce said in a monotone.

I noticed no Ben in the class. I felt relieved.

"Precisely," Mr. Scarborough said, pumping his fist to accentuate the word. "Writing, you see, is an exploration. You start from nothing and learn as you go. That's a quote from the writer E. L. Doctorow, who wrote . . . ?"

No one spoke for a while, until a kid in the back said, "Books?"

Mr. Scarborough laughed, and then we did. It was my first class on the first day, and I got the sense that students here took their cues for how much they could get away with from their teachers. Mr. Scarborough was tall and thin and young-looking, maybe just a bit out of college, though he wore a beige blazer that made him look old. Still, he was cute — for a teacher, anyway.

"Fair enough. That's a little much to expect. E. L. Doctorow wrote *Ragtime*, which became a movie, and *The Book of Daniel*, among others. He's one of our finest American authors. He said, and I repeat: 'Writing is an exploration. You start from nothing and learn as you go.'"

I wrote that sentence down on the page, which was blank other than the date and the title

MR. SCARBOROUGH's WRITING SEMINAR

I had always loved writing. It was my favorite subject. Not to brag, but at Rangeview I was considered one of the best writers in the school. I hoped that would be the case here.

"I want to start with an exercise here in class," Mr. Scarborough said, prompting a few groans. "I know, I know. You've hardly shaken off the rust of the summer, and here you are, eight-thirty on the first Monday of school, and you have to work. Just humor me. This won't be that challenging.

"I want you to fastwrite on the following subject: someone you've hurt in your life. I'll repeat. Someone you've hurt. When I ask you to fastwrite, I want you to simply put words on paper. Don't worry about editing, or how it's going to read to someone else. This is about getting your feelings down and not allowing form or the editing part of our brains to get in the way."

One of my favorite parts of writing is that *aha* moment you get when you know what you're going to write, and it propels you to start writing. I got mine right away: Claire Olivia. That would be an easy one, since I had, actually, hurt her.

Claire Olivia and I had been best friends forever. Our families were friends, and my first memory of her was my parents talking about her name. Her parents were typical Boulder loonies, sort of like my folks. My parents had met at Oberlin College, which is this liberal paradise in the middle of Ohio, and Claire Olivia's had met at Reed College, Oregon's Oberlin. The name they chose for their first daughter, Claire Olivia, sounded perfectly nice. But here was the deal: Her last name was Casey. Her mother spoke fluent Spanish for her job. They named her Claire Olivia so they could call her Claire O. Casey.

Which was supposed to sound like *"Claro que sí."* Which means, *But of course.*

Claire Olivia rebelled — *but of course* — once she was old enough to realize her name was also a joke, and she insisted on being called Claire Olivia ever since. We now referred to the incident as an NWI: Naming While Intoxicated. Which should obviously be a crime.

I would know, since I, Seamus Rafael Goldberg, was another victim of an NWI. I always got a lot of "Oh, is your mother Irish?" on the first day of school each year from my new teachers.

"Nope," I'd say.

"Your . . . father?" they'd ask as a hopeful follow-up. I could see the combinations and permutations flutter through their minds. This was Boulder. It could easily be two moms. Two dads. A dad, a mom, and an orangutan. Three Amish hipsters and a transgendered Aboriginal mermaid.

"Nope," I'd answer. "My parents went to Oberlin."

And the teachers would nod, usually. Sometimes they'd creep backward, slowly. Often they wouldn't respond at all, just go on to the next name. Everyone knew about Oberlin.

So Claire Olivia and I bonded over horrible names as kids. We were inseparable through elementary school, junior high, and the first two years of high school. The spring of eighth grade, she was the first person I told about being gay. She was like, *Wow, shocker.*

When I decided I wanted to go to Natick, she was in denial, while I just wanted to leave. So we never really talked it out until the good-bye party my parents threw for me at Barker Reservoir. We had snuck a couple bottles of Corona and sat on one of the concrete benches that faced the water.

"You psyched?" Claire Olivia asked. She was wearing all black — mourning, she explained.

I took a swig, swished the beer around in my mouth, and swallowed. "I dunno," I said, rubbing my knees together. "Kind of psyched."

She snorted and gulped down more beer. "You're abandoning me for *kind of*?"

"I'm psyched," I said.

"You don't sound psyched at all."

"Well, it's just weird, you know? I'll be, like, the one new junior, and the rest of the kids . . ."

"Guys," she corrected, looking at me through narrowed eyes. To Claire Olivia, even the idea of an all-boys boarding school was misogynistic.

"Guys," I repeated. "The rest of them will already know each other, and I'll be this outsider freak."

I hadn't told her about the main reason I was going to Natick. I knew she wouldn't understand.

Claire Olivia put the beer bottle against her forehead. I wondered if it was still cold, so I did the same. Lukewarm. We were silent for a bit. I listened to the way the water lapped against the concrete barrier, the faint sounds of the party my parents were throwing.

"Well, aside from the fact that I will be totally alone for the next two years," she muttered, rolling the bottle back and forth, "I guess I'm glad for you."

"It's only two years. I'll see you in college. I promise."

"You suck," she mumbled.

We made brief eye contact and she quickly looked away. My gut churned. I put my hand on Claire Olivia's shoulder, even though we were not touchy people. She looked over at it as if it were an exotic parrot. I took it off, and we sat silently, looking out at the reservoir. She sighed.

"I'm just not happy," she said, and she picked up her beer bottle and threw it at the concrete bench about ten feet away. It nicked the edge and shattered. Beer gushed into the grass.

We both stared at the broken bottle.

"Did you just throw a bottle?" I said.

"I think I did," she said.

"That's, like, what you do when you're unhappy now?"

"Yeah."

"Well, I'm not happy either," I said, and I tossed my half-full bottle at the bench too. It missed, thudded against the grass, and spun before settling and leaking onto the grass.

"God, I'm gonna miss you," she said.

"Yeah," I said back. "Me too. Miss you too."

"Is that how you talk now that you're an East Coast prep student?"

"Is yes," I said.

So I had hurt Claire Olivia by leaving. Now, as I scribbled words as fast as I could, trying to write something that was the complete truth while avoiding certain other truths, I realized something I hadn't allowed myself to see before: I had been so focused on leaving that I had completely brushed her off when she wanted to talk about it. She must have felt totally abandoned. For all the grief I'd given her about how everything was always about her, at the most crucial time, it had been all about me.

And now maybe we'd go to the same college — we'd try — but it was hardly a given that we'd get into the same places. A lump grew in my throat.

The problem, as I was writing, was all that I had to leave out. Instead of going right into our strange but weird friendship (a guy has sleepovers with a girl, who happens to be his best friend?), I had to write less and hope that my words conveyed something.

"Who will read?" Mr. Scarborough asked.

A kid I hadn't met yet, with a mouth full of braces, read. His piece was pretty good, about a time he'd been on a seesaw with his sister, and he was high in the air, and as a joke he'd jumped off, and she'd flown down and smacked her mouth against the metal bar. I could actually smell the blood and see the chipped tooth, which is one way I know something is well written.

"Good, good," Mr. Scarborough said. "What I'd like you to think about, Curtis, is culpability. You didn't mean to hurt her; it was an accident, as you said. I'd like you to add to your homework a short piece like the one you wrote, but in this one I want you to reflect on a time when you purposefully hurt someone else. We can learn so much from seeing our own character flaws. I want to see that from you. Excellent work."

My gut churned. I knew that if he could find a flaw in that piece, mine would surely be flawed too, and I didn't like the possibility. I hoped I wouldn't have to read.

"How about our new student?" Mr. Scarborough said, smiling at me. He looked down at his attendance sheet. "Rafe?"

By sixth grade, I'd figured out that you have to get your parents to insist that your name is written as *Rafe* rather than *Seamus Rafael* on attendance sheets. *Seamus Rafael* isn't the kind of name kids just let go by.

So I read what I'd written.

> Claire Olivia was the kind of girl who could keep up with me on the slopes, even on the moguls. She laughed at all my jokes, even the unfunny ones. She coined the word craptacular. Her eyes smiled, even when she was crying. She was always beautiful, especially without makeup. When I told her I was coming to Natick, she looked up and to the left, like the answer was up there. I knew that it made her cry, but she never cried in front of me. I knew, because she always texted at night, and that night she didn't. And the next morning she wouldn't look me in the eye. When you hurt someone you care about, it's like a part of you dies inside. If you can't talk about it, the death goes unnoticed. I was never able to go there, and I'll always regret that.

"Wow. In-ter-est-ing," Mr. Scarborough said, not taking his eyes off me. "Great details. Looking up and to the left — class, that's the way you use singular detail, the way to show a lot with a little. But

40

there was something else, a few other things, actually, that I noticed about that piece. Anyone?"

"Sentence length," said Bryce, not looking at me. "Scads of short sentences."

"Yes!" Mr. Scarborough cried. "Precisely. Did anyone else have a feeling as though it was hard to breathe, listening to that piece? Extremely tight, clipped, controlled. That can be fixed by varying sentence length. Anything else?"

Some other kid said, "Why the hell would someone leave their hot girlfriend and move across the country to an all-boys school?"

The room got really quiet, and it was like I could hear all my internal organs turning over inside me. I scanned what I'd written. *Girlfriend?* I hadn't said "girlfriend." And then I wondered if a part of me wanted them to think that.

"Well, that's a question for a different time, perhaps," Mr. Scarborough said, clearing his throat. "But I think you make a valid point. Are we getting the full story? What's missing here? Where is Rafe's focus, emotionally?"

No one had an answer for that one. Everyone just sort of stared, brain-dead-like, and I felt this sinking sensation in my chest and I wasn't sure why.

I thought about when I was training for Speaking Out, the gay advocacy group that Mom talked me into joining last year, which got me speaking engagements at high schools across the state. They taught us this game that we took to the schools. You ask everyone to write down three major facts about themselves. Then you put the kids in groups and ask them to introduce themselves without mentioning any of the three things. The exercise is supposed to help kids understand how hard it is for gay people when they are told, like, "It's okay if you're gay, just don't talk about it."

That exercise sometimes worked, sometimes didn't, depending on the crowd. But sitting in Mr. Scarborough's writing seminar, it occurred to me that this was that lesson in action.

The bell rang, and we started packing up.

Mr. Scarborough said, "Before you go, I wanted to announce that I'm the advisor for the school literary magazine, and we're looking for new staff people, so let me know if you're interested. As for this class, you'll all keep journals. I'll read them. I will not share them with other students, and I will not ask you to read from them. So you may feel free to write whatever you feel is important. But it must be about you. Your life. Tell me who you are."

Great, I thought. How the hell was I going to do that?

At our first soccer practice, Mr. Donnelly lined us up against a wall in the gymnasium. He was our dorm adviser at East and a history teacher. Maybe thirty or thirty-five, he appeared to be going for older; he wore big wire-rimmed glasses that seemed like they were meant to look bookish. His black hair was parted on the side and combed over the top of his head.

"The Romans dominated the world for hundreds of years. Does anyone care to guess why?" he asked as we sat in front of him on the gymnasium floor.

I almost raised my hand. Legions, right? Military strategy and organization? I didn't remember a ton from tenth-grade history, but I knew a few things still.

42

"Leg strength," he said. "No one had thighs like the Romans."

That was not what I'd expected to hear. It got me interested, at least.

"The proof was in the famous marathons, discovered by the Romans, as you might recall. Did you know that the first Roman army ran all the way from Damascus to Constantinople? The French, and the Germans, and the . . . Danish . . . couldn't keep up. Those Romans had stamina. Do you know what that means? Do you?"

I looked around. Were there hidden cameras somewhere? Were we being punked? Even I knew the Greeks had invented the marathon. I looked over at Steve, but his expression was totally blank. I caught Ben's eye, and he looked away, but not before a flicker of something crossed his face. I smirked. I wasn't the only one thinking this guy had a few of his facts wrong.

"All's I know is the following: Stamina means never having to give up. Stamina means your body never builds up lactic acid. We're going to get stamina this year, boys."

I made a mental note to look up the word *stamina* later.

He had us lean up against the wall in a sitting position. I was fine for about thirty seconds, even when some of the other guys began to grunt. Then I felt it. The shaking, in my quads. I closed my eyes as Donnelly kept walking back and forth in front of us. He yelled, "Be like Mark Anthony and, uh . . ." Even with my quads throbbing, I almost laughed as he struggled to think of another name. "And all the other Roman leaders!" A few more painful seconds. "C'mon. Don't you dare give up. First three to fail are doing laps the rest of practice. Hear me?"

You can do anything for five minutes. This was something my

dad used to say, and it was true. When I took swimming lessons as a kid, I hated the cold water of the lake we swam in. But if I didn't pass, we wouldn't be able to go Jet Skiing. Dad said: "Five minutes is nothing. You can do anything, *anything*, for five minutes." So I did. I pretended I had a wet suit on, that the freezing water against my sides was a second skin, protecting me from the elements. And I started the crawl stroke and I didn't stop until I heard the whistle.

"And then there were four," I heard Donnelly say, and I opened my eyes and realized I'd tuned things out so much that I didn't know how long it had been. My legs shook something fierce, but I decided to keep going. I could win this. I could be the best. I could . . .

"Nice try there, Goldberg. All's I know is that's a nice effort by the new guy. Way to show up on the first day."

I picked myself up off the gym floor, my quads still throbbing. I watched Steve, Ben, and Robinson, the final three. Robinson crashed soon after I did, and then there were two. Ben's eyes were closed, and I saw a bead of sweat travel down the side of his face. His legs were like horse legs. His calves, grapefruit sized and finely matted with light hair, bulged and trembled. I wasn't surprised when Steve fell first.

"Ben Carver. He outplayed, outwitted, outlasted you all," Donnelly said.

Wasn't that the *Survivor* TV show motto? I'd have to ask Albie and Toby later. Nah, probably not the right kind of survivor show.

We went out to the soccer field. Natick has some of the best athletic facilities around, and that includes a gorgeously manicured soccer field surrounded by a track. I worked out with the midfielders. I'd always liked to run, and they did the most running.

We scrimmaged. The ball came my way, and I dribbled up the sideline. Steve came over to defend. I knew I couldn't get around him, so I faked as if I were going to try, and when he bit, I kicked the ball across the field. I had no idea whom I was passing to, but at least it seemed like the right thing.

As luck would have it, Bryce was there. He stopped the pass by catching it with his chest, dribbled around a defender, and hit the top of the net, easily past the diving goalie.

"Beautiful, Bryce. Great, great pass, Rafe. That's the way," shouted Donnelly.

I was glad I'd made a positive impression, even if it was dumb luck. I was clearly not the best player, but I tried hard, and I wasn't the worst either.

I found Ben as we walked back to the locker room. "I think some long-passed Natick history teachers are turning over in their graves right about now," I said.

He smirked. "Wait until he starts using World War II analogies. He gets the Axis and the axis of evil confused."

"Sounds excellent," I said as I held the door for him.

"Some of the more disgruntled upperclassmen made a big stink about it last year. Natick is famous for pushing these sorts of things under the table. We win games, so why worry about the miseducation of the soccer team?"

"Were you one of the disgruntled?" I asked.

"Nah. I was gruntled."

That cracked me up. I liked Ben. He was smart. So was Bryce, who had used the word *scads* in our writing class. I hoped I could make them see that we should be friends. And just as I was thinking up a good comeback, he was gone, hustling down the aisle to his locker.

As I started to get undressed, I saw the first few guys head into the shower area. I felt my heart beat faster as I glimpsed my teammates walking by, some wrapped in towels, some with towels draped over their shoulders. In Boulder, as the gay guy, it was an unspoken rule that I wouldn't gawk at my fellow athletes. That would be considered rude, you know? And, basically, I just figured it was a tradeoff: They accepted me, I didn't stare at them naked. It worked.

Here, no such unspoken pact had been made; why would there be? And I felt a little guilty and a bit tingly, entering the sacred shower room with my fellow straight teammates.

The thing about Natick guys was this: They really were genuinely nice. I had never been in a shower room that wasn't filled with name-calling and insults. Once *faggot* had been taken away from my Boulder teammates, they'd found other ones — dumbass, shit breath, dick face — that they used with abandon. Here, the guys were mostly talking about, of all things, soccer.

"We gotta be better this year," Steve said. "Schroeder's gone, but Bryce is our boy."

I looked over at Bryce. It was almost like he wasn't there; Steve had spoken about him in the third person rather than the second. It was weird.

"Add Rafe and his speed and we got a serious shot to win it all, right?"

Steve turned to me and smiled, which made my heart spin even more, since he was just about perfect, physically. It gave me a chance to look at him, since he was looking at me. He had a six-pack, the kind I was not quite muscular enough to have.

I looked over at Ben. He was silently soaping and rinsing. His torso was thick — not fat, just bigger — and well sculpted. The curve of his back was graceful, his neck strong. *Teen People* would probably choose Steve, but something about Ben made me think he was even more attractive.

Steve continued to work the room, and I realized it was basically his space. Whatever Steve said or did, people listened. I'd never been part of a group like that, so it was interesting, like a National Geographic special on wolves that I might watch with my dad.

And I was part of the pack.

Albie and Toby came into our room while I was reading *A Separate Peace* for lit class that night.

"Hey," I said, pretending to be engrossed in my book, even though my interest in Gene and Finny was pretty low. I had gotten along with Albie and Toby over the weekend when we'd been in the room together. They were weird but harmless. Albie said strange things and never laughed, which made me a little uncomfortable. Toby said even stranger things and laughed a lot. I hadn't seen either of them much out of the room, and when I did, a nod was all I'd give them. I liked them fine, but clearly if I had to choose between my jock friends and these two, it wasn't going to be a tough choice.

"Greetings and salutations," said Albie.

I saw he was wearing huge camouflage shorts, and what happened next was not exactly expected. He dug four Styrofoam bowls out of his desk drawer and put them on the desk. He then stood on his toes and proceeded to turn his pockets inside out. Lucky Charms poured into the bowls. Each pocket seemed to fill two bowls to the rim. There was some overflow that landed on the floor, and without thinking, I stood up to go over and clean up the spill, but Albie put out his hand to stop me. He then bent down and picked up the cereal bits that had landed on the floor and placed them in the garbage.

"Progress!" I said, smiling, and he bowed at me.

"Here goes nothing," Toby said, and he walked over to the windowsill, where a single, wilted rose drooped in a clear glass vase. Toby picked up the vase and poured the clear liquid — water, I supposed — into the Styrofoam bowls. The cereal pile got higher.

"Ew," I said, unable to suppress my disgust. As if Lucky Charms weren't disgusting enough, adding *flower water*?

"Puts hair on your chest," Toby said, grinning. "Want some?"

"I'm afraid to ask," I said.

"Don't ask, don't tell," he said.

"Vodka?"

Toby nodded bravely. "They kick you out for this," he said. "Hence the vase."

"Lucky Charms with vodka?"

"Frosted Russkie Charms. They're Bolshevik delicious!" Toby sang. "Think of it like an after-dinner drink, a dessert wine."

"Actually, it's more like an alcoholic dessert," Albie said. "It's not a drink."

"It's more like an alcoholic's dessert," I said, and Toby giggled.

I passed on a bowl. Albie shrugged and said, "More for us," and we three sat there, a strange trio.

"So what's your thing, Rafe?" Toby said, rolling marshmallows around in his mouth before crunching on them.

"My thing?" I asked.

"Tweaker, womanizer, historical reenactments, poetry slams, model airplanes, VH1." Toby listed these choices as if they were the only possibilities.

"Um," I said.

"Weed whacking, porcelain doll collecting, Ferris wheels," added Albie.

I just stared at the guys, totally speechless.

Albie looked at Toby, and for the first time since I'd met him, he dropped the aloof act, smiling.

"He doesn't know what to make of us," he said.

"Good," Toby said, smirking. "I like to be a mystery."

In Boulder, I'd be friends with these guys, I realized. Maybe not the *Survival Planet* stuff, but they were funny. They said things that surprised me constantly. I decided to play along. What Steve and Zack didn't know wouldn't hurt them. Plus, it would be fun to go against the label they'd given me. Blow their minds a little.

"I like the Yeah Yeah Yeahs and taking photographs of nuns on Segways," I said.

I was thinking back to the time this summer when Claire Olivia and I had seen these three nuns riding on Segways in the Pearl Street Mall. The rest of the crowd was being very Boulder, very "nothing to see here" laid-back, so Claire Olivia and I followed the nuns and waited until they parked their Segways and sat down on a bench. Then we went and talked with them and found out they were an honest-to-God (no pun intended) group of local nuns who traveled on Segways. For fun. They liked us, and, of course, I got to snap several pictures of Claire Olivia riding on a Segway amidst a group of nuns. (A *cloister* of nuns, we later decided, when we got to talking about words meaning groups of things, like *a gaggle of geese, a murder of crows*.)

"That's two of the rules of comedy right there," Albie said, picking up the bowl he'd emptied of cereal, lifting it to his mouth, and slurping the vodka. "One: Nuns are always funny. Two: Segways are always funny. That's comedy gold."

"I'm a regular Tosh.0," I deadpanned.

Toby laughed. Albie frowned. "He relies on profanity and sex innuendo," Albie said. "Very much in violation of the rules of comedy."

"Albie loves rules," Toby said, rolling his eyes. "Rules and of course survival shows on television, and thinking up new ways to abuse and humiliate jocks. Present company excluded."

"I never get to use them, though," Albie said. "I don't like being killed."

I looked at Albie, who was not looking at me, and I realized he was nervous about being around me. His bravado and humor aside, here I was, this supposed jock he was rooming with. He had no way of knowing that I'd been anything other than a jock all my life. I felt bad for him, so I decided to say what the old Rafe would say. Pre-Natick Rafe.

"I hear ya. In Boulder, my best friend and I used to come up with ingenious plans about how to make the FBITs pay."

"FBITs?" Albie asked.

"Frat Boys In Training."

He looked at me, sized me up again. I could tell he was sort of thinking I was one.

"We call them Jockheads," Toby said. "Rhymes with *blockhead*?"

"Yes, I got that," I said. "Extremely clever."

This made Toby laugh.

"Well, anyway, this school is all FBITs," Albie said.

"I had dinner with them a few times over the weekend. Steve and Zack?"

Albie raised his eyebrows. "Impressive," he said. "I mean, in a very unimpressive way."

"I like them," I said.

"I gotta piss like a racehorse," he said. "And by that I mean while galloping." He galloped out of the room.

So there we were, me and Toby, alone in the room. I crossed and uncrossed my legs. Toby kept eating his Frosted Russkie Charms. He had an earring in his right ear, and he wore a tight white T-shirt. His voice wasn't effeminate, but he was definitely different.

"I guess if you've talked to the Jockheads already, they probably told you about me," he said, squirming in his seat. "I'm gay. Everyone knows and I'm fine with that."

I swallowed. "No," I said. "They had not told me that."

"Oh," said Toby. "Um . . . awkward."

All summer, I'd gone over every scenario in my mind in terms of gay stuff at Natick. I had firm plans in place. I was going to be label-free. *Don't ask, and I won't tell.* The only way I would actually lie was if I were asked directly, "Are you gay?" In that case, I'd say no. But even then I wouldn't go on about being straight. I didn't want to lie; I just wanted to not be the guy whose main attribute was liking other guys. Been there, done that. So anything less than a full-on, direct question would receive a deflection of some kind.

If people assumed I were straight — they call that heterosexism, I'd learned in my Speaking Out training — I'd let them. I wouldn't go on and on about it, but I'd let them.

If someone asked if I had a girlfriend, the answer was no.

If someone asked if there were some girl I liked, or if they tried to set me up with some girl at a party, the answer was "I'm focusing on getting into a good school." That way, I wouldn't have to pretend to be interested, but also I wouldn't be saying no, which would obviously make people wonder.

If something came up about someone else being gay, I'd go for Liberal Boulderite. *That's cool*, I'd say, totally unconcerned.

I'd say as little as possible about sex and focus on other stuff.

I'd even thought about what I'd do if another gay kid told me he was gay, so I was ready for this. I was ready for anything.

"I had gay friends in Boulder. I'm definitely cool with that," I heard myself say to Toby, and held back a grimace. How many times had people said that kind of thing to me? Like I'd be so grateful to know they liked other gay people. *Gee, how awesome of you*, I'd always thought when people said shit like that.

He smiled. "Good. Although I have to say," he said, and suddenly he got a little coquettish, his eyes batting a touch. "I was hoping maybe you were, you know."

I blushed. My "don't ask, I won't tell" plan didn't have a contingency for a follow-up question. I tried for another deflection. "Must be tough to be gay here," I said, averting my eyes.

Toby just stared at me. He wasn't buying my deflections. This was not good. Not good at all.

Oh, well. So much for no lying. "Yeah. Sorry. I'm not."

He sighed dramatically. "All the cute ones are straight or married," he said, looking away. I laughed, though I'm not sure if and when my blushing ever really stopped.

Albie neighed and threw his head back as he returned to the room. When he sensed the awkwardness, he turned to Toby. "So you told him?"

"Ya," Toby said.

"Your team, or my team?"

"Yours," Toby said, mock dejectedly.

"Oh, well. Sorry, little buddy. Someday your prince will come. C-O-M-E, I mean, because I'm not about the sex innuendo. That's the lowest form of comedy." Then Albie appraised my mood. "You are not extremely uncomfortable."

"I am not," I responded.

"I thought maybe you would be."

"It's not a big deal."

Albie seemed to digest this. Then he got mock serious, sticking his hand out at me and lowering his voice. "Welcome to the squad, young man. Good to have you, good to have you."

"Um, thank you. Thank you very much," I said, mimicking his lowered voice. And then we all laughed, and I wondered if these guys might actually be great friends to have.

In the comfort of our room, anyway.

"**Now** don't kill me," I said when the voice at the other end said hello. "I know it's been too long. I've been really busy settling in."

"Who is this?" Claire Olivia said. "I don't recognize the voice."

"I'm sorry," I said. "I'm sorry, I'm sorry, I'm sorry. It won't happen again."

"Damn right it won't. What's with not calling me back for almost a week? What am I, chopped liver?"

"Are you still going for the whole Jewish grandmother thing? Because I thought we'd talked about this? You're Irish, girlie girl. It's not working."

"All I know, Seamus Rafael Goldberg, is I haven't heard your sweet voice in way too long! What's going on, Shay Shay?"

"Oh, you know. Got married. Divorced. Became a drunk. Moved to Reno."

"You are NOT getting away without giving me a full report. I've MISSED you, Shay Shay! Seriously. You cannot not call like that. I'm having Rafe withdrawals!"

"I know, I know," I said. "I hate that I've been such a suck-ass friend. What's wrong with me?"

"We do not even have time for you to get all self-pityish. We have way too much to cover. After all, my life is going to serious hell."

I lay back sideways on my bed and kicked my legs up against the wall. I knew Claire Olivia well enough to know that I was about to hear a drawn-out story. And I was glad. It *had* been too long, really. "Tell me, tell me," I said.

She took a dramatic breath. "Thank God. I absolutely have to tell someone who will actually understand. So I'm with Courtney and her boyfriend, Sam, and You-Know-Caleb at the Laughing Goat."

Claire Olivia called this guy Caleb "You-Know-Caleb," because that's how everyone mentioned him to me. He was the only other openly gay kid in our grade at Rangeview. If I had to describe him, I'd say he was, well, bitchy. I hate to stereotype, but he was. Anyway, almost every day someone said to me, "You know Caleb?" — like we must be close, since we shared a sexual orientation. It made me a little crazy. We definitely didn't hang out.

"So this is like Monday, after school, first day. And we're just hanging out, and this serious cutie is with his friend, he's wearing a burnt-orange ski hat and has the most insanely beautiful blue eyes and cheekbones up to the ceiling, and he keeps looking over. And it's like, at me. I mean, he's looking. So I smile at him, and Caleb, of course, you know he goes over. . . ."

I looked at my skinny legs and then studied the ceiling. I was used to Claire Olivia going on and on; that was our thing. I did it sometimes too. It was just that so much had happened since the last time we'd done this. Back in Boulder, it wasn't unusual for me to go weeks talking only to my parents and her. Now I had a lot of people in my life whom I talked to, and it felt different. I imagined her on a raft at Barker Reservoir, floating off into the distance, floating, floating.

". . . And so that night we text a hundred times, and it's obvious that he likes me and I like him, and he finally says, 'Wanna hang out Friday?' And I didn't even play coy, because it wasn't needed. I just wrote yes. And he's like, 'Cool. I'll call you.' And then Tuesday and Wednesday, no calls, no texts. And I finally text him on Wednesday night with something appropriately snarky, like, 'Are you dead?' And get this: no reply."

I suppressed a yawn. How many boyfriends had I been through with Claire Olivia? How many bad dates? And that was the thing. How many had she gone through with me? I hadn't said much to her about the only so-called dates I'd ever had because, frankly, there was nothing much to say. And now I had lots to tell her, and, granted, it was my fault she didn't know some of the stuff that was going on, but even if she had known, would I have gotten the chance to go first? Or would we be having this same one-way conversation?

". . . And I call Caleb and we talk about it for an hour, and even he's like, 'Enough, you've known this guy like a day,' and I said, *'But we texted,'* and Caleb is like, 'Two out of three psychologists say that texting is not an actual date.' But, anyway, the guy totally blows me off.

"So, like, Friday, yesterday, after school we go back to the Goat. It's me and Courtney and You-Know-Caleb again, we're like this trio now that you have ABANDONED me. We go there and we're having Italian sodas and guess who walks in?"

There was a pause, and it occurred to me that it was my line.

"The guy," I said.

"The guy," she repeated. "Whose pathetic name is Pete. Pathetic Pete. And he's all smiles, and he comes and sits with us."

"Wow," I said, trying to straighten my legs to be at a ninety-degree angle with my torso.

". . . And he says, get this: 'I'm just not into you in that way. But you're a really cool chick. Can we be friends?'

"Um, no! So I told him in no uncertain terms that we could not. Okay. That's a lie. I said I had to go to the bathroom, and then I waited in there until Courtney came, and she totally was there for me and she said she'd make sure he was gone before I came out. She's a really cool girl. You would have liked getting to know her better if you had NOT ABANDONED ME HERE."

"Have you sold the film rights?" I asked.

"I know you did not just say that, Shay Shay."

"Tee hee," I said. And the thing was, I was only half kidding. It was a decent story, but we hadn't talked in over a week, and I was at a new school. Surely if our roles were exchanged, I would not have gone off on a pointless story like that, would I have? And then having that thought made me feel a little guilty, because it was Claire Olivia, and she was my best friend in the world.

"That guy is a jerk," I said, hoping it would make up for my snarky comment.

In the slight pause she gave, I could sense that she got that our connection was a little off. "I know, right?" she said.

"Totally," I said.

"So other than my catastrophic life, what's going on with you in Rhode Island?"

"I'm in Massachusetts, girlie girl," I said, a little irked.

"I know, Shay Shay. But to be honest, I'm pretty sure the East Coast is not really a place. I think it's all a Republican plot to create this make-believe liberal place so that they can claim the rest of the country and be like, *You have your place.* So given that it doesn't exist, I refuse to believe in state lines and artificial boundaries. So I'm going to call it Rhode Island or North Carolina or Delaware, or whatever occurs to me at the moment. 'Kay?"

"'Kay."

"So what's going on in Vermont?"

"It's cool. I really like it here. I'm having a blast."

"Have you met any guys?"

"It's an all-boys school. I've met tons of guys."

"No. I mean, like, dateable guys."

"They're all dateable for someone."

"Evasive much? You're pissing me off."

"I've met a lot of great people," I said. "I'm not looking to date right now. I just want to hang out, you know?"

She was silent for a while. So I was too.

"I miss hanging out at the Laughing Goat with you," she said.

"Me too." I did. I missed sitting in a diner with her and deciding which of the patrons had been in prison, and which guys were wearing women's underwear, things like that. I didn't have that easy relationship with anyone at Natick.

"You've changed, Rafe."

"Have I?" I said, a little anxiously. The truth was, I hoped I had changed. And I wanted her to tell me exactly how.

"I don't know if I like it."

"Just give me some time, okay? I'll be back. I promise."

I could hear the sulking at the other end of the line. I imagined her lying on her bed just like I was, her legs above her head, her stockinged feet against the wall.

"But you won't be back."

What would that be like? I thought. To never return to the person I was before. To never again have to stand out as different, to fade into the crowd, to be this new, uncomplicated Rafe forever? The idea made me shiver.

"I'll be back," I said, and my voice cracked a little as I said it.

"You won't be the same," she said.

"Maybe not," I replied.

Sept. 17

My name is Rafe, and I have insane parents.

(Hi, Rafe.)

I don't use this term lightly. Well, actually I do, but so far as we agree to define <u>insane</u> as seriously unusual rather than in need of hospitalization, my parents are indeed insane.

My mother does naked yoga. In the summer at our home in Boulder, when I hear either John Lennon music or the Moody Blues pouring from the outside speakers, I know that I need to close my window shades, unless I want to see a show that no son should ever see. She says that naked yoga allows her to get in touch with her "inner priestess." She talks like that. It's horrifying.

On the plus side, before you start thinking I'm stereotyping her, she glows. Her skin always has a sheen of something shiny on it, and I am convinced that it's not sweat, not grease, not suntan lotion, but something inside shining through to the surface of her face. Mom is one of the happiest people in the world, and I'm pretty sure that's because she holds nothing in. When she feels something, she'll let you know it. It can be off-putting. When she told my friend Claire Olivia that she thought her favorite pink blouse was trashy and "beneath her" this summer, I thought Claire Olivia was going to freak. But while she was taken aback, she appreciated my mom's candor and now regularly asks her for fashion advice. Claire Olivia is on the same Hippie Chick path as my mom.

My father raps. Karaoke raps. When he's not <u>boogying</u>. Yes, he uses the word <u>boogying</u>. He teaches at CU Boulder, in the English Department, and at their annual picnic last June, he got up and did karaoke to Eve's "Let Me Blow Ya Mind." You have not lived until you've seen your father rap, "Drop yo' glasses, shake yo' asses," in front of a bunch of English professors.

I so wish I was kidding. And what's even stranger is that people go along with it. The head of the English Department, who is maybe sixty and my dad's close friend and happens to be African-American, stood up and sang the chorus with him even though he's not, well, a singer. At all. It was odd.

My dad does these sorts of things all the time. When we drove across the country to school here, we went to this cheesy restaurant that serves crab legs in Moline, Illinois, and when the waitresses started doing a line dance to the annoying song "Come On Ride the Train," my dad got on his feet and leapt to the center of the floor and danced with them, even though he didn't know the steps.

I wanted to die. This is not something I could ever do in public. I'd be afraid everyone would laugh at me, and I was sure they'd laugh at him. But by the end of the song, everyone in the restaurant was on their feet for him. And I felt like, what would it take for me to be that comfortable in my body, to express myself like that? Even once? I'm pretty chill, I'm pretty comfortable, but there's a difference between normal comfortable and being forty-something and shaking your backside to a bad hip-hop song in an Illinois restaurant full of strangers.

At the bottom of the page, it read:

B+. See me.

I went to Mr. Scarborough's office during my free period and sat across from him. I threw the essay onto his desk, maybe a little arrogantly.

He picked up the essay, scanned it, grinned once, and put it back down.

"Good start," he said. "You are a bit all over the place, but the voice, it's intriguing."

No one had ever told me that my writing was all over the place. I could feel heat spread across my face and into my ears. Take away my labels, fine. Take away part of my identity, fine. Just leave me the things I know I am, like being a good writer.

"I was trying to be amusing," I mumbled.

He smiled. "I got that. The way you started was a bit generic, with that lame AA joke, but, otherwise, quite amusing."

"At my old school, they loved my sense of humor," I said, crossing and uncrossing my legs.

He took a sip from his orange ceramic coffee mug and leaned back in his chair. "I liked it, Rafe. To me, a B plus is what it deserves. It's clever, but I don't feel this piece ever really comes together the way it would need to for an A piece. You bring up some good questions without really reflecting on them."

He picked up the essay and leafed through it.

"You say here that you would love to be as free as your parents. What do you think is stopping you from being that way?"

"I don't know," I said, my ego still bruised, thinking, *What are you, my shrink?*

"You don't need to know the answer. But I don't think it would hurt for you to be a bit more self-reflective about it. Anyhow, that's actually not why I called you in here."

"Oh," I said, reclining in my chair a bit.

"I hope you'll accept what I'm going to tell you in the manner in which I am offering it to you," he said. "I don't think it takes much reading between the lines to know that perhaps you are . . . well, you're different. I wanted to let you know that you can be that here. Different. For instance — we have a GSA. Did you know that?"

I took a deep breath.

"I'm the faculty adviser, actually. We have several boys this year."

"Oh," I said, taking in those pieces of information.

We stared at each other.

"Wait. I'm different?" I asked.

He nodded, this time with a supportive smile on his face, and I just wanted to wipe it clean off him. Who the hell was he to intrude? What if I was, like, in the closet, deep in the closet, and I didn't want to be out? Wait. Was I in the closet? No, not exactly. But how was that his business? I gripped the handles of the chair.

"What do you mean, 'I'm different'? Where are you getting this from? I've sat in your class for a week. Are you asking me if I'm gay? Because that's kind of inappropriate, don't you think?"

He pursed his lips and looked down at his desk. "Actually, I got that from your mother."

I raised my voice. "What?"

He cleared his throat. "Your mother called the school about a week before classes. She asked to speak to me, as the head of the GSA. She told me about her work with PFLAG, and I have to say, I was excited to have you join us. But . . . you haven't joined us, have you, Rafe?"

"My mother called you?" She was way out of line. Way out.

"She did. Nice woman."

I could feel the veins pulsing in my forehead, the skin pulled tight by the angle of my neck. Why couldn't she mind her own business, even one time? I sighed, dropped my head back, and studied the ceiling.

"This is so extremely typical," I said.

He didn't answer. I stared at the ceiling for maybe a full minute, knowing that at some point, I'd need to say more. Finally, when I was pretty sure I was calm enough that my head wouldn't burst, I raised it again.

"You want to hear a story?" I asked. "You'd be the first to hear it."

"Sure," he said, looking a bit concerned.

So for the first time since I'd come to Natick — the first time ever, really — I explained what I was doing. And you know what? It felt pretty good, having a confidant. Letting my secrets go. Having a secret feels exciting at first, but it seems like it always winds up being more of a weight than anything else.

Mr. Scarborough listened intently, not taking his eyes off mine as I explained what label-free meant to me, and why I'd felt the need to try to start anew.

"Interesting," he said, once I was done.

I blinked expectantly. Wasn't he going to have any advice for me? I wouldn't mind, I realized, some sage words from someone older and wiser and not my parents. Who, I knew, would be less than thrilled if and when they heard the details of my plan. I'd been

66

evasive with them every time we'd spoken, and that wasn't going so well. My folks were not fans of evasive.

He broke into a grin when he saw that I expected him to say something.

"Sorry, Rafe. I don't know what to say other than I'm glad you told me. You're on an interesting ledge, and I'm curious to hear about your explorations. So no GSA for you, I suppose?"

"Nah," I said.

"What about the literary magazine? You're obviously interested and talented."

"Soccer," I said, shaking my head. "Sorry."

He waved off the apology. "Do what you need to do," he said. "And as for your experiment, please feel free to write about it. Okay? In fact, that's what I'd like you to do. Your journal. That's your assignment this semester. Write about why you've done what you've done."

"I wouldn't know where to start," I said.

"Start at the beginning, then," he said. "We have all semester."

I thought about what it would feel like to write everything out. I wasn't sure he was going to like everything I wrote. "Sure," I said.

He smiled again. "I'm reminded of the ancient Chinese proverb — well, in fact, the origin is unclear: May you live in interesting times."

"Thanks, I think," I said.

He tapped his orange coffee mug and stared intently at the handle, lost in deep thought.

"I guess we should be happy that you have the choice today," he said. "Ten years ago? Twenty? I'm pretty sure this situation wouldn't happen. That's something, isn't it?"

"Up to five now!" the kid with the black do-rag yelled. His face was red, his eyes unfocused, and I felt like I might as well be looking in the mirror because I was seriously doused too.

I picked up the shot glass, got myself set so that I didn't fall over onto the kitchen floor, and looked around the room. Everyone was a stranger, and for a moment I wondered where the hell I was. And then I remembered. Saturday after the first week of classes. Shawn Something. A Joey Warren kid, aka a townie. Parents out of town. Whole soccer team there.

And I was leading the way.

It was a tradition. Every Natick School class would find a way to get in with some of the kids from Joey Warren. They didn't exactly love us, but they tolerated us, especially if we'd bring alcohol to their parties, which we always did. Every few years, a new kid inherited the long-standing fake ID business at Natick, so getting booze was never a problem. And I'd been told the girls liked the Natick School boys. A lot. Almost every year, there was some sort of scandal in which a Natick boy got a townie girl pregnant.

It was unlikely to be me.

Steve was my partner for the drinking game we were playing. He'd passed four with flying colors, and now I got to do five with him as the pour man.

They called it Spinner, which sounded like *Spinnah* to my ears. The interesting thing about hanging out with the townies was that I finally heard that Boston accent that everybody jokes about — *Pahk yah cah at Hahvahd Yahd*. The Natick School kids didn't seem to have it. I wondered if it was a class thing.

The rules of Spinnah were simple: teams of two, start with one guy downing one shot. Then you'd be up to two, and the other guy had to drink one, spin, and while he was spinning his teammate poured another shot. The first guy had to pick it up without slowing down from his spin, and he couldn't miss the shot glass or even fumble it a little. Then he'd down the shot in one fluid motion. Any jerkiness and everyone would yell "Bawk!" like it was a baseball game and the guy was a pitcher making an illegal motion. And if you got a balk, your team was out. You also lost if you fell down, which happened with the other team on four. If we made this one, we'd win.

The drink was butterscotch schnapps, which made it easier *at first*, because it tasted like candy. Of course, that didn't help too much once it was in your stomach, rolling and lurching around like a syrupy wave.

I was drunked up.

"Ready, set, go!" screamed a bald kid, and I quickly downed shot number one. It hit the back of my throat like cough syrup. I spun in a counterclockwise circle, reveling in the screaming and shouting around me. They were watching me. They were rooting me on. Me.

I tried to make sure the spin wasn't too fast so Steve had time to pour and make sure the shot glass was in an easy place for me to grab. When my hand hit the counter again, about three-quarters of the way through the turn, I opened my palm and tried to focus my eyes.

The tan liquid in the shot glass was right where I wanted it. Me and Steve, we were a machine. I swiped it up and swigged it down. I felt the liquor burn my esophagus and leak into my sinuses.

"That's two," someone yelled. "I say four and he's on the floor." *Flaw-ah.*

I made a smooth spin, my eyes unfocused until I sensed it was time to swipe up the shot glass again. And there it was, and I swiped it up, and I drank it down, and the clapping was music to my ears.

Four was tougher. My head was spinning right and my feet were spinning left and I had already had four and three shots and that was too much, and my feet forgot how to shuffle, and I slowed down in my turn, and when I was back around to the counter, I saw the shot glass, I reached out for it, but my vision, my perspective were all messed up. It clinked against my hand and spilled over, and I knew I'd lost it. I heard a major coed "Aw!" and for dramatic effect, I collapsed in a heap.

"Rafe rocks!" a voice said, male, I didn't know whose. The room spun and I closed my eyes, savoring the sensation. My stomach was really, really unhappy with me in a sour way, but the rest of me was all blissed out.

I smiled. Then I felt breathing on my face, and a girl with brown hair in a ponytail was kneeling over me. She put her hand on my head and smoothed my hair.

"You okay, cutie?" she whispered, and I looked into her eyes, which were mega-unfocused, and she leaned down and put her mouth on mine.

Stomach, sour. Lips, on mine. I dry heaved. She sensed it moments before it happened, moments before the contents of my stomach began to rumble, and then I was a geyser, Old Faithful, spewing upchuck up and out.

All those shots. Too much. The girl jumped out of the way, and she had this terrified, horrified expression on her face, and then all the guys started screaming with laughter, and I somehow knew that the joke wasn't on me. And while I felt bad for the girl, I figured that was an occupational hazard when you kneel down and try to kiss a drunk guy.

Steve took me to the upstairs bathroom and helped me get cleaned up, all the time replaying how awesome it was that I almost ralphed on this chick who was trying to kiss me.

"Dude, that was awesome. You're all right, Colorado."

I mumbled an affirmative while I leaned down to the faucet and washed the acid taste out of my mouth. My head was pounding a bit, but it still felt great to be part of this group of guys.

"Yo, Benny!" Steve yelled, when we were back out of the bathroom and somehow in an upstairs bedroom. My spinning pupils located Ben, sitting in a rocking chair in the corner. On the other side of the room, a Joey Warren couple was having a gentle conversation, and Ben looked like he was just chilling.

"Benny. Keep an eye on this one," Steve said. "Way, way too much to drink. On the positive side, we won at Spinner. I did four."

"The folks at AA will be so proud," Ben deadpanned. He took a swig of his Diet Coke, and Steve headed back downstairs to drink some more. Personally, I was glad to be taking a break. I sat on the floor against the bed, facing Ben's rocking chair.

"Urinal Guy," he said, and I cracked up. He'd called me that in practice a couple times now.

"Oh, my God, the urinal. That was out of control," I said.

"It was certainly special" was his response. "Having fun?"

"I threw up when a girl kissed me," I said, before I could even attempt to switch into intelligent mode. And then I realized, fuck it. There was no way, with this much alcohol in my system, that I'd be able to seem rational and intelligent.

Ben laughed, though, like it was a totally normal thing to say. "You get her?"

"Missed, thank God," I said.

He laughed again, rocked, and took a slow swig of soda.

"What are you doing up here?" I asked.

He rolled the Diet Coke can against his meaty left leg. "Designated driver. Anyway, I'm more an observer than a partay animal," he said.

I laughed and raised one eyebrow. "I think you're only allowed to say 'partay' if you're, like, wearing a lamp shade on your head."

Ben looked around the room. Then he stood, crossed over to the other side, and took a lamp shade off a floor lamp. He put it on his head, came back to the rocker, and sat back down.

"Partay, partay, partay," he said. "So there."

72

"Yep, you can say it all you want now," I said, closing my eyes and lying down on the floor. "Why did I drink that much?"

"Same reason I even come to these things," he said, taking the lamp shade off and placing it on the floor next to him. "Pure stupidity."

"You're a good guy," I said. "I really like you."

He laughed. "Oh, good. I was afraid this was going to be awkward, like at the urinal."

I thought that was hilarious, for some reason, and I couldn't stop laughing. And I think Ben liked that I thought he was funny, because then he said some other things that were equally funny that I can't even remember because I was sloshed.

"I wish I was more like you," I said softly. I could hear the squeaking of the rocking chair. "You aren't ridiculous."

I could hear him sighing. "You're not ridiculous, Rafe. Just a little . . . I dunno."

"What?" I said, sitting up so quickly that my head spun and I had to drop down to the floor again.

"Drunk," he said, and I laughed.

I pondered what I was a little of for what felt like a couple seconds, but the next thing I heard was: "Rafe? I think you passed out."

"I'm not usually like this," I mumbled, feeling incoherent.

"Should we get you back?"

I felt sick to my stomach. "Yeah," I said.

He helped me to my feet. Ben was strong. Very.

"I just need to check on Bryce before we go, okay?"

"Why?" I said. "What's wrong with him?"

"He gets sort of intense, and alcohol is not a big help," Ben said as we left the bedroom and headed downstairs.

We found Bryce leaning against the fireplace, beer in hand.

"Hey, buddy," Ben said.

"Hey," Bryce answered, listless.

"You remember Rafe."

"I just watched him puke on a girl," Bryce said.

"Yes, I've heard tell nigh on three times in the last twenty minutes," Ben said.

"Nigh on," I repeated. "You crack me up."

Ben ignored me. "You wanna come back?"

"Nah. I'll stay," Bryce said.

Ben hesitated. "You sure?"

"I just don't feel like being in that godforsaken dorm yet."

Ben sighed. "I'll come back to pick you up," he said. "Call when you're ready, okay?"

"Okay," Bryce responded.

I tried to focus on Bryce. He was a nice-looking guy, really smart. The kind of person who probably would be cool to talk to.

"I wanna get to know you," I blurted.

Bryce considered this. "Okay," he said, and I couldn't tell if it was an okay like "Okay, this guy is a moron," or "Okay, this guy is a fraud," or "Okay."

"Okay," I said. "I will look forward to that, Bryce Hixon."

And Ben laughed, and Bryce smiled a little, and I knew I'd struck the right note as the earnest drunk guy.

Ben drove an old Chevy that smelled a little like vinegar inside. We listened to jazz music and watched the Natick night float by as we drove.

"Vomit is verboten in Gretchen," he said.

"Gretchen?"

"I call her Gretchen," he explained, patting the dashboard, and I snorted. "So. No throwing up, okay?"

"I promise," I muttered, as the streets rolled by. "Gretchen."

We were silent, listening to the strange chord progressions of the trumpets and saxophones. I was never a big jazz guy.

"I can't quite figure you out," I finally said.

"Huh," Ben said, after a short silence. "What's to figure out?"

"Where you fit in, in the general, um, scheme of things at Natick?" The car was spinning, and I knew I was saying stuff I wouldn't say sober. It felt good, in a way. Less guarded. "You're quiet like Bryce. And also Robinson is quiet. I guess it's okay to be a jock and just not say anything. Steve and Zack talk all the time and everyone listens to them, but they're not smart like us. Maybe I'll be the quiet type like you and Bryce and Robinson."

"Why do I have to be a type?" he asked.

I shot up in my seat. "Exactly!" I exclaimed, and then I hid my eyes, because the spinning was too much. I could hear Ben laughing.

"You're a mess," he said.

I ignored the comment. "Exactly about the types. I am not a type. I am so tired of being a type."

"I hear you," he said, exhaling. "I guess at first look I'm a jock, right? Except on the inside, I'm about a million things before I'd even get to the fact that I can throw or kick a ball. Like, who in their right mind would ever label themselves because of something so meaningless?"

"Right," I said, working extra hard to stay with him because he was saying interesting things and I was shitfaced.

"In New Hampshire I was labeled a nerd because I got good grades and I liked to read books. No one out there really cared if I was a good athlete. It was like, Ben Carver is a nerd because he talks about ideas. I was born in the wrong place, I guess. And then I come here, and I get labeled something else, and because it's not negative, I buy into it, you know?"

"I know!" I shouted, and then I covered my mouth because I was afraid I was actually going to do the one thing he told me not to do in his female car.

He shot me a warning look.

"I'm good," I said. "I promise."

"My parents had no idea in the world Natick even existed. I did all this. Well, my uncle helped. He was pretty much my saving grace growing up. Unlike my parents, who don't believe in talking about anything, he was a talker. He really taught me how to share my feelings, if that's not too weird to say."

"Not too weird for me," I replied.

He glanced my way again and nodded. "Well, anyway, he understood why I had to get away. My dad's a farmer. If it were up to him, I'd follow in his footsteps. But that's not for me. So I put up with all this upper-class bullshit because you know what? I deserve a chance at a good education and a good life. You know?"

I nodded and nodded and nodded. We had so much in common and I couldn't even tell him. I also had done the footwork to get to Natick. I too had come here to shed a label, and been given another one that didn't fit, and been okay with the mislabeling because at least it wasn't negative. And I wanted so much to tell Ben my story, because he seemed like the kind of person who would be totally okay with it. But I also knew that doing that would change everything. And I didn't want to change everything. So I said nothing. Well, nothing about that, anyway.

"I know. I'm so tired of being a type," I repeated.

"Bryce and I, we always talk about that. He always says that if Natick is a microcosm of this country, we might as well still have separate but equal facilities. And it's not just a black and white thing. Jock. Geek. Stoner. No one is considered just a human being, it seems like."

I couldn't help myself. I turned to Ben and latched a hand on his shoulder. "I want to be just a human being," I said, with great urgency in my voice.

"You're drunk off your skull," Ben said.

"No. Really. That's what I want. I'm always trying on labels, and I want to be entirely label-free."

"Now that's interesting," Ben said. "But is it possible?"

"I am going to find out," I said as we pulled into the parking lot behind East Hall.

"Let me know how it goes," he said, and I felt a pang in my heart, because I didn't want the conversation to end.

"The main thing I need to stop doing is caring who likes me," I said, and I wasn't sure where that thought came from, but in my drunk state, it made a ton of sense. I flashed back to the spinning room and Spinnah, and I knew it was true.

He turned off the ignition. "Ya think?" he asked.

A History of Rafe
Part I

LIKE MOST MAJOR moments in my life, coming out was totally random. Spring of eighth grade. I was up in my room on a school night, thinking about Garth. Garth was this kid who also ran cross-country at the time. He's since moved to California. We weren't really close friends, but he was pretty chill, and we'd say hi, that sort of thing. But I totally liked Garth. And I was okay with that. I'd been thinking about Garth for weeks, and before that, Mason. And before that, Corey Westerly, who was the first guy in our class to lose his virginity, back in sixth grade. So it wasn't like I was sitting up there and I had this epiphany: *Wow! I'm gay!* I had known that for a long time. I guess if there was an epiphany, it was like, *I've got a feeling, and no one else knows about it. Maybe I should tell Mom and Dad.*

So that was it. No major breakdown, no thoughts about whether I'd be homeless. More like, I could *enjoy* chocolate ice cream, but I prefer strawberry. I should tell the folks so they stop buying chocolate. I walked down the stairs, not scared, exactly, but surprised. Because I didn't wake up that day and think: *Today I'm going to tell Mom and Dad I'm gay.*

I simply walked into the kitchen and told them.

There weren't any huge emotions on either side. Just a nice sit-down discussion. Mom, Dad? I want you to know I'm gay. Oh, sweetie, that's wonderful! We're so glad you told us!

I wasn't surprised that they weren't surprised. But I did want to know how they knew.

"Oh, sweetie," my mother said. "You're our son. We know who you are."

We hugged, and my dad cried a little. I don't have a macho-type dad, who hunts and fishes and collects guns. He's sensitive and caring. He drives me crazy most of the time, but I do admire that he's not afraid to show his "feminine side."

But for me, that's when the trouble started. I figured I'd come out to my parents, get my first boyfriend, and then just live my life. No. Instead, it was like this thing had happened, and now we all had to mobilize. (I should have known. My mom is a mobilizer.) Suddenly there were six books I had to read about what it's like to be gay. I said to her, "Mom, can't I just be gay, and not read about it?" But she explained — and Dad backed her up — that we need to know history. Those who don't study history are doomed to repeat it, blah blah blah.

Do you know how you get the urge to clean your room, and it's no big deal? But when your mom tells you that you have to clean your room, you don't want to? That's me, anyway. So maybe if I had found all this stuff on my own, I would have really enjoyed learning about it. But instead, I got a pile of books from Mom, and now it was like I had gay homework from my mother. I was like, *Thanks for making this exciting new thing a chore, Mom. Awesome.*

So I read this book about the gay rights movement. And it was interesting, I have to admit. I didn't know that being gay was this epic struggle, and that it came with all these "responsibilities." My best friend, Claire Olivia, came over and read some of the books with me, or more like, we went through the books and read random parts to each other. One was about sex, and I was like, *Please tell me my mom didn't just give me a book teaching me how to give a blow job.* But of course she did. Claire Olivia thought that was excellent. She was like, "This is so great, Shay Shay! Maybe one day you can send her pictures!"

The next weekend, Mom and Dad were being extremely weird about going out to dinner. They wanted to go down to Denver. We almost never do that, but they wouldn't let it go, so I just got in the car with them and off we went. We parked in front of this place called Hamburger Mary's. We went in, and first of all there was this life-size cutout of a busty waitress at the entrance, winking and blowing us a kiss. Her picture was on all the walls and on the menu. It was way gay in terms of clientele, which was cool, but also there were Grandma Chloe and the rest of my extended family, and Claire Olivia, and her parents, and they were all wearing tacky cone-shaped birthday hats. On the hats it said: *Yay! Rafe Is Gay!*

It was APPALLING. I would have slid right under the table if I could have done it without Mom saying something like, "Oh, is that what gay kids do nowadays?" or something equally humiliating.

"You're trying to kill me," I said to her, and Mom's face was so shocked that I started to laugh, because throwing someone a party is generally not synonymous with killing them. And I WAS laughing, but inside I was pissed because it's like nothing is ever enough with my parents. Just one time, I'd like them to let something go, and not throw a big, outrageous party, or sing, or dance, or whatever weird thing they're feeling. After a few minutes I loosened up a little. I even let them sing me "Happy Birthday" along with the waitstaff, even though it was pretty clear from the hats that this was no birthday party.

There are definitely fun moments having parents whom you can't possibly shock. But it's a mixed bag. On the major plus side, I never for one moment felt like my parents were embarrassed about me or grossed out by me or disappointed in me. So who cares if Mom is more ready for me to have a sex life than I am? These are pretty minor concerns, considering.

Rafe,

So much interesting stuff in here! Yet as well-written as this is, I want to ask you about your process as a writer. Remember the E. L. Doctorow quote. Did you go into this piece knowing where you wanted to go, or open to uncovering new questions? Also, what do you mean when you write "nothing is ever enough with my parents"? Would you really have preferred them to not mark the occasion of your coming out? I'm just asking for you to think about it. Good job.

— Mr. Scarborough

"Up for some scanner pong?" Toby asked when I got back to the dorm and placed my knapsack on the bed.

It was a Friday afternoon, the end of my third week, and I was used to weirdness in my room by now. Toby was always there, at least when he wasn't missing in action. In the past week, there had been several periods when he disappeared completely. Albie referred to these as alien abductions. It was pretty clear there was a guy in Toby's life, but he wouldn't share the details.

On the positive side, our room was cleaner now. Albie was trying. A couple times I'd come back to find that he had actually swept. Miracle.

"Say again?" I asked.

Toby repeated, "Scanner pong. It's a drinking game."

I watched as Toby pulled an open can of Budweiser out from under the desk.

"Cool," I said. "How do you play?"

Albie bent down and pulled his own beer from under the bed, and then turned the scanner up. "You playing?"

"Why not."

Albie leaned under his bed again and pulled out a third beer. He contemplated throwing it to me, and then opted to walk it over. It was warm; I didn't care. I opened it and was about to take a sip when he gave me a startled look.

"No!" he said. "You have to pick your word!"

He explained the game. In scanner pong, you hang out and listen to the scanner, and anytime your chosen word is said, you drink.

"So where does Ping-Pong come in?" I asked.

"Ping-Pong?" Toby said.

"As in *pong*?"

"Don't be absurd," he said. "It's a drinking game. Hence the *pong*."

I didn't have the energy to explain to him the derivation of the phrase *beer pong*. Instead, I said, "So what's my word?"

"I pick! I pick!" yelled Toby. "Um . . . *suspect*!"

"Good call," Albie said. "I'm *Caucasian*."

"I'm *suspicious*," Toby said.

"I think you're both suspicious Caucasians," I said.

Toby snorted. "You funny fella," he said in a weird, fake Chinese accent.

Since the channel we were on seemed to be coming from a low-crime area, there was a ton of sitting around in scanner pong. Which gave us a chance to talk, a lot. Toby finally talked about the mystery guy he was dating, and how annoying it was that they couldn't be open about it, and Albie went on and on about some kid in his math class who dared to question a solution Albie had come up with in class on the board. The teacher had accepted it, and then, out of nowhere, this Joseph kid is all "Mr. Braddock! That's wrong. The *dy* and *dx* are switched up. Look." And the kid got up and corrected Albie, and in the end it turned out Albie was wrong. And then the teacher used Albie's carelessness as a lesson to the class, even though he'd been careless himself.

I realized there was a lot of talking in this game, not a lot of drinking. I mentioned that.

"Yeah, we've both had one sip so far," said Toby.

I busted out laughing. "What kind of drinking game is this if you're not drinking?"

Albie shrugged. "Sometimes it's better. I won last time."

"What word did Toby give you?"

"*Murder.*"

"What was Toby's?"

"*Natick.*"

"Nice," I said.

I finally got them to just drink, and we each had a sip of warm beer. That's when the voice over the radio came through, after a lengthy silence.

"We have a naked Caucasian woman wandering around Bacon Street," the female voice said. In response, two or three officers shouted, "I'll take this one!" Then there was a lot of laughter while they decided whom to dispatch.

Albie's eyes lit up. "Mmm, bacon. Are you thinking what I'm thinking?" he said, looking at me.

"That you need to drink? They said *Caucasian,*" Toby said.

"Shut up. We're going to find her. Let's do this!"

"At least one of us will get a thrill," I said, and then I realized what I'd said and that it was too late to go back. Luckily neither Albie nor Toby were good listeners, because neither of them even reacted like they'd heard it, and I followed up with "I'm game."

We hid our mostly full beers beneath the beds and headed out the door.

"We need aliases," Toby said as we descended the stairs. "I'll be Detective Pollard, the spiky-haired detective with the hidden identity not yet discovered."

"I'll be Justin Auerbach, lover of wandering naked ladies," said Albie.

"Can I just be Detective Goldberg?" I said.

"Boring," Toby yelled from half a flight below me.

"What? All Albie did was change his name. He *is* a lover of wandering naked ladies."

"So change your name," yelled Toby.

"Fine," I said, putting on an accent that started out Indian and then, as I went on, somehow turned British. "Warren. Warren Wilson, visiting from London."

"Perfection," Toby said.

At that moment, I saw Ben starting up the stairs. I froze, afraid I'd just broken the dork meter. But then I remembered our conversation in his car, and I was glad that he saw me being something other than serious and bland. When he passed he smiled at me, and I smiled back. And by the time I'd done that, he was already behind me, and I couldn't see his reaction.

Albie drove a light blue '93 Toyota Celica that he had nicknamed Sleepy because of its tendency to not want to start up in winter. I hopped in back, Toby took shotgun, and off we sped to Bacon Street.

On Main Street, Albie turned on his right turn blinker, and we yielded to oncoming traffic on Central.

"Okay, now what do we say when we're about to merge?" Albie asked.

Then Albie hit the gas, and the two of them screamed: "MERGE!"

And once we were merged, nothing more was said about it.

"We have rules," Toby explained. "For instance, if Albie drives through a yellow light, you have to kiss the ceiling." He put his fingers to his lips, kissed them, then touched the ceiling.

"I wonder what you'd do if he went through a red light. Would you have to fuck the ceiling?" I asked.

Both Albie and Toby laughed. "Yes," Toby said. "Yes, you would."

As it turned out, Bacon Street in Natick is fairly long. We turned left onto Bacon from Marion, and by the time we were at Park Avenue several blocks later, we still saw no sign of a naked lady. Toby was looking left, I looked right, and we had to keep telling Albie to keep his eyes on the road, because the car veered several times as he looked for Wandering Naked Lady.

As we passed Tyler Street, Toby yelled, "There she is!" Albie slammed on the brakes, I turned to my right, and there, sure as shit, was a woman, sans clothing, running down the street. She was not young. She was, in fact, older than my grandmother, with gray hair and pasty, white skin. Albie pulled the car up so that we were right in front of her, and then slowed down.

"Perv!" I yelled. "She's, like, ancient."

"We should help her," Toby said, and before either me or Albie answered, he was rolling down the window. "Excuse me, ma'am, can we help you? Are you okay?"

The woman looked at the car, an expression of panic across her face.

"Stop harassing me, Buzz!" she yelled, and then she put up her middle finger at Toby.

Toby tried to explain. "No, ma'am, I'm not Buzz. We're here to help. Are you lost?"

The woman knelt down and scooped up some red, brown, and orange leaves piled along the sidewalk. "Stop it, you!" she yelled, throwing the leaves at us. They barely traveled two feet before fluttering to the ground.

"We should just go," I said.

"Wait," Toby said. "She needs help."

"Not from us she doesn't," I said.

Albie hadn't moved the car, and I noticed I was easing up on a pretend brake pedal at my feet. If I could have made the car go myself, I would have.

"Can we drive you somewhere?" Toby asked.

That's when the woman charged at our car, screaming at us. "Traitors!" she yelled. "You're all traitors. Buzz sent you!"

That's when Albie realized he probably ought to drive. He started to pull away, and the woman started smacking the back window. Her face was creased like a witch's, and she looked directly in my eyes. I couldn't help it. I screamed.

"Traitors!" she yelled. "Evil traitors!"

Albie peeled off, and we sped down Bacon Street, away from the crazy woman.

We drove in shocked silence for a few minutes, and then Albie glanced back at me.

"You scream like a girl."

"I know," I said back. "It was totally innate. She looked like a Disney witch."

"I like that," Albie said. "You're a jock who screams like a girl."

Yes, it was a stereotype. But it was also true. One time last year, I ran over to Claire Olivia's house early one morning to tell her what had happened. Basically, this cheerleader girl from school I barely knew had chatted me up on Facebook. We talked about normal things for a while, and then she was like, "If you let me, I could switch you."

I was like, "Switch me?"

She said, "Yeah. It's cool you're gay. But I could make you bi."

It was way awkward and I said my own version of *thanks but no thanks*. But then I went to sleep and had an honest-to-God sex dream about the girl. And it kind of worked for me. Or at least it wasn't frightening. So I was running over to tell Claire Olivia that maybe I was bi.

Her parents let me go upstairs, which was pretty normal since I slept over a lot. I knocked gently and opened the door, and Claire Olivia was sleeping on her back. When she saw me, she sat up, and the sheet dropped, and there were her tits, staring at me.

So I screamed like a girl.

Claire Olivia covered herself up, and we had a good laugh.

"So what was so important that you had to barge in and wake me up?" she asked.

"Never mind," I said. "It's over."

But I definitely couldn't tell Albie and Toby that story.

"She reminded me of my grandmother," Toby said wistfully.

"Your grandmother was a crazy naked lady?" I asked.

"Well, yeah," he said.

And for some reason, that struck all of us as pretty hilarious.

A History of Rafe
Part II

FOR ME, the whole coming-out thing was about finding a boy-friend. I mean, why else would you come out? Because it's so much fun to be oppressed? No, you come out because you want to find love. But it didn't really work that way for me. Even in a place like Boulder, finding a boyfriend just wasn't that easy. It was like, where do you look?

The only other kids at my school who identified as gay were more friend material than dating material. I liked guys who were laid-back and chill, and my choices were You-Know-Caleb, who was the opposite of chill, and a guy named Marshall who was a year above me. He was okay, but not really my type. I tried this online chat site for gay youth, but I got bored with it pretty fast. Typing isn't exactly my idea of a fun way to spend a Saturday afternoon, thanks very much.

Meanwhile, my mom had a totally different idea of what coming out was all about. Maybe a month after the coming-out party that my father had dubbed my "cotillion," my mother urged me back into the car for another surprise trip. It was a Thursday night and I had a biology test the next day, but my mother told me this was "more important."

She drove the Prius down Thirteenth Street toward Pearl, and she turned on Spruce. I said, "Please tell me you're not taking me to your Shambhala Meditation Center place again." One time the previous summer, she got it in her head that I needed more serenity. Serenity is apparently like a great, big fabulous party, except without food or people or talking or fun. She was not amused when I told her afterward that if she'd wanted me to shut up, she could have just stopped by my room and told me to shut up.

"Better," she said as she parked in front of a church. She explained that we were going to this group she'd been attending for the past few weeks: a PFLAG meeting.

PFLAG is short for Parents, Families and Friends of Lesbians and Gays, and it's long for a place to spend a few quality hours talking about what your gay son or daughter likes to eat for breakfast. There was only one other kid there, and he was wearing a polka-dot tie. Also not my type. We passed a feather around a circle, and when it was in your hand, you had to say something about yourself. "It's a good time to locate yourself," the leader, a woman with Sideshow Bob hair named Martha, had said.

God, did I try to locate Rafe. Everyone was so earnest and cheerful, and I didn't want to be the jerk, so when the feather came to me, I said, "I thought we were going for ice cream, but other than the fact that I don't have any candy-cane ice cream with white chocolate bits mixed in, this is kinda cool." People laughed. When I added, "I love my gay son," people didn't laugh, and my mother shot me a look that said either, "I will kill you when we get home" or "Comedy is not really for you, is it?" I'm not sure which.

She kept going, I didn't, and about four months later, around fall of my freshman year, my mom came home one night and told me and my dad that she had fabulous news.

"I've just become president!" she shrieked.

It needs to be said that sometimes my mom forgets important details when she talks. Like the time she told us she was considering leather (couches, it turns out), or when I was little and she said, "Here's a napkin to put your balls in" (the Atomic Fireballs that I was eating, she meant).

So my dad and I waited a bit, and finally she added, "Of PFLAG!"

I congratulated her, but inside I knew this was maybe not the best news. I hadn't loved the one meeting, and did this mean I would have to go back now?

It meant worse. Suddenly, every dinner conversation centered around oppression. I don't think I'm a really insensitive kid. I cried when I saw that old movie *The Color Purple* when Oprah Winfrey was hauled off to jail, and when I saw *Milk* and Sean Penn got shot because he was gay, I sobbed. So you can't say I'm not down with the oppressed. But every dinner conversation? Homophobia, heterosexism, genderqueer? Really?

It was sort of like Mom was the gay one now. Me, I was basically the same kid I'd been the year before. Still a virgin. Still not dating. Still texting with Claire Olivia until one in the morning almost always.

Was I missing something? Was there, like, a welcome packet

that arrived once you'd come out, and had my mom taken it for herself when it came in the mail?

She asked if I wanted to come out publicly when I started high school. I figured, well yeah. I mean, how was I going to get a boyfriend if I didn't come out?

I'm not totally stupid. I know that this is supposed to be super-traumatic stuff. But growing up in Boulder is like growing up in a bubble. I kinda always knew it would be okay.

And it was. Mom set up a meeting with the school principal and the head guidance counselor, Rosalie. The four of us sat in a room, and I felt like a freak sitting there, with the principal overcompensating by making sure he looked directly at me every time he said something, and this Rosalie lady, who was way too excited about the fact I liked boys, grinning at me like I was her favorite pet.

They told me about the GSA, and also that they had strict policies in place to deal with homophobia and bullying. And those things didn't happen to me. I came out by telling some people, who told other people, and there we were, a school with gays and straights, and no one died in the process.

Rafe,

It sounds like you thought coming out was a small thing, but your mom and the rest of the world treated it like it was huge. Why do you think she reacted like that? We'll read an excerpt from Edmund White's autobiographical novel A Boy's Own Story in class later this semester, and I'd love to hear your further thoughts about oppression and being out after that.

—— Mr. Scarborough

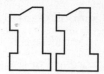

The annual Fall Classic was a Natick School tradition, pitting the juniors against the seniors in a softball game on the final Saturday afternoon of September. Bragging rights were a big deal at Natick. Last year the juniors got them when they beat the seniors. The stakes were high, and I'd been hearing about it all week. On Friday afternoon, Steve stopped by my room while Albie and I were studying.

"Hey, Rafe, how'd you do on the calc test?" Steve asked, totally ignoring Albie.

"A minus," I said. "I hate calculus."

"You and me both," he said. "You can join our study group if you want. Zack is acing calc. Throw some differential equations in there, and he's this genius. Otherwise he's a dumbass."

"You gotta be honest," I said, and Steve smirked.

"Exactly. Hey, we got an extra ticket to see B.o.B in Boston. You wanna go?"

"Uh, sure!"

He smiled that amazing, perfect smile of his, and I felt my

insides turn to jelly. It wasn't so much that I was in love with him; I was just in love with being included. Being chosen.

"So you gonna be out there with us? Tomorrow?"

"Uh, yeah, sure," I said again, afraid to mention that I hadn't actually touched a softball since I was maybe eight and playing T-ball at school. And even then it was something I had to do until people saw how much I sucked at it and said, "You know, you might really enjoy soccer."

"You got a glove?"

"Yeah, somewhere" was my muffled reply. *In the garage back in Boulder,* I left out.

"Well, we'll find you one. Righty?" Steve asked.

"Lefty."

"We'll head over around two. See you then?"

"Awesome."

"Awesome," he said, smiling.

Once he left, Albie said, "Thanks for asking, Steve! It's been a fine start to the semester. Why, yes, this is a new black T-shirt, how astute of you to notice!"

I shrugged, feeling bad for him, and wondering how this was going to continue to work, being a popular jock who also enjoyed hanging out with the misfit guys.

Saturday was sunny, and the junior team — which was basically all the soccer guys — walked across the quad toward the field. We were bonding pretty well as a soccer team. We had four wins and a tie in our first five games, and it seemed pretty important to everyone that we win at softball too. All week, I'd been hearing strategy talk that I barely understood — we'll play our fourth outfielder in short center, let's use Kenny as our extra hitter to get his bat in the lineup — and now that we were on our way to the game, it escalated.

"Bryce at first, Zack at second, Morris at short," Steve said. "Benny at third, Joey behind the plate. I'm on the mound. For the outfield, Rafe, you play outfield? You're fast."

"Yeah," I said. "Right field."

"Okay. Rodriguez in center, Robinson in left. And Standish as a fourth. Kenny's the extra hitter."

A fattish kid I'd seen mostly on the bench at soccer practice nodded. I could see that in the grand pecking order of things, he was just happy to be along for the ride.

We strutted across the quad, feeling like rulers of the campus. Underclassmen either meekly said hey as we passed them, or averted their eyes.

"You want to warm up?" said Robinson when we got to the field.

I'd barely spoken to him, even though we hung out in the same circle and his locker was right next to mine. He had a mole on his cheek that I always tried not to look at and the hairiest butt I'd ever seen. The guys called him Gorilla Butt in the showers. He didn't seem to really mind.

"Okay," I said, practicing snapping the glove Steve had lent me. It felt old and raggedy, and I wondered how I'd be able to catch the ball with it if it came to me. Robinson walked onto the grass and jogged backward about ten feet. Then he tossed the ball at my head.

I raised the glove and opened it, deeply concentrating while trying to look nonchalant, and the softball lodged in the pocket.

Robinson grinned. His front teeth were exceptionally large. "Next time, try it without the kick."

"What kick?" I threw the ball back at him.

"When you caught the ball, you kicked up with your right knee. You were protecting yourself. The ball won't hurt you." He had a really deep voice, very manly. He seemed older in a way.

I didn't realize I had been doing that. So when he threw again, I tried real hard to stay still. Then, at the last moment, I realized I hadn't raised my glove. I barely got it up in time to deflect it away from my mouth.

He laughed again, that mole shaking as his mouth moved. "I mean, it won't hurt you as long as you catch it in the glove."

I had to laugh. I mean, I'm not an idiot, but this throwing and catching thing was like a muscle I hadn't used before. I ran over, picked up the ball, which had landed about ten feet away, and threw it back to him, sidearm. It felt good.

"You've got a good arm," Robinson said. "I guess you haven't played much softball, huh?"

"We were more into, like, skiing," I said.

"Cool."

As we warmed up, I saw Ben and Bryce deep in conversation. I almost went over to say hey but decided not to because they looked serious. When Steve called us all in to announce the lineup, Ben cuffed Bryce on the shoulder. Bryce's face looked pained. I thought back to how he seemed at the party, and I wondered what could make a kid look that upset at a softball game.

We were up first as the away team. Right before we sent our first hitter up, Bryce called everyone over. As he spoke to us, he looked down at the dirt.

"I'm having a hard day," he said, almost a mumble. "Just take it easy on me, okay?"

The guys all looked at one another, as if needing a cue on how to react. I felt like nodding and saying, *Sure, of course*, but I didn't want to stand out. I looked over at Ben, and it seemed to me that he probably could have said something supportive. But I guess I wasn't the only one afraid of standing out.

"Oh-kay . . ." Steve said, as if Bryce were a crazy person. "Sure thing, buddy." And it amazed me, how the words were all Natick positive, like *all for one, and one for all*, which was the kind of team-first mentality I was so used to hearing from the guys. But his tone was a lot of things, and none of them was positive at all.

Bryce kicked the ground in the same way I would have if someone had said something that hurt my feelings. And then Zack went up to the plate, and it was like none of that conversation ever happened.

My turn to bat came up in the first inning. The guys were all pretty good, hitting the ball into the outfield every time. As I stood on the dirt circle where I could take warm-up swings, I thought back to probably the last time that I had swung a bat . . . again, third-grade T-ball? Joey, our catcher, was batting before me. He stayed back on his right leg, watched the arc of the ball, and then swung hard, shifting his weight with a big step forward. I was a lefty, so I figured I would just reverse everything. Joey made an out by hitting a high ball to the first baseman, and I came forward.

"Hey, you need to get in the box," said the senior team's catcher.

My face flushed. "I know," I said, looking down in front of me. There was a crudely drawn rectangle in the dirt surrounding home plate. I stepped into the box and extended the bat to make sure it would reach over the plate. It would.

Then the kid on the mound lofted an underarm pitch. As it started to come down, I thought about swinging, but I would have had to swing up over my head, which didn't feel right. It landed in the catcher's glove, right about waist high.

"Ball one!" the umpire shouted.

"Cool," I mumbled.

Then the guy threw one that was a little lower. I was about to swing, but then I didn't.

"Strike one!"

The third pitch came in a lot like the second one, and I just put all my weight into it, stepping forward and taking a huge swing.

Contact! The ball jumped off my bat and went toward the third baseman. I watched for a second, saw the third baseman put his glove down because it was a low shot, and then remembered I was supposed to run. I sprinted as fast as I could. I focused on first base, figuring the ball would probably get there before I did, and I'd be out.

It didn't. I crossed the bag and looked back over at third. The guy was holding his shin and writhing around on the ground.

"Nice shot," said the first baseman. "I think you killed our third baseman."

"I did?" I said, flushing with pride from the fact that I had actually gotten a hit.

I ran around the bases when the guy after me, Kenny the extra hitter, hit a long fly ball past the right fielder. When I crossed home plate, the guys slapped my butt, and one cuffed me on the shoulder.

"Not bad for someone who obviously has never played softball before," Steve said.

I reddened. "That obvious, huh?"

"Oh, yeah," he said. "How are you with the glove?"

I pointed to Robinson, who I'd warmed up with. He was standing nearby.

"He's brutal, Steve," he said. "Seriously bad."

"We'll switch it up, then," Steve said. "Kenny. Take right field, okay? We'll use Rafe as the extra hitter."

I nodded, sure that meant something to someone. I figured they'd tell me where to stand, and I'd stand there. And, anyway, I was having a blast.

It turns out that the extra hitter gets to sit on the bench while the rest of the team is on the field. Kenny, whose belly made him look like a pregnant lady, shot me a dirty look as he waddled to the outfield.

"You better study up, Colorado," he yelled back. "We need your speed out there."

In the third inning, with us leading 5–4, I got another chance at the plate. This time, I was a bit jacked up. I swung as hard as I could, and the ball went really, really high. Just not far. The pitcher barely moved and caught my ball easily.

I jogged back to the bench, a little red in the face because I'd just made an out. I sat down next to Ben and fished out my water bottle.

"Where are Albie and Toby?" he asked. "How come they're not watching the game?"

I laughed, but he didn't. I just figured he was kidding, since the likelihood of those guys hanging with the jocks was about the same as Kenny being a swimsuit model.

"You guys looked like you were having fun the other day," Ben said as I took a swig of water.

"Well, we were," I said, swishing the water around my mouth. "I know they're weird, but they're good to hang with."

"Cool," he said, surprising me.

"Yeah," I said. "I guess."

Ben poured some sunflower seeds into his palm and threw them into his mouth. "What were you doing, anyway?"

"Oh, we went to see a crazy naked lady running down Bacon Street."

"Ah," he said, his eyes narrowing. I could tell he was trying to gauge whether I was messing with him, whether this was my sense of humor.

"That's actually a true story," I said. "Hard to explain. Involved a police scanner and drinking."

"Of course," he said, and we both laughed.

We watched as Steve stepped up to the plate and took a few practice swings.

"So Toby?"

"Toby what?"

"Wanted to go see a naked . . . lady?"

"Peer pressure," I said, and we both laughed again.

"So what do you think of them?" I asked. I wiped the bottle across my forehead; even on a day in the seventies, it was humid here.

"Different," he said. "Albie's real smart. Toby is gay. You know that, right?"

"He told me," I said. "Not a big issue."

Ben nodded. "It used to be pretty bad for him," he said. "The guys could be really mean. I mean, not me and Bryce. But some of them were. And then, last year, this gay guy came and spoke on Diversity Day. He used to play college football. That really changed things. All of a sudden, the whole soccer team starts talking about homophobia like it was this issue that had always concerned them, you know? And Steve started making a point of sitting with Toby at lunch a couple times a week. He would always say hi to him and make sure no one was bothering him. And no one has."

"That's cool," I said, finding it hard to swallow. "But they totally ignore him now. And sometimes they say shit behind his back."

We watched as Bryce swung the bat and hit a high pop-up to third for an out.

"Well, yeah. But not gay stuff. That was this huge topic at dinner one night last year. Could you make fun of someone who is gay for something other than being gay? We decided that yes, yes, you could."

I laughed. "You're kidding, right?"

"Sadly I'm not," Ben said as Zack got a hit to center field. "But the upshot is, no one rides Toby about the gay thing, so that's good."

"That is good," I said. But I was thinking, *Wouldn't it be nice if we lived in a world where no one thought being gay was even something to ride someone about?*

"And Toby lucked out. The head of student life got this idea that perhaps an openly gay kid should have his own dorm room, a single. So he got one."

"Ah. Why he's not roommates with Albie now makes sense," I said. "Well, all's well that ends well."

"Ben, you're on double deck," Steve yelled.

Ben stood and grabbed a bat. I stood too, and walked with him.

"Yeah. Of course, there's plenty of other stuff about Toby. I mean, he's not the most sensible person of all time," Ben said.

I was going to let it go, but I decided if open conversation was the thing at Natick, why not go for it? "Isn't that homophobic? Like a gay stereotype? Like all gays are flighty?"

"No, it's a fact. It has nothing to do with him being gay."

"Okay, it just sounded like it could be homophobic, like the one gay kid is not very sensible," I said, crossing my arms.

"One guy in the on-deck circle, Colorado," Steve yelled. "C'mon!"

I moved back but not before Ben leaned in toward me. "Last year, the fire alarm went off in the middle of the night. It was January and freezing out, and everyone bundled up and went outside while they checked things out. And out comes Toby in a pair of shorts and a T-shirt, with an honest-to-God bow and arrow. Everyone's staring at him, and he's saying: 'There are probably wolves out here. I'm not going outside in the pitch black without some sort of protection.' The idiot nearly got frostbite, and Mr. Donnelly had to break the drill and go in and get him pants and a jacket."

I tried to think of some comeback. I had nothing. Ben saw it and smiled this great, goofy smile, with his two uneven front teeth sticking out just slightly under his top lip.

"Okay. Not so sensible," I said, allowing myself to smile back.

I grounded out in the fifth inning, and then, in the seventh, I came up with us leading by one run with two runners on base. My heart was pounding in my ears, and as I approached the plate, I kept saying to myself, *Don't screw up. Don't screw up.*

"Let's see it, kid," Steve yelled, and I could hear the team clapping for me.

I took a deep breath, stepped into the batter's box, and raised the bat.

The first pitch was perfect, right over the plate, and I concentrated as hard as I could to swing level so it wouldn't be a high pop-up like the last one. The contact felt good, clean, sweet, and the ball jumped off my bat in a way it hadn't before. I swung all the way through and then started running as the ball screamed past the pitcher's glove.

It went into center field, hitting the grass just in front of the outfielder, who dove for it. He scooped it up on a short hop and threw as hard as he could to home plate. The throw was too late, though; I was on first, Ben was on third, and Standish was across home plate, giving us a 9–7 lead.

I could feel the applause in my bones, my joints, this reverberation of sound and celebration. I smiled as wide as I could remember smiling. Steve yelled, "Outstanding, Colorado. Outstanding."

When our half of the inning was over, I sat on the bench, watching the final at bat by the senior team. They got a runner to first, then someone grounded out and the next guy popped out, and suddenly we were one out away from winning, with a runner on second.

The guy who stepped up to the plate, I remembered, was not that good. He had struck out one time, and another time he hit a weak ball to third base. We were going to win and I was going to be part of the celebration, and this alternate universe I had chosen just couldn't have been more surprising, or better.

Steve lobbed the ball over home plate. The guy looked up at the ball as it hit its apex, and then he started his swing.

He hit a soft grounder, this one to Steve, on the pitcher's mound. Steve caught the ball in his glove, turned, and tossed underhand to Bryce, who was waiting at first base with his glove outstretched.

It was like tunnel vision then, because I saw it happening.

It seemed like the ball hung in the air for minutes. I saw the concentration and the despair in Bryce's face as if he were right next to me, not across the diamond. Almost like I could taste the sweat dripping from his forehead.

The ball hit the pocket of his glove, and Bryce moved his glove slightly, like he was trying to close it. But his muscles must have miscued, and he pulled his arm back instead of closing his hand into a fist. The ball jumped out to the edge of his glove, and I watched his face fall as he couldn't seem to figure out how to make this simple play happen.

The ball fell to the ground, the runner crossed first base, and the other team's bench exploded in cheers because they still had life.

I watched Steve walk over to first, staring at Bryce. I couldn't see his expression, since he was facing the other way, but Bryce bowed his head, and Steve knelt down and swiped the ball up like he was a teacher snatching an exam off the desk of a cheating student. He walked back to the mound, muttering to himself. The rest of our infield was yelling at Bryce, and it was the first time I'd seen a crack in the unity façade since getting to Natick.

Only Ben wasn't screaming. He just stood at third base, his arms crossed, his head down.

The next batter hit a double, scoring a run to make it 9–8, us. The batter after that hit a towering fly ball to right. Kenny had no chance to catch it as it sailed over his head. Two runs scored on the home run, and the seniors won the game, 10–9.

It was quiet on the bench as we packed up our things. The deflation was palpable, like tar had settled over all of us, and we were trudging under its weight.

"All you had to do was close your glove," Rodriguez said finally. "Just close it. We win. What's wrong with you? You can't close your glove? You need a new hand or something?"

"Now all year we get to hear them jaw it out," Steve said. "It's on you, Bryce. We didn't lose. You lost."

It occurred to me that there were two labels that mattered more than almost any other at Natick: winner and loser. Why did they care so much? And why didn't I?

I watched Bryce, who didn't look only pained; he looked devastated, like someone would look if you told them their parents were killed in a car crash.

"Leave him alone," Ben said, his voice quavering. "It's just a softball game."

Bryce walked off then, trudging off with his bat bag slung over his shoulder and his head bowed so heavily, it looked like you'd need a crane to lift it. Ben followed him, and I felt torn, wanting to go with them, but afraid that if I did, I'd lose my standing with Steve. So I continued packing up my stuff and walked back to the dorm silently with my teammates, who seemed to be lost in the fog of a celebration that never quite happened.

Later that night after dinner, while Albie and Toby were playing scanner pong and I was reading about the building of suburbs in 1950s America for my Monday morning history class, a chirp from the scanner piqued my interest.

"Can you repeat?" said a male voice.

A female voice said: "Disoriented black male, outside Natick School. Can we get a car out to check on the situation? Over."

"I'm on it," said a male voice, and then static.

"Awesome sauce!" Toby yelled, and he jumped to his feet, spilling his Red Bull on the carpet as he jumped. Albie grabbed him by the shirt.

"Slow down, Detective Pollard," Albie said. "It's late. I don't want to miss curfew. Plus, this one sounds dicey."

Toby put his hands on his hips. "Racist! Besides, I don't know who this Detective Pollard you speak of is," he said. "I am Ryan Giles, famous crime reporter . . . with a mustache." And then he reached into his pants pocket and pulled out a fake mustache, which he stuck on his upper lip.

"You have a fake mustache in your pocket?" I asked.

He nodded, like this was a normal thing to have. Albie didn't say anything, so I figured he might have one too. Yeah.

"We're not going," Albie said. "Now sit down and drink your Bull."

Toby sat, sulking, his arms crossed tight across his chest, like a little boy denied cotton candy at the fair.

"It's probably some Joey Warren kid. Maybe he swam across Dug Pond. He thought he'd swum back and forth and was back at Joey, and now he's disoriented because the campus looks all different," Albie said.

"He's a spy," Toby said. "His disguise is . . . well, he's disoriented as a disguise."

"Yeah," Albie said. "I'm sure he disguised himself as black, seeing as there are SO many black people at Natick School. This way he wouldn't stand out."

I was only half paying attention to the Albie-Toby circus. My mind was buzzing. What if it was Bryce? He looked pretty down at the softball game; it didn't take a genius to put two and two together. I excused myself and hurried over to Ben and Bryce's room. I knocked on the door.

"Oh, hey," Ben said. He was wearing a red flannel bathrobe, sweatpants, slippers, and black horn-rimmed glasses. If he wasn't obviously seventeen and built like a truck, he could have been a middle-aged English professor.

"Hey." I fidgeted my fingers and couldn't look him in the eye. "Is, um, Bryce here, by any chance?"

"No," he said. "I'm actually a little worried about that." I could see creases around his eyes.

I said, "You know how we have that police scanner? I just heard something about a disoriented black male or something outside Natick School." I wondered if it sounded racist, equating that with Bryce.

But Ben instantly sprinted off down the hall, in his robe and pajamas. I was too stunned to go after him. I looked at my watch. It was 10:45, and Saturday night curfew was in fifteen minutes. Hopefully Ben could find Bryce — if this was, in fact, Bryce — and get him back on campus within that time, not to mention before the police got involved.

I stood by Ben's door for a moment and then I went into his room. Ben and Bryce had made their room kinda comfy, like a home. One desk was lit by this old-looking lamp, like something out of an antique shop. Under the lamp was an open copy of Walt Whitman's *Leaves of Grass*. Ben's, I figured. In front of that desk, instead of a typical wooden chair, was a cushioned burgundy chair with a high back. On the wall next to his desk was an Escher print, the one with a never-ending rooftop staircase where all these hooded men are ascending and descending in pairs and it appears they could do so indefinitely and stay in the staircase loop. On the opposite wall, above Bryce's desk, was an Albert Einstein photo.

I sat down in the burgundy chair. Plush. Comfortable. I could smell a faint tinge of garlic; it wasn't altogether unpleasant.

Five minutes later, an out-of-breath Ben returned, looking panicked.

"He's not in the library. He's not anywhere around the quad. I don't know what to do here. Help me figure out what to do," he said.

"Okay, okay," I said, standing and pacing the room. "Where do you think he went? He looked really upset after the game."

"Well, wouldn't you have been? He dropped a ball, for Christ's sake. He didn't kill anyone! The guys made him feel like dirt. Lower than dirt."

"You don't have to tell me," I said, feeling defensive. "I thought it was terrible the way they treated him."

Ben seemed to take that in. "It's worse than that, though."

"Worse?"

"If I tell you something, do you promise . . ."

"A hundred percent," I said. "You can trust me. I promise."

He swallowed and took a deep breath. "Bryce has this big problem with depression."

"Ah. That makes sense. How he was at the party," I said.

He nodded. "He definitely has a problem and he hates taking those pills. Says they make him feel weird. Anyway, over the summer, his folks back in Rhode Island took him to a doctor and they diagnosed him as clinically depressed. I wasn't completely shocked, because I've known him a couple years now and he can get pretty dark. But this year, it's been different. Like scary different."

He sat down in his chair and I sat down on Ben's bed.

"A couple nights ago, he just sat there in bed, staring at the same spot on the wall for hours at a time. I'd wake up and there he was, still staring. I'd go and sit next to him, and it was like, no response. I told him I was going to get the school nurse, and he begged me not to do that. He said he was scared they'd lock him up. That's his biggest fear. So I didn't do anything, and maybe I should have. And then the softball game, and it's just, this is not good, Rafe. Not good. I'm really scared."

"Okay, well, we'll go look for him."

Ben was staring out the window. "There's more," he said. "Bryce has two strikes already. Twice now he's skipped curfew. Both times on weekends. He just totally disregarded the eleven o'clock curfew and sailed in around one A.M. And you know, three strikes and you're out here. Coach Donnelly let him know that the next time he'd be suspended, or worse."

We both looked at the clock on Ben's desk. It was 10:56.

"Shit," I said.

"Yeah," responded Ben. "He has a car. He could be anywhere."

"C'mon. I have an idea," I said, standing and leading him out of the room.

"So he's somewhere, maybe messed up, and he's missed curfew, or he's, like, in trouble," I explained to Toby and Albie.

"We should just tell Mr. Donnelly," Albie said crisply. I could see he was not comfortable with Ben in the room. To Albie, I guess, Ben was simply another jock. "This is too serious to mess around with."

"This could get him kicked out," said Ben. "No way we're telling Donnelly."

"Look," Albie said, "I'm sorry. And Bryce is a nice kid. But I don't see how this has anything to do with me. Us."

Everyone was quiet. The awkwardness was palpable. So was the static from the scanner.

Toby was staring out the window, as if he was deep in thought.

"He's like me," he said, breaking the silence. He still had his fake mustache on.

Ben and I looked at each other. I raised an eyebrow, and Ben shook his head.

"Bryce isn't gay," he said. "I happen to know him really well, and he's definitely not gay. He won't stop talking about girls sometimes. It can actually get annoying."

Toby frowned. "I mean, he's different, like me. He's different, and that can be really, like, depressing. Really depressing." He turned to Albie. "Remember last spring?"

Albie nodded solemnly.

"That could have been me. I was, like, so close to running away from here, it's not even funny."

We all considered that for a moment. I thought about what Mr. Scarborough had asked me, about coming out being a big deal. Hearing about how even Toby had felt depressed about being different made me realize that maybe it was a bigger deal than I'd thought. For everyone.

"That sucks," Ben said. "Sorry."

"Well, it's not exactly a bucket of ice cream to be different around here," Toby said, a little vehemence in his voice.

"A bucket of ice cream? Who puts ice cream in a bucket?" Albie said.

"Shut up, Albie," Toby said.

"You shut up," he replied. "And put your shoes on. We have a mission to accomplish."

Sneaking out of East wasn't that difficult. Donnelly, aside from being an enemy of grammar and the minister of disinformation at Natick, was notoriously lax about security, occasionally leaving the front door unlocked after curfew, not setting the alarm, that sort of thing. And everyone knew about the window to the first-floor bathroom. It was fairly easy to open, and so long as you didn't mind landing momentarily in a shrub, and didn't mind, later, shimmying around the shrub and hoisting yourself up, it was not an issue.

Toby went first, being the only one of us who had actually done this before. Ben wasn't a rule breaker, I was new, and Albie, well, Albie would have been happy to spend every night of his life in our room or the TV lounge. Plus Toby was agile, so hoisting himself up and out was not a problem. I found it pretty easy too. Ben helped Albie from the inside, and Toby and I caught him on the outside.

Once we were behind East, we snuck around the floodlights and out to the parking lot. It was cold inside Sleepy. Ben and I took the back, and Toby sat up front with Albie, the fake mustache hanging precipitously from his face.

Albie turned on the motor, opting to leave the headlights off until we got out of the parking lot. But then we had no idea where to drive.

"I know his favorite diner," Ben said. "It's twenty-four hours."

"That sounds like a good place to start," I said.

Toby pressed his fingers on his mustache like he was thinking deeply. "Crime reporter Ryan Giles thinks we need to develop a secret plan. . . ."

"Shut up," I yelled. "What the hell is wrong with you? This is a real person we're looking for here."

Toby removed his mustache and put it back in his pocket. "Sorry," he said.

"It's okay," I said. "I like joking too, Toby, but let's just get serious for half a minute, okay?"

"Sure," he said. "That was dumb. Stupid. I'm a retard."

"Enough," Albie said. "We love you. You're not dumb."

"That's right," I echoed. "You're loved." And as I said it, I instinctively wondered if Ben would judge me. But when I glanced up, the creases on Ben's forehead told me he had more important things on his mind.

Ben directed us to Sparky's, a diner in downtown Natick. We parked on the main street, jumped out of the car, and headed in. It was loud. The jukebox was playing some rock ballad from before we were born, and groups of high school kids were hanging out in the booths. Probably Joey Warren kids.

Every time I saw someone with dark skin, my heart jumped, hoping it was Bryce. It never was. Ben checked the bathroom but came back alone. Bryce just wasn't there.

We drove in silence down the semifestive streets of downtown Natick, looking for any sign of him. None.

I looked at my watch. It was 11:20.

"What do we do now?" I asked.

No one had an answer for that.

"Bryce liked going to Boston," Ben said.

Silence again, finally broken by Albie. "Did you call his cell?"

"No answer," said Ben, who bit his lip.

"Because Boston is a big place," Albie continued.

"I know," Ben said, annoyed. "I know. It's not gonna work. It just feels hopeless going back now. I mean, he's out here somewhere."

"I guess we need to go to . . ." Albie said, hoping someone would fill in the blanks so he wouldn't have to say it.

"I'd say the police and then the hospital," Ben said, his voice full of fear.

I put my hand on his shoulder and squeezed. It seemed like the right thing to do. He didn't seem to mind, so I left it there for a few moments, just to let him know I cared.

The police officer we spoke to at the station claimed he didn't know anything about a Bryce Hixon being picked up. We drove to the hospital and pulled up at the emergency room, each of us wondering which was best: to find him there, or not.

"I can't give out that sort of information," the woman at the information desk said, glancing at each of us as if searching for one who would understand.

"Please. He's our friend, we're worried," I said.

She pursed her lips, and that was the moment I knew something was wrong.

"Don't you have a dorm adviser?" she said, her face wrinkled with concern. "Go and talk to your dorm adviser."

My pulse soared. I looked at Ben and opened my mouth, but nothing came out. There was nothing I had said that included where we went to school. We'd just said Bryce's name.

She knew something. I nodded thanks and took off, running, down the corridor toward the parking lot. I could hear the others as they followed behind me.

We jumped in the car, and in silence Albie sped back to the

dorm. It felt like we were in the middle of a nightmare. I didn't even know Bryce. Bryce. Poor Bryce.

Albie turned off the lights, turned into the parking lot, and coasted as quietly as possible into a spot before shutting down the engine. We crept across the parking lot and back behind East Hall, the late-night nip shivering our necks.

"Why don't we just use the front door," a voice said. We looked up, and there, in the floodlight, was Mr. Donnelly.

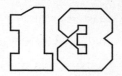

Mr. Donnelly walked us back into East through the front door and kept walking toward his room, which also served as the dorm's office. Once there, he closed the door behind him and pointed to a dated-looking green fabric couch. The four of us bunched together on it and nervously waited for whatever was coming.

"Got a call from some lady at the hospital, told me four young men were out searching for their friend," he said, sitting down behind his desk across the room. "Don't do that ever again, boys. Ever. I don't even want to know how you got out."

He continued, "Bryce is in the hospital, but he's going to be fine. He had what they call a major depressive episode. In layman's terms, that's a depression." I felt Ben fidget next to me on the couch, and Mr. Donnelly went on, "Bryce wandered off campus and was incoherent when the police picked him up. He didn't cohere to the rules of the campus, in other words. And when they asked if he was a danger to anyone, he said, 'Just myself.'"

Ben took a deep breath.

"So he's under observation at MetroWest. They will observe him and see what to do next, through observation. But if you asked me, I don't think he'll be coming back here. It's a terrible tragedy, not to mention for the soccer team."

I could almost feel Ben wanting to pounce on Donnelly. How could you get to be an adult, much less a teacher, and think that was something to say to kids about their friend?

"All's I know is that his parents are on their way. My best guess is that they'll take him back to Rhode Island."

"Why didn't you tell me?" Ben erupted. "Why didn't you come up and let me know? I'm his best friend."

"I tried, Carver," Mr. Donnelly said. "Around eleven-thirty. No one answered. I knocked on some other doors, and no one knew where you were. I know you're not one to sneak out, so I figured you'd show eventually. Then the hospital called."

"I'm sorry," I said. "This was my idea. We heard on the scanner. . . ."

Mr. Donnelly looked at me funny. "You guys have a police scanner?"

Albie raised his hand, guilty, and Mr. Donnelly broke into a bit of a grin. "Well, there's a lot worse you could be up to than listening to a police scanner in your room. That's not a punishable offense in my book. But please, guys. Use your common senses."

"Can we go now?" Toby asked.

Mr. Donnelly nodded. "Please don't do this kind of shenanigans again. You're the types of boys who should be the least amount of trouble, not the most. Just promise, no more sneaking out, okay?"

We promised. The four of us walked upstairs in silence and stopped at my room. Toby looked over at Ben, his eyes averted. "I'm really sorry about Bryce," he said. "And I'm sorry that I was such a jerk. I don't think sometimes."

Ben nodded. "That's okay," he said. "Thanks."

Albie opened the door and he and Toby went inside. I paused outside. "I'm gonna hang out for a bit, if that's okay." I looked up at Ben.

"Sure," he said. "I could use the company."

We went into his room, and my heart started thumping again. What if I didn't say the right thing and offended Ben somehow? But then I calmed down. I'd been on campus three weeks so far, and nothing disastrous had happened yet. Maybe I just needed to trust myself.

Ben flopped down on his bed, and I sat on the floor, facing him. I picked up a single sock next to me and listlessly began to pull on the elastic until I realized what I was doing. I looked up to see if Ben had witnessed me playing with a stranger's (probably dirty) sock, and he had. He was half smiling again.

"Having fun?"

"In Colorado I used to spend all my Saturday nights doing this. I'd go to the laundromat and steal single socks out of different dryers, and take them home, and pull on them. It's pretty much my favorite thing."

Ben jumped up, went to a refrigerator in the closet, pulled out two orange sports drinks, and tossed me one. I was pretty parched from running around all night, so I opened it and took a long swig.

"Bryce and I used to mix this stuff with vodka," Ben said. "He called it a plastic screwdriver, I guess because it's like a screwdriver but the juice is, I don't know, not real."

I sat up. "Do you have any . . ."

"Hmm," Ben said. "I think Bryce does. I guess if he comes back, I can explain."

He crossed the room and rummaged underneath Bryce's bed, pulling out another stray sock, like the one I had been playing with.

"He called these orphans. When he folded his laundry, he always called the matching of socks Sock Mahjong, like the computer card game."

I picked up and examined the sock I had been touching. "I wish I knew him better. He sounds funny."

"He was funny," Ben said, pulling out a bottle of Absolut from deep under the bed. It was about three-quarters full. "Is. Painfully funny. Like way too funny for the people here."

He filled my bottle of sports drink, which was half full, with enough vodka to make it three-quarters full. "You're sort of like that too," I said as I closed the top on the bottle and shook.

Ben chugged down his own drink until it was also half empty, then he filled the bottle with vodka. "I'm a better listener than talker, more of an audience for good comedy than a comedian."

I took a sip of my drink, and it was pretty good. I liked the way the sweetness quieted that vodka bite. Truth is, I don't really love drinking. I just do it when I have to. To fit in.

"Plastic screwdriver good," I said, in a weird Russian accent.

He sipped his and agreed, in an equally bad accent. "Plastic screwdriver very good."

Then Ben told me all about Bryce, about how he could do perfect imitations of almost everyone at the school.

"Did he do me?" I asked.

"No, not yet. But if you'd given him a little more time, I'm sure he would have."

I flinched, trying to imagine what that would sound like.

We both finished our bottles, and Ben, now a little wobbly, went and got two more sports drinks. We swigged them partway down and filled them again with vodka. This time, we toasted. I pulled up a chair, and he lay on his bed, facedown. When he spoke, he lifted his head toward me.

"You would not believe his imitation of Coach Donnelly," Ben said.

I laughed, imagining.

"Run as fast as you can," he said, trying to sound like what Bryce probably sounded like imitating Donnelly, but failing. "Like the French did in the Civil War, when they eluded the Greeks on their way from Charleston to Nashville."

"We knew the only way to attack the axis of evil was by storming the beaches at Normandy," I said back.

Ben started laughing louder than I'd ever heard, and I figured some of that was the vodka. But that just made me laugh harder too, and my head was feeling it as well.

"Taking out Saddam Hussein was wrong. We should have gone after Hitler. He was the real danger," Ben said.

"Yes. And the Iranians, when they bombed Nagasaki."

We were in fits now, Ben cracking up and rolling on the bed and me with my head in my hands, practically snorting. And we just let the laughter flow until we were both tearing up. My chest started to hurt, and I had to breathe deep so that I could get my lungs back.

Ben dried his eyes with the back of his palm. "I should have said something this afternoon," he said.

The change was so abrupt that it caught me off guard, and I had to work hard not to break out laughing again.

"No, no," I said. "You didn't do anything wrong."

"I didn't do anything right either," he said. "And I will never forgive myself for that. If Bryce doesn't come back, I will never forgive myself."

And then Ben really started to tear up, and I was drunk enough that I did what any good buddy would do. I went over to the bed and put my arms around him and hugged him while he cried onto my shoulder.

"He's my best friend. He's made this place bearable for two years. What's going to happen to him?"

"He's gonna be fine," I said, not sure if that was true or not. "He'll be fine. He'll be back here again, I just know it."

"I just . . . Bryce was the kindest person I've ever known. Last year when my uncle died, Bryce came to the funeral. And not just to get out of classes. I mean, he really wanted to be there for me, make sure I was okay. I was close to my uncle, you know? Real close, and Bryce was there for me."

"He sounds like a great friend," I said.

Ben sniffled into my shoulder, still holding on. He smelled like butter and alcohol and garlic, and the combination made my insides melt. I realized, with my nose against his shirt, that I hadn't ever talked to a guy like this.

"Why didn't I just stick up for him?"

I said, "The same reason I didn't. We were afraid."

Ben thought about this, and the sniffling decreased. We kept hugging each other. I was kind of drunk, and Ben was too, and it was all okay.

"You're a really good person, Rafe. I was wrong about you. You're not like those other guys."

"You think?" I asked.

"I know," he said.

"Thanks," I said.

"I think I like the Rafe I saw tonight with Albie and Toby better than the one at football and at the party. Sorry if that hurts your feelings."

I kept my face against his short brown hair, my eyebrow against his ear. "It doesn't," I said. "I like that Rafe better too."

I let go and went back to the chair, and part of me was relieved, because as much as I had enjoyed being on his bed with him, hugging, it was getting a little close there.

We finished up our plastic screwdrivers, and soon I was yawning. I looked over at the clock. It was 3:17.

"Getting too late for me," I said. "Time to go to bed."

Ben sat up then, and leaned toward me.

"I don't want to sleep alone tonight," he slurred.

I wondered how drunk he was, and how much of this was an act. Either way, my heart accelerated.

"That's sort of, I dunno," I said. "I mean, it's a small bed. . . ."

He cracked up. "In Bryce's bed, you maniac," he said.

I laughed and nodded. Sure, I could sleep there. And I went over to Bryce's bed, took off my pants, and climbed under his covers. It felt weird being under someone else's sheets. I could smell him, Bryce, the faint musk of his sweat.

"G'night," I said.

"Thanks for staying, friend," he said.

"You got it, friend," I said back.

A History of Rafe
Part III

I'M NOT REALLY a believer in fate, or that everything happens for a reason, or that we have soul mates or whatever. I mean, if there's a God and everyone has a soul mate, why doesn't everyone find theirs? Does God put some people's soul mates in another country, just to be cruel? And if only some people have one, why? What did the others do to piss God off? I think stuff happens, and then people try to figure out why, and then voilà! Fate and soul mates.

I write that because I definitely never thought Clay was my soul mate. I thought he was just a decent guy who could have been a passable boyfriend.

The first time I saw him was outside of chemistry class. It was about a month into sophomore year, and I had never noticed him in class. I was the last to leave the room that day, because I had to ask Mr. Stanhouse a question about the upcoming test. When I got into the hallway, there Clay was, this unassuming, quiet-looking kid with light brown hair, a little bit of acne on his chin and left cheek. A nerd type, I thought. When I looked at him, he nodded.

"Hey, Rafe, you're good at this chemistry stuff, right?"

I shrugged. "I guess."

"Would you help me with it? I don't get it."

I was confused. Did he mean right then and there? Another class period was four minutes from starting.

"Sure . . ."

He looked relieved. "I could come over to your house."

"Oh," I said, like I had been pinched on the butt. "Sure. Okay."

"Thanks," he said. He averted his eyes, and I noticed them. Maybe hazel? Cute nerd. He wore a pine green Lacoste shirt that was too short for him, and a pair of generic jeans with no belt. Terrible taste in clothing, not stylish at all, but cute. Definitely not out.

"Um, when?" I asked.

"Today?"

I knew this was kind of weird, but I was interested in the same way you get interested when a Facebook friend you barely know comments on a random picture in your photo gallery. You know they've been paying more attention to you than you have to them, and you want to know why.

"Sure, I guess," I said. "Um, who are you?"

He looked down at his shoes. "Clay."

"Hi, Clay."

"Hi."

At lunch, I saw him again, eating at a table with some other guys, all bookish types. I tapped Claire Olivia on the shoulder.

"Whatever you do, don't make it obvious," I said. "But will you tell me if you know the kid with the green shirt, at the table two behind us to your right?"

Good old Claire Olivia immediately turned the opposite way, and looked three back, and made a big deal about it, so anyone watching us would think I had just asked her to check out a person at that table. She always did that. Throw them off the trail. Then, once she was done with that, she surreptitiously looked where I told her to look.

"Never seen him before in my life. Maybe the most generic boy in the history of Rangeview."

"Thought so," I said.

So Clay came over to my house that afternoon. My mom was home, and she was pretty surprised to see this boy with me. Usually I was with Claire Olivia or no one. I saw her raise an eyebrow as we went up to my room, and I just wanted to tell her to PLEASE. BE. NORMAL. For once.

It was my first time having a boy in my room. Clay sat at my desk, and I went over the three types of radioactivity. He was close to me, his nose near mine. I could actually hear his breathing in my ear. It was all a little surprising.

That's when I felt it.

One thin finger. Gently touching my thigh.

I kept talking about how alpha loses two protons and two neutrons, like his finger wasn't on my thigh. And I think he liked that, because he kept asking questions, as if his finger weren't on my thigh.

Nobody had ever touched me that way before, and even though my mouth kept motoring, I felt a little bit under a wave, maybe, water rushing everywhere and the shock of chill and the sound. It was

128

almost deafening, the sound of us not talking about it, and I loved the dizziness it gave me.

That was as far as it went. It was just a normal tutoring session, and at the end of it, off came the finger, and both of us pretended like it hadn't happened. I asked what subjects interested him in school, and he said, "I want to be an engineer."

And I was like, *An engineer, asking the writing kid for help in science?* That's when I fully accepted that Clay had come over with a specific purpose in mind, and that purpose consisted of laying one digit on the meatiest part of my thigh for somewhere between twelve and eighteen minutes. I was definitely okay with that.

"Do you think you'll need help again?" I asked.

"Yeah," he said.

"Cool."

Rafe,

Nice job of showing us Clay (and Claire Olivia) without telling us too much! It would be easy to just say that Claire Olivia has a way with words, or that Clay is an awkward character, but you do a nice job of demonstrating it through their dialogue and actions. In your opinion, does self-expression get easier once you're out of the closet? Do you think it would help Clay?

— Mr. Scarborough

I waited to call my mom until Albie packed up his bags and went off to the library. It was hard enough avoiding the subject of my sexuality with her; I didn't need to be worried about how it all sounded to him too.

"Hey, Mom."

"Darling! How are you? How is Massachusetts? How do you like the school? Are you making friends?"

"Whoa, one at a time, please," I said. "I'm fine. School's good. It's totally . . . different than Boulder. In a good way."

"That's fantastic, Rafe. Fantastic. I can't wait to see it in person!" she said.

"Yeah, that's hilarious."

My mother's tone changed. "Hon. You know that Parents' Weekend is not this weekend but next, right? Did you really think we wouldn't come?"

"Oh, right," I said. "Um, yeah, no, I totally figured you'd be here."

"Oh, Rafe, you're such a bad liar."

"Fine. No, I didn't know." I rested my forehead on my desk, my mouth far enough away from the mouthpiece that I could say an inaudible "fuck" even though I was alone in the room.

"Well, now you do," she said. "We can't wait to see you."

"Are your tickets refundable?"

"Honey! Did you really think we'd send you to school across the country and then not check up on you? We want to know that you haven't run off and joined the circus. We'll be there, Rafe. Count on it."

I cradled my head in my left hand, holding the phone with my right. "I'm kidding, Mom. I'm looking forward to it."

"Well, you better be. I wouldn't want your father to get it in his head that you need to be embarrassed."

"Mom! Please. Please tell me you'll bring his leash."

"I never leave home without it," she said. "Now tell me, who are these new friends of yours? Have you found a boyfriend?"

". . ."

"Darling?"

"Mom . . ." I said softly. Maybe communication *was* a lot harder when you weren't out, like Mr. Scarborough said, because I felt like I had to choose each word supercarefully.

She said, "What? It's a perfectly normal question."

"I'm not looking for a boyfriend, Mom."

"That seems like a strange choice . . . at an ALL-BOYS SCHOOL! I mean, come on, darling, who do you think you're talking to? You know, when your dad and I went to Oberlin, well . . . Oh, for God's sake. You know you can talk to me."

"You really don't want to know," I said.

"Well, now that you say that, I really do, Rafe. I really do want to know. What's going on?" I could hear an edge in my mother's voice.

"Mom. I'm not gay at Natick."

"You're . . . straight?"

"No."

"Bi? Bicurious? Genderqueer?" she asked.

"Stop it, Mom. I'm just not gay."

"Just not gay," she said, as if she were reading some odd item off a menu.

"Right."

"But you are still gay."

"Duh."

She raised her voice a bit, which was unusual for my mother. "Oh, I do NOT think this is a situation that calls for a *duh*. I don't get it. You're back in the closet?"

"Not exactly, Mom. I'm just not telling anyone." It was more like I was in the doorway than actually in the closet, I thought.

"Seamus Rafael. For goodness' . . . That's the closet, honey. You've been through this. Why would you go through it again?"

"The closet is when you say you're not gay," I said, standing and moving over to my bed. "I'm just not saying one way or the other."

She sighed. "It sounds like you're lying, honey."

"Not telling is not lying."

"Well, what's going to happen when you make a close friend?"

I lay down, turned on the speakerphone, and placed the speaker next to my head. "I already have," I said, thinking of Ben. "And I'm not telling him."

"Why would you do that?" She sounded so exasperated.

"I'm tired of it. I'm so tired of being the gay kid. I don't want this anymore. I just want to be, like, a normal kid."

"Oh, honey. There's no such thing as a normal kid."

I closed my eyes. "You don't get it."

"That's true. Explain this to me, Rafe. I must be lost."

I took a deep breath. "Back in Boulder, when people saw me, they saw the GAY kid. It was like, every second of my life, I had to be aware of the fact that I was different."

"Oh, sweetie," my mother said, her voice full of compassion in that inimitable Opal Goldberg way.

"When I went to soccer practice at Rangeview, I knew they were not talking about girls in front of me because it was awkward having me there. Did you know that in history class, Ms. Peavy asked me for the gay perspective on the civil rights movement?"

"I'm sure Ms. Peavy was just trying to support you," my mother said. "Surely you could have told her how this made you feel. Told anyone, really. This is the first I've heard of this."

"But that's part of it. It was like, I'm so special, my feelings are so special. I wanted to get my feelings hurt sometimes and not have Mommy come to school."

"Well," my mother said, her voice sharp.

I said, "I know, Mom. You're awesome. Dad is awesome. I just — I just wanted something different, is all. I just want people to see me."

"You don't have any idea how lucky you are, do you?"

I closed my eyes. "Yeah, I do."

"No, you don't. If you had been born just ten years earlier, you would have been torn apart for being openly gay."

I exhaled. "I know, Mom. . . ."

"Twenty years ago, you might have had to quit school. There would have been violence."

I repeated myself in the exact same tone. "I know, Mom. . . ."

"Now you're able to be exactly who you are, and your friends love you for it, and everyone seems to respect you, and you've thrown that all away," she said, her voice full of emotion. "I really don't understand you, Rafe. I don't understand this."

"Well, I guess you don't need to," I said.

"That's your answer?" she asked.

I sighed. "I just, you don't get it. If it's so different being gay these days, if I'm such a *new case*, then how can you expect to understand what's going on inside me?"

She was silent for a moment. "Well, I don't have an answer for that one, Rafe. But I don't like this."

"I'm sorry, Mom. But this was what I wanted to do."

"And when we visit?" she asked.

I sat up. "You'll need to go along with my choice. Sorry, but you will."

"Oh, no. No, no, no," she said, her voice trembling now. "I am not liking the sound of this, Rafe. You're telling me that I have to go back in the closet too! And your father. How could you not think about that?"

"Why do I need to worry about your reaction to my life?"

"Rafe, you are really being a brat right now," she nearly shouted. It was so unusual for her to raise her voice that a part of me was enjoying getting her riled up.

"Okay, if this is where this conversation is going, Mom, I'm hanging up," I said, staying calm.

"Rafe. Did you expect you could just tell me this and it would immediately be fine?"

"I expected not to tell you at all."

"Wow. I am just so . . . disappointed. I don't know how to react to you doing this."

"You don't need to react in any way. Just be my mom."

"Be straight Rafe's mom, you mean," she said flatly.

"Why does it need to be labeled one way or the other?"

She sighed, still sounding exasperated. "It's called heterosexism, honey. You used to talk about it when you spoke at schools, remember? You're assumed to be straight if you're not openly gay."

"Fine. Then, yes. You're the mother of straight Rafe, if you have to put a label on me."

There was a long silence.

"I just HATE this, sweetheart. Hate it. But if this is what you want, I'll speak with your dad. We'll do the best we can, I suppose. But please do not blame me if we screw this up. We're not perfect, you know."

"I'm counting on you," I said. "I need you to please try your hardest. Please."

"Ugh. We'll do our best. That's all I can promise."

"Thanks, Mom. You are the best. Really."

"You know, I'm beginning to think perhaps I am."

A History of Rafe
Part IV

CLAIRE OLIVIA, not my mother, was the one who talked me into getting involved with Speaking Out.

One day after school we were at the Laughing Goat, a cool coffee shop on Pearl Street, the kind of place where they proudly announce that their napkins are made from 100 percent recycled hemp. Claire Olivia was talking about this guy Willy in our school. He was a Mormon and he came from this huge family that was superstrict. His dad fully expected Willy to wear that special Mormon underwear and go on a mission for two years when he was nineteen. Willy was superartistic, like incredible at painting and stuff. He was a nice kid too. What he definitely wasn't, though, was a lumberjack type. He would never wear flannel, and he would totally look ridiculous holding an axe.

Claire Olivia was talking about how in homeroom, out of nowhere, he started crying, and it turned out that the night before, his dad found Willy on this emo website. It wasn't even a gay thing; it was just emo music and chat. But his dad got furious and threatened to "put an end to this GD misfit stuff." He said if Willy went on that site again, he'd be sent to a place called Exodus, a church camp where they turned guys like Willy into "real men."

As I said, it wasn't even a gay thing. But it made me think of how hard some kids have it with their families. Me, I could show up as Lady Gaga dressed as Little Red Riding Hood, and Mom would be like, "How was your day, honey?" That's just not the case for most kids.

I told Claire Olivia about my mom's idea that I should join this group in which I'd speak at high schools about what it was like to be gay, to be, like, a good role model, and Claire Olivia's eyes lit up.

"Oh, my God, Shay Shay, you should totally do that," she said. "You would be seriously awesome at that."

Maybe I'm a praise whore or something, but that was enough for me. I volunteered. My mother was so proud of me that she started to cry as she gave me the e-mail address of the woman to contact.

I had to go to three Saturdays' worth of training, where I basically learned how to speak to big groups, and how to make sure not to say anything that could get Speaking Out in trouble, and how to handle all sorts of gay questions. You become an expert on gay issues in a way, because they keep throwing numbers at you. Like, did you know that LGBT kids are 8.4 times more likely than straight kids to attempt suicide? And 50 percent of LGBT kids are rejected by their parents? That between 20 and 40 percent of homeless teens say they're gay, lesbian, or transgender, and that up to 50 percent of the guy teens have sold their bodies to support themselves? Well, that's the kind of stuff I learned, and not having those issues made me feel like the luckiest guy in the world.

The first school I ever spoke at was Niwot, which is about twenty minutes north of Boulder. My mom drove me there, and she was sitting in the back of the auditorium while I talked.

"What was it like, telling your mom and dad?" this big blond girl with a butterfly barrette in her hair asked.

"Well, my parents are awful, so . . . oh, hey, Mom," I said. "My mom is here, actually, so I can't give you all the dirt."

There was polite laughter from the audience.

"It's kind of unusual, my situation," I said. "I mean, my mom and dad always talked about how some people were straight and some were gay, so it wasn't, like, shocking that when I told them, they were totally fine with it."

This kid, maybe fifteen, raised his hand. I remember I was smiling, thinking that it was good that I was keeping things light and humorous. It really helped straight people deal with gay issues if you fed it to them with a little humor, I'd learned.

"What would you do if, like, you had a friend? And your friend was gay? And his parents were, well, they don't like gays at all, and they said they'd disown him if he turned out gay?"

The room got silent. I got it immediately. I could see it in his drawn, tired, sad face. And I felt bad, suddenly, that I'd been acting like being gay isn't this big thing, when for a lot of kids, it totally is.

I wanted to say to him: *Stay strong. Don't ever let that light inside flicker out, because your situation, it's not ever going to be easy, and it's probably going to get worse before it gets better.* But I couldn't say that to a kid who was talking about "a friend." So instead, I said, "Outside support. Tell your friend to find some youth groups, or a gay hotline where he can talk to someone. And be a good friend to him. Please. He needs good friends."

The kid nodded blankly and sat down, and I don't remember anything else from that day, except how my mom and I drove in silence most of the way home, and I reached out at one point and took her hand, and I could sense the tears dripping down her face without even looking.

Rafe,

Lots to like about this piece! It made me cry. I cried not just for the boy who asked the question, but because I feel pain here. That tells me that you did a good job of showing the scene and not just telling us about it. At the same time, this feels brief. Could you have gone further? Are there places you fall back on exposition when you could have stayed in scene? Take a look at the paragraph where you write "I felt bad, suddenly, that I'd been acting like being gay isn't this big thing." What other choices could you make there, and how would they change the piece?

— Mr. Scarborough

"I want to talk a bit today about respecting and understanding differences," Mr. Scarborough said as he sat down on the corner of his desk and faced us, crossing his loafers. He had become my favorite teacher, and I had spent several free periods in his office, just talking about writing.

"I'm sure there are a lot of feelings going on about your classmate Bryce Hixon, who is no longer in school with us. Now, the word around school, I understand, is that Bryce suffered from depression. Fine. But I want to talk about the invisible elephant in the room.

"Bryce is black. How many other black students are there in the junior class?"

Everyone looked around. The answer was obvious.

"None?" I said.

He nodded. "Oftentimes here at Natick, we talk about being color-blind. But I want, for just a moment, for you to think about what it might be like to be the only black person in the room. Would color blindness then be a good thing, or a bad thing?"

Again, we were quiet. There was awkward foot shuffling.

"Depends?" a kid in the back said.

"Sure. Depends," Scarborough said. "What else?"

"We're a pretty tolerant place," Steve said, an edge to his voice.

"Ah, interesting word. Tolerant. What does *tolerant* mean?"

"It means we tolerate," Steve said, flat. "We accept people."

"Actually, tolerance and acceptance are different. *To tolerate* seems to mean that there is something negative to tolerate, doesn't it? *Acceptance*, though, what's that?"

I thought about that. It reminded me of the excerpt from Edmund White's *A Boy's Own Story* that Mr. Scarborough had assigned us. White had talked about the strange sort of tolerance his roommates had had for him back at his boarding school in the 1950s. I remembered underlining the word *tolerance*. I mean, if you accept something, you take it for what it is. Tolerance is different. Less. So is acceptance at the top of the pyramid? Is that what everyone wants in the best of all possible worlds? Acceptance? I rolled the idea around in my head. It didn't feel right, somehow.

No one was saying anything.

"*Acceptance* also has a bit of negative to it, doesn't it?" I finally said.

Scarborough looked over at me. "Yes! Tell me more about that."

My face reddened. I knew everyone was looking at me. I didn't want to stand out in this conversation, but I did have something to add. I took a shot.

"Well, if you need to accept something, that means it's not like it should be, right? Like you accept something as it is."

"No," someone said, from the back. "You get accepted into college. It doesn't mean you aren't as you should be. That's stupid."

"Not stupid," Scarborough said. "Stay with me here. That's a slightly different form of the word. And yet, colleges accept students who are otherwise rejected. Acceptance is an affirmation that you're good enough."

We were quiet. I looked around. A lot of the kids, Steve included, seemed to be writing that down, and I almost laughed. It was like, *This isn't going to be on a test, dummies. Listen. Stop worrying about memorizing things you don't even understand.* I turned my eyes to Scarborough, and I watched as he saw the same thing I did. I could see that the class's silence was even more disappointing to him. His expression was sad, and then he caught me looking and put on a poker face as quickly as he could. It made me feel good to know I wasn't the only one concerned about the lack of intellectual curiosity within this group.

"It's hard to be different," Scarborough said. "And perhaps the best answer is not to tolerate differences, not even to accept them. But to celebrate them. Maybe then those who are different would feel more loved, and less, well, tolerated."

The writing continued, and I looked at Scarborough, thinking: *That's never gonna happen with this bunch.* And damned if he didn't look back at me and sigh.

As I walked back to East Hall after class, I noticed something out of the corner of my eye. A flicker of color, near the tree line. When you walk across the quad toward the dorm, the woods are to the left. There are some dirt paths into the woods, and everyone knows that some kids go there to smoke weed. Infamous. And way risky at Natick; if you get caught with weed, you get kicked out. It's that simple.

I turned my head, and what I saw surprised me. It was Robinson, emerging from the woods. He was half walking, half jogging toward East Hall, turning his head left and right to see who was noticing. He saw me, and he didn't freeze exactly, but he slowed his pace and looked down, as if that were somehow going to make him look less guilty. I almost sped up to catch him and say something like, "Busted!" but I didn't know him well enough to joke around about something that could be serious. And I hadn't really taken him for a stoner type.

So I pretended I hadn't seen him or didn't care, which was basically true. What he did was his business. I just kept walking, a good fifty yards behind him. But about a minute later, I saw another flash out of the corner of my eye, and this time, what I saw sort of was my business.

Toby, exiting the woods as well. Heading toward Academy Hall, the building with all the classrooms, where I was walking from. He didn't see me.

Toby and . . . Robinson? In the woods, alone? Robinson was Toby's mystery boyfriend? The idea made me laugh. Robinson the Jockhead? Gorilla Butt? No way. Robinson was like the weirdest, most random choice. Not that I was surprised that maybe he was gay or bi; lots of people you'd never think could be gay or bi actually are. I knew that, everyone knew that. But . . . Toby and Robinson? For reals?

We had four wins, two losses, and two draws going into our game with Exeter. And we knew we were going to lose to them. We always do. The question was, how badly?

Well, without Bryce, 6–1 badly.

I had started for the first time, as the left midfielder. They had to move Rodriguez to the position that Bryce had played. The left midfielder needs to be fast and in shape, and be able to dribble the ball upfield and pass to our best offensive players.

I wasn't great but I wasn't bad. I definitely don't think we lost because of me. It's just that Exeter is superfast and strong, and we couldn't quite keep up.

"Listen up, boys," Coach Donnelly said after the game. "I generally don't praise a loss. Especially a loss by five goals. But I must say, you showed heart out there today. As a team, we have an enlarged heart, and by and large that's a function of your effort."

Ben and I walked to the locker room together afterward.

"I'm very concerned about this enlarged heart we have," I said.

"Me too," Ben said as he held the locker room door open, and we were hit with the stench of sweat. "We can probably fix it by trying less and relaxing more."

"Yes. We should send that in to the medical journals. We'll be saving lives."

In the showers, it was low-key. The loss had taken the wind out of a lot of the guys' sails, and that included Steve, who, as striker, had really not gotten the job done. So we soaped and rinsed in silence, listening to the sound of water slapping tile.

I had gotten used to taking a shower at the far end, where I could turn around if I got shy. Showering in the middle of the room seemed like a dangerous thing to do, especially since there was the possibility I could get excited by all the bodies surrounding me. It hadn't happened to me yet, but there was no telling when, especially since having no room of my own to "take care of things" had begun to weigh on me. I wondered if storing up semen would have a health impact on me, positive or negative, like shinier hair or weight gain.

"Hey, Steve, did you hook up with Melody?" someone asked. I think it was Zack, but I wasn't sure because of the sound in the shower chamber.

"Shut up," said Steve. "Why do you wanna know? You want to hook up with her?"

"Maybe," Zack said. "She's seriously stacked."

"Well, then, yeah. I did. Hands off."

There was laughter, and then Zack did this thing in which he wet his hair and then shook his head like a dog, getting everyone else wet. It didn't make a lot of sense to me, since we were already, you know, in a shower. I made a mental note to ask Ben about this phenomenon. He was becoming a very good source for long, philosophical discussions about all things less than brilliant at Natick.

"Stop it, freak," Steve said, wiping the water from Zack's hair out of his eyes. "You know Robinson's getting laid. Always off somewhere. You got a babe somewhere?"

"Yep," Robinson said.

My face flushed, embarrassed for Robinson. I figured he meant Toby. And if he did, here was someone who was actively lying about who he was. Did he feel like he had to? What did he think would happen if his buddies Steve and Zack knew about him and Toby? And why didn't he come out last year, after the college football player came and talked? I looked over at him, and it was like I could see inside him, inside his rib cage, all the intricate muscles and veins and bone and the same heart that everyone else had. Was it twisting in there? I felt sorry for him.

"Man, I would not want to see that hairy ass of yours in motion, you know," Steve said, and then he mimed pumping in and out, which, I have to say, was not so bad to watch. Everyone roared with laughter. Robinson just took it. Didn't really react in any way.

"Zack needs to get laid," Steve continued. "What about Amber?"

"Amber is a fucking slut," Zack said.

"Awesome," Standish said. "Would she do me?"

"No," Zack said.

It was customary, this naming of girls from Joey Warren. And yet every weekend at our parties, the soccer guys would stand in one corner of the room, looking all preppy and uncomfortable, until finally one of the girls broke the ice by talking to one of the guys. And then it was like the uncomfortable beginning of the party never happened.

"Is Amber the one who got splattered when Colorado threw up?" someone said.

Lots of laughter. I was glad I was under piping hot water, because that way, they couldn't tell that I was blushing.

"Yo," Zack said. "She leans over to kiss him and he's like . . . blat!"

"Off the hook," Steve said. "Nice, Colorado."

"I aim to please," I said.

"You didn't want her?" Standish asked. "She's crazy hot."

"I was shitfaced" was my response.

"Yeah, true. I had to take him upstairs or he was gonna pass out in his own puke," Steve said as he lifted his arm and washed the pit. "You have a girlfriend, Colorado?"

I'd thought about this moment all summer. The moment I was finally asked if I had a girlfriend. I'd decided that I'd say no. After all, not all straight guys have girlfriends. I'd skirt the question and remain one of the guys by being more of a listener than a talker. A follower. The quiet guy.

Standing there among my teammates, though, the silence became loud. I felt as if every second I remained quiet, my entire life at Natick was ripping apart. And I couldn't let that happen. Sometimes, reality makes you ever so slightly shift your plan.

"Yup," I answered.

"Back home?"

"Yeah. Claire Olivia." My jaw felt tight.

"Oh, yeah, you read something about her in English class," one of the guys said.

"Is she hot?" Steve asked.

"Incredibly," I said, turning to face the shower spray.

"She blow you?" This was Steve, again.

This time I didn't answer. I looked over at Ben, who was definitely minding his own business. I noticed that he didn't partake in the trash talk, the girl talk. I liked being part of the soccer posse, but I had to admit, there were about a thousand things I liked better than this part, in which we talked about women like they were just things. I tried to imagine what it would be like if gay were normal and all of us were gay. Would we objectify men in the same way?

My head felt so noisy. The thoughts were rapid and loud, and I put my head under the streaming hot water, trying to wash it all clean.

"Man, you must miss that shit. Why'd you leave?" Steve asked, for some reason taking my silence as a yes.

"Good college," I said. "I mean, I can probably get laid at Harvard or Yale, right?"

"Fuckin' A," said Steve. "Those Harvard girls are off the hook."

"Yeah, like any Harvard girl would give a moron like you the time of day," Zack said, and everyone laughed. I joined in, because at least it wasn't about me again.

I looked over at Ben again. He caught my glance and rolled his eyes, and at first I thought he was judging me, that he knew what I was doing. But then I realized he was rolling his eyes at the conversation, and I smiled, grateful I had a friend who didn't need me to be someone I was not.

When I called Claire Olivia later, I felt like I'd dragged out naked pictures of her and showed them to the guys. It felt like I'd crossed the line. But there was no way I could explain that to her, so I went in another direction.

"My mother is driving me crazy," I said.

"What now, Shay Shay? Did she actually send you those hemp pillowcases?"

"Nah, she gave up on that. But now she's all about coming to visit on Parents' Weekend, and you know she's going to embarrass me. She lives for that. They both do."

"Sigh. Parents. They're the worst," she said.

"Totally."

"So how's the boyfriend front?"

"Nonexistent. I'm just studying all the time."

She asked, "How's Ben?" I'd mentioned my new friend a few times, and I had told her about the time we'd gone looking for Bryce, and then how he'd cried on my shoulder and asked me to sleep over. I didn't tell her that I thought about Ben a lot these days, because that would bring up all sorts of issues I wasn't ready to talk to her about, such as the fact that Ben didn't know I was gay.

"I think you're in love with him," I answered, laughing.

"Me too. Maybe I'm just jealous that he's your new me."

I said, "That doesn't make any sense."

"He's, like, your gal pal, or your guy pal, whatever. And I think it's so cool, the whole straight and gay buddies thing. He just sounds, you know. Cool."

"He is," I said.

"You know, you haven't said even a single word about the GSA or what the gay scene is over there. It's a little weird," she said.

"I'm just not focused there," I said. And that was the truth.

"Okay, whatever. I want to go on record and say that if you become some celibate monk or something, I am so going to want pictures of you in any frock they make you wear."

"I'm not becoming a monk," I said. "Although some of those frocks are very flattering."

She laughed. "Why can't You-Know-Caleb be less of a bitch and more like you?"

"It's one of the mysteries of the universe," I said. "Why can't all gay guys be exactly the same so that Claire Olivia doesn't have to adjust?"

"You're such an ass."

"Love you!"

She laughed again. "I love you too, Shay Shay. I just can't wait to see you. You'll be back for Thanksgiving, right?"

"Definitely."

A History of Rafe
Part V

MY FRESHMAN YEAR at Rangeview, two seniors on the football team dressed up as Shakira and Beyoncé for Halloween. One wore this midriff shirt that showed off his hairy stomach, and he kept shaking his butt in people's faces, and the other wore huge hoop earrings and this tight red dress. It was hysterical. So for Halloween sophomore year, I got this idea. I told my mother, and she took me to this cool vintage clothing store where we got me a leather miniskirt and black leggings. She made me up that morning for school, and Dad couldn't stop laughing when I came downstairs as an eighties rocker chick, with this stupid plastic electric guitar thing around my waist. I wasn't pretty, exactly. If anything, I looked kind of butch.

But when I got to school, the weirdness began. Kids looked at me and then quickly looked away, as if they were seeing something delicate and secret about me. In history class, Ms. Peavy used my outfit to talk about Stonewall, which was this big riot during which drag queens fought cops in Greenwich Village in New York City. It turned out to be the beginning of the gay rights movement.

"When Rafe wears that outfit, it works on two levels," she told the class. Everyone was staring at me, and suddenly I was a red-faced rocker, wishing I were just about anywhere else in the world. "It's fun, and at the same time it reminds us of the powerful role drag queens played in the gay rights movement."

I wanted to say, *Um, I'm not actually a drag queen. Drag queens impersonate women. Wait, am I a drag queen?* I didn't even know anymore. All I knew was that suddenly everyone was looking at my outfit like it was a political statement, or proof that deep inside I really wanted to be a woman. Not funny at all.

When the two football guys wore women's clothing, I'm pretty sure nobody called them drag queens. I remember that day at lunch this kid at the table next to mine asked his friend if he'd seen the two jock transvestites.

Drag queen. Transvestite. Very different, I guess. And apparently, an openly gay guy can only be the former.

It was a way awkward day, and I will definitely never do that again.

A few weeks after that, after a soccer game at Gateway, this huge high school in Aurora, Jordan Kemp came up to me in the locker room.

"Hey, Rafe," he said, his head down. Jordan and I had probably exchanged two words ever. His eyes were really close together, in the way mentally challenged people's eyes are often too close together.

"Hey," I said. "Good game." Jordan had scored two goals. I'd done nothing to help the team at all.

"Lemme ask you a question," he said, furtively looking around the otherwise empty row of lockers.

" 'Kay," I said.

"I'm definitely not gay, but if I was, would I be considered hot?"

I tried really hard not to laugh, knowing that if I did, it would close this little honest window that had opened.

"Um, yeah," I said. "Kinda hot."

"Should I get, like, a different haircut?" He touched his dark blond hair. It was short on the sides and front, not neat and not styled, but short, almost like he should have a mullet, except he didn't have the party in back.

"Maybe use some gel," I said, having no idea.

"Cool," he said, avoiding my eyes, and then, with a quick, impersonal nod, he was off. I don't think Jordan ever said another word to me.

A couple of weeks later, I scored my first goal of the season. The goal happened to help us beat Niwot, 3–2.

Afterward, a reporter for the school paper, Roger Jones, came up to my locker with a notepad and a digital recorder, which he shoved in my face.

"The gay guy won the game!" he enthused, as if that were a question. I froze.

We stared at each other for a few seconds until it got uncomfortable. "Do you have anything to say?" a rattled Roger asked. I was like, *No, not really*, and he went away, and the article came out, and the headline had the word *gay* in it, as if who I was attracted to had anything at all to do with kicking the stupid soccer ball. So Rosalie, the guidance counselor, went and had a talk with Roger. Because it was Boulder, we had to have this big meeting where I sat uncomfortably in the background as Rosalie lectured the newspaper staff not to make a big deal out of someone's sexuality unless it was relevant. And all the time, I sat there wondering: *When is it relevant? When I get a boyfriend?*

Rafe,

Think about what I said to you earlier this semester about going deeper. This is nicely done but it feels rather rehearsed. I want you to get more comfortable NOT having all the answers. To me, this reads as if you had several pieces of evidence and you wanted to lay them out as reasons for why you felt frustrated about being "out." Fine, but what are YOU learning from writing this?

That's quite the question here at the end. When is being gay relevant? My question back to you is this: Has your answer changed here at Natick, now that you're not "openly gay"?

— Mr. Scarborough

"So, are you up for something insanely stupid?" I asked Ben when he opened the door.

It was late Saturday morning, a week before Parents' Weekend. He stared at me, wiping the sleep out of his eyes. He was in his sleeping shorts, his thick legs making it hard for me to look up at his face.

"So, something insanely stupid?" I said again. "You game?"

"Wow, that's quite an offer. I'm guessing this is not a two-person outing?"

I laughed. "Did the 'insanely stupid' part give it away?"

"Yeah," he answered.

"I actually have no idea what this outing is. I just have a strong sense that it will be odd, since it's an Albie-and-Toby production."

"I'm in," he said.

Later, we four walked to the parking lot, me and Ben wearing normal clothing, Toby wearing his usual skinny jeans and hoodie, and Albie wearing pants with arguably the biggest pockets I'd ever seen. It looked like you could fit a family of squirrels in there. When

155

I asked him about it, he said, "You always want to be prepared for the unforeseen." And that's when I started really having doubts about this outing.

Steve Nickelson was in the parking lot, getting something from his trunk. As we approached, he had a weird look on his face. I knew it was because Ben and I were with Toby and Albie. Then, as we got closer, the look turned to a smile.

"Hey, guys," he said.

"Hey," Ben said, and I saluted.

We continued on in silence toward the car.

"You know, the way Steve and all of them are so nice," I said, "there's something menacing about it."

"Nice? When is Steve Nickelson nice?" Toby said.

"He's almost always nice," I said.

"Yeah, if you're on the inside," Albie said. "Otherwise, he's a flaming prick. And not in a good way, Toby."

Toby said, "Thanks for clarifying."

"But wasn't Steve nice to you after the guy . . ." and then I realized this might be a delicate area. I mean, Ben told me about how Steve hung out with Toby after the gay speaker came in, and if I'd been publicly gay, I might have been free to talk about it. But since I was supposedly straight, I had to watch what I said so that I wasn't (A) too knowledgeable about gay things or (B) insulting to gays. It was exhausting. Don't try this at home.

"Yeah," Toby said. "For like a week after that football guy spoke, he was all over me. I was like his pet. Like, oh, look, how cute. A homosexual of our very own. And then he was, like, gone. I haven't talked to him since, and he ignores me in the hallways if I say hi."

I was having trouble thinking of Toby in quite the same way ever since I saw him leave the woods after Robinson. I just was having trouble . . . picturing it, exactly. Toby, first of all, was like the least sexual person in the history of the world for me. Too skinny and spiky haired and quirky. And Robinson was the least talkative person ever. No personality at all. What did they talk about? Did they even talk? Maybe that's how it worked at Natick: Take what you can get. So far, I had made getting laid at Natick an impossibility for myself, so who was I to say?

We got into the car in our previous formation: me and Ben in the back, Albie driving, Toby shotgun. I had no idea where we were going as Albie pulled Sleepy out of the parking lot and onto Green Street.

"Give me a hint: Does this trip have anything to do with the end of the world?" I asked.

Albie and Toby looked at each other as they pondered the correct answer.

"In a way, yes," Albie said.

"Oh, good," I said. "I'm sorry in advance, Ben."

"Hey, I'm here on my own volition," Ben said.

Even though I liked hanging out with Steve and his posse, I was equally happy spending time with Albie and Toby, a fact I hid from my jock friends — except Ben. The few times we walked as a foursome, Ben didn't seem to give a crap what people thought of him hanging out with Albie and Toby. It made my opinion of Ben even higher.

Five minutes later, Albie turned on his right turn signal and we pulled into a place called Dowse Orchards.

"Huh," I said. "I was not expecting this."

"No. Me neither," said Ben.

"How is this related to the end of the world?" I asked.

"Well, if the world was going to end, an apple orchard would be a reasonably good place to camp out. Food, shelter of the big trees," Albie said.

"Ah," I said. "Of course."

Albie broke into a rare smile. "I didn't say it was the BEST place to be should the apocalypse hit. That would probably be a cave stocked with nonperishables and enough ammunition to survive the inevitable postapocalypse riots."

We walked over to the farm stand where the owners were selling apple cider.

Toby said, "Hi, my name is Bailey Hutchinson, and I am an apple enthusiast. Might we pick apples at your orchard?"

It took everything I had not to laugh.

The woman, maybe forty, with curly brown hair and lots of freckles, smiled. "So long as you pay for 'em, I don't care what the heck you do here," she said. "Want a picking pole?"

"Indeed," Toby said. "Indeed we do."

"And a couple of buckets?"

"Four, please," Toby said.

She studied us before turning around and getting us four buckets and a pole with what looked like a birdcage on top of it.

"Now, you look like nice boys. You behave, hear?"

"I promise. I'll keep an eye on them, or my name isn't Bailey Hutchinson," Toby said.

We each grabbed a bucket and headed back to the orchard, the smell of apples suddenly lodged in the back of my throat. I'd never really noticed that apples had such a sweet smell before.

"What possible trouble could people get into at an apple orchard?" I asked as we passed through an open field.

"Oh, you'd be surprised," said Albie. "Haven't you heard of apple gangs?"

This cracked Ben up, and Albie seemed pleased.

"Absolutely. There are drive-by apple throwings. It's a dangerous world."

"Not to mention the terrible things that can happen when rival gangs wear the wrong colors. Like if the Golden Deliciouses wear red, or the Honeycrisps wear green," said Toby.

"I wonder what they'd call an apple orchard gang?" I asked. "The MacDaddies? Like Mac-Intosh? That's not bad."

"Eh," said Toby. "We can do better. You don't like the Golden Deliciouses?"

"Would you be offended if I said that sounded really gay?" Albie asked.

"I would take it as a compliment," Toby said, and Ben laughed again, so I did too.

"Are we forming some kind of apple gang now?" Ben asked.

"Sure," Toby said as we reached a clearing with a bunch of picnic tables. All around us were groups of trees and signs about what harvests were available and where to find them.

"The Apple Dumpling Gang?" Ben asked.

"What the hell is the Apple Dumpling Gang?" asked Albie.

Ben said, "The Apple Dumpling Gang. Wasn't that like an old movie or a cartoon or something?"

"It does sound kind of familiar," I answered. "I like it. We're the Apple Dumpling Gang."

Toby giggled. "It's perfect. Scary, but not too scary. Cartoonish, but not too cartoonish. Sexy, but not too sexy. You don't mess with the Apple Dumpling Gang." He struck a pose, his arms crossed in front of his skinny chest, and attempted a serious, menacing expression.

"Yeah, but what does our gang do?" Ben asked as we approached a sign for Jonathan apples.

"We maintain order among the different apple breeds," Toby explained. "We make sure the Jonathans and the McIntoshes don't get into it. And, of course, we defend our territory. This, friends, is our territory."

"I want the pole," I said.

"I figured Toby would say that," Albie said.

I turned crimson.

"Come on, be nice," said Ben, which made my face and neck flush even more.

"Oh, please," Albie said. "You should hear the things he says to me."

"It's true," Toby said, turning around from where he was standing guard, defending our territory. "I'm horrible to him. And he deserves it."

"You guys are like an old married couple," I said. "Are you sure you're not gay, Albie?"

Albie put his arm around Toby. "If only. Wouldn't this be a nice trophy wife or husband or whatever? The only problem is that I find boys about as attractive as I find hamsters."

160

"Yes, if you don't dig hamsters, that's a problem," I said, looking over at Ben, who was smiling at me. And I got the idea he was thinking the same thing I was: *We're nice, comfortable straight guys. That's cool, right?*

Ben and I went and actually picked apples, which wasn't super-exciting, exactly, but was mildly entertaining. We took the pole, and it was fun trying to get the apples high up in trees to fall into the birdcage thing. We succeeded about half the time.

"I've never had a gay friend before," Ben said, and my heart skipped a beat until I realized he meant Toby.

"Yeah," I said. "I mean, I have. But it's the same. People are people."

"People are, people are," he said, and I cracked up because he was so adorable — Ben the apple orchard philosopher. I could get used to walking through apple orchards with Ben.

We came back with a whole bucket full of Jonathan apples and found Toby and Albie filling their buckets with shiny red and green fruit. "Nice job protecting our territory," I said.

"Thanks," said Toby.

Just then an old lady walked by. She smiled at us. I smiled back. Then Toby stepped forward, crossed his skinny arms again, and tried to look tough. The woman looked at him, did a double take, and walked away, shaking her head.

That made Ben howl. I definitely had never heard him howl, but I guess something about Toby scaring away an old lady from our gang turf was funny to him and he doubled over. That made me laugh, of course, and soon we all were, and I kind of felt sorry for the old lady, but mostly I felt like it was hard to breathe because I was laughing so hard.

"Stop," Toby said, once he recovered and went back into character again. "You're killing our reputation as gang members. We're the toughest gang in this entire apple orchard, and you can't show weakness."

Albie kept laughing, and Toby picked up an apple and kind of tossed it at him. It hit Albie in the forearm hard, though.

"Hey!" he yelled.

Albie picked up the apple, and Toby started running. So Albie chucked it as hard as he could, but he couldn't reach the sprinting Toby.

"You need someone with an arm," Ben said, and he picked up an apple and threw it high and far. Toby was now facing us, a good one hundred feet away, and the apple was in the air for a long, long time. Toby watched it as it approached and stuttered in his shoes, unsure of which way to dodge. He was still standing in the same spot what felt like minutes later, when the apple smacked him on the shoulder.

He fell over. Which just about made us die laughing.

I grabbed a bucket and ran over to Toby, who at first was afraid but then got it — I was going to protect him. Apples started flying in both directions as infighting overtook the once solid Apple Dumpling Gang. I took one from Ben on the shin, and it really hurt. But I got him in the back, and he yelled, "Shit!" and even though we were involved in a painful apple fight, we kept throwing. Fortunately, none of us had real good aim.

"Boys! Excuse me! Excuse me! Boys!" the woman yelled, running up the hill toward the clearing. "Stop this right now! You will pay for all those apples, you know. Are you crazy?"

"We're sorry, ma'am," Toby said. "We apologize. There was a gang war."

It took everything I had not to bust out laughing again.

It cost each of us twenty-one dollars to pay for the apple carnage. We wanted to take some home, but the lady confiscated them and told us never to come back. I couldn't help it; my face got red from getting yelled at, but also from having the most fun I'd had in an afternoon, maybe ever.

Back in the car, we just drove around for a while, not sure where to go. Then Albie reached into his pocket and pulled out one shiny Jonathan apple.

"Hungry?" he asked us.

"How'd you do that?" I asked, wondering when he'd had time to pocket an apple.

"Oh, I have four of them," he said, patting his megalarge pockets. "Next time you won't laugh when I tell you to watch *Survival Planet*."

"So a guy gets into a terrible car accident, and his body is okay, but he's brain-dead," Ben said.

"What kind of car was it?" I said, turning my head to look at him. He punched me in the arm.

We were lying on his floor, studying. Him philosophy, me World War II.

"So he's brain-dead, but his body — fine. At the same time, another guy gets into a separate accident. His body is totally mangled, but his brain is intact, totally fine. There's a transplant. The healthy mind and the healthy body are merged. So who is the person?"

"James?" I asked. Ben didn't even look over and punched me again.

I rubbed my arm, closed my eyes, and pondered. I'd never had conversations like this with a friend, since Claire Olivia wasn't the philosophical type. This was like exercising a muscle I hadn't ever used before. I liked it. "I guess the mind," I said at last.

We were facing opposite ways, our heads near each other, close enough that I could not only hear Ben's breathing but sync mine with it. "So you think you are your mind?" he asked.

"I think so. I mean, the body gets told what to do by the mind," I said.

"Yeah, but if you didn't have a body, you wouldn't exist."

I had to think about that one for a second. Could I be just a mind without my body? The idea made my head hurt, but in a good way.

"So you think you are your body?" I asked him.

"See that? You're doing the Socratic method without even trying," Ben said.

"Cool beans."

He laughed. "This is the kind of conversation people have in the movies when they're high."

I nodded. My voice sounded pinched when I spoke, and that made me think maybe I was high, in a way.

"Have you ever been?" I asked.

"High?" he asked.

"Yeah," I said.

"Once," he answered. "You?"

"Yeah, a couple of times. Medical marijuana has been legal in Colorado for a while now, so it's easy to get. I didn't really like it, though."

"Yeah," Ben said. "I like my brain to be in control."

"Because you are your brain," I said.

"I didn't say that."

We laughed. I could hear his head move, so I turned my face to the side. Our eyes met. His were literally a foot away from mine, and

165

I got this amusement-park feeling in my stomach, this whirling, tumbling, delightful sensation in my gut. I felt suddenly disoriented, like I was seeing his eyes for the first time. They were pale blue and kind, like a lazy Sunday afternoon nap. I felt at home looking at him from so close, and his eyes, they were open. To me. They were letting me in.

I didn't look away. I couldn't. I couldn't tell him, but this, this was better than sex. Or at least better than the one time I'd had sex, sophomore year with Clay.

"That Hitler. He sure annexed most of Europe," I said when the silence finally became too awkward.

Ben laughed and looked away. "Philosophy's more interesting," he said as he went back to his book.

"Agreed," I said.

Later that night, not yet quite asleep in my bed, I realized that I couldn't go even one more minute. I hadn't jerked off since the night before I left Boulder, and now it was October 21. Seven weeks. Given my usual schedule, that was six weeks and five or six days too long.

I crept out of bed, careful not to wake Albie, well aware that my boxers were totally bulging. Some guys joked about jerking off while their roommate was asleep, and some even talked as if they knew when their roommates were "slapping the salami." But I was as likely to do that as I was to become a serial cat murderer. I needed my privacy for this kind of thing.

The bathroom was empty, so I took the stall farthest from the door, closed the toilet seat, and sat down. Lotion would have been good, I realized. But there was none. So spit would just have to do.

I thought of Ben's shaggy brown hair, the way his mouth curled down at the bottom and made every smile that much more rewarding, the way he used language, the way his voice sounded when he said "perchance." I imagined us naked together, writhing. That was the stuff, that was . . .

The bathroom door swung open. I froze, throbbing below, literally seconds away from the finale. Even though the door was closed and no one could see, I felt like I'd been caught.

"Yo," the voice said. "Who's in there?"

"None of your damn business," I grumbled.

"Colorado! Nice," said whoever it was. I couldn't tell. It didn't matter. "Takin' care of business."

For a moment I thought he knew exactly what I was doing, and then I realized he meant taking a crap. I didn't understand why anyone would talk to somebody else while in a bathroom stall to begin with. It's a private thing, you know? So I didn't answer, and when I started hearing sounds I didn't want to hear, I flushed, waited five seconds, and got the hell out of there.

I'd have to find a place sometime very soon to finish myself off. This wasn't healthy for anyone.

A History of Rafe
Part VI

"SO POLONIUM TURNS into lead. Cobalt turns into?" I asked Clay. He was sitting on my bed and I was sitting on my desk chair, really wanting to sit on my bed with him. I didn't think of myself as a shy person, and it wasn't like Clay was so incredible that he made me feel starstruck. I just couldn't quite figure out a way to get there without seeming insanely eager. Without his finger on my thigh, I was suddenly a little unsure.

He looked at me blankly, and I couldn't help it. I had to laugh.

"So do you actually not know this?"

He looked hurt. "Know what?"

"What cobalt turns into? The difference between alpha and gamma radiation?"

He averted his eyes and I could see that his feelings were hurt. "Clay. What's up? Because, like, I don't mind having you over here, but I'm not that excited about talking about chemistry. Seriously, you're going to be an engineer. Don't you know this stuff already?"

Clay hadn't looked back at me yet. He was glancing around my room.

168

"When my dad was our age, he lived on a reservation for a while," he said.

"Huh?"

"My granddad used to teach. So they moved a lot and for a while they lived on the Cheyenne reservation in Montana. I always liked it when he talked about that. It was like watching a movie in my brain."

I didn't know what to say. A lot of sarcastic comments occurred to me. *Non sequitur much, Clay? Guess what, Clay? I'm having reservations about how much chemistry we have.* That sort of thing. Luckily, I kept my stupid mouth shut.

"When my dad died last year, I decided I have to be an engineer. He was one. Worked for Ball Aerospace. He designed instruments for the Hubble space telescope. He died of skin cancer. My dad always wanted me to be an engineer, but I'm not really very good at science. I'm good at English and history mostly."

I instantly felt so bad about his dad and terrible for doubting him. I rolled my chair over and put my hand on his knee. Clay looked down like there was a tarantula on his leg. I started to take my hand off.

"No," he said, not taking his surprised eyes off his knee. "You can keep your hand there."

So I left it there and Clay stared at my hand as he told me more about his father. Clay could say amazing things, surprising things, for a guy who at first seemed to be about as exciting as our chemistry textbook. He told me about how his dad used to take him out to his work area in the garage. He would show Clay blueprints for different machines he was creating. One was meant to change lenses

169

on the telescope so quickly that you could take two distinct images of the earth just about simultaneously.

"My dad was my best friend," Clay said, his eyes still on my hand, and I squeezed his knee, and I could almost — almost — see a reaction in him.

And I felt radiant, which I know is weird. Because Clay, he was not exactly captain of the football team or even some major thespian. He was just this random guy. But something about feeling like I was getting through to him, breaking through that big wall he had built around himself, made me feel good about myself.

This was becoming something. The more Clay talked, the more I was sure of it. Clay. My boyfriend.

As I listened to his monologue about his dad, and then about his mom and her painting, I realized: Here's this incredible person, and I would never have even guessed that based on his exterior. Clay was sensitive and interesting and somehow getting cuter by the second. And the thing with the finger on my leg, that was his only way to let me know that he was interested. In me! This was not how I expected to find a boyfriend, but this, this will work, I thought.

We talked for a long, long time. Maybe a full hour, nonstop. And not a single word of it was about me.

But I was okay with that. Because Clay, he seemed to need it. And isn't that what boyfriends do? They listen.

Rafe,
Bravo! Such a nice improvement here. One of my concerns earlier this semester was about you being "all over the place." This feels much more focused. At the same time, I still wonder how much of this is, as Doctorow would say, "an exploration"?

Are you really starting with nothing? What does "starting with nothing" mean? How open is Rafe, as an author, to learning new things about Rafe? One other thought: Have you reflected at all about how you had labeled Clay before you knew him? How correct was that label?

— Mr. Scarborough

"So tell us about you," my mother asked Ben. The four of us were sitting in Peace o' Pie in Boston, on Friday night of Parents' Weekend. "Rafe doesn't tell us anything. Before tonight, I'd pictured you as a leprechaun."

Ben and I looked at each other. I liked how he immediately understood that my parents were not to be taken too seriously, that it was okay to share a look with me in front of them. And I could tell that my parents liked that he wasn't a bullshit artist.

"Well, I used to be a leprechaun," Ben said. "My parents are, actually. But I decided to change. You know the saying: A leopard can't change his spots, but a leprechaun can."

My mom cackled. Her laugh is always extra loud, and I looked around the restaurant, totally embarrassed. But the half dozen other aging hippies feasting on gluten-free crust and lactose-free mozzarella pizzas didn't even notice her. I'd apologized in advance to Ben, both for my postprime hippie parents and everything embarrassing they were going to say, and also for the food, which was going to make our cafeteria's "Natick meat-loaf special" seem downright tasty.

172

The one comment everyone always makes when they se
mom is that she looks happy. I guess that's a compliment, and I know
she'd take it that way. Mom has red hair that she wears long, sometimes in a ponytail, sometimes not. She's also big into suspenders
and tie-dye, and I hadn't seen her in a dress maybe ever. Tonight, she
was wearing a T-shirt that said IMPEACH BUSH, which she'd been
wearing since I was in fifth grade.

"And you're from New Hampshire?" my dad asked.

"Yessir," Ben responded.

"Live free or die," my dad said, as if it were a command.

"I didn't realize how far Natick was from Boston," my mother
said. "I rather pictured you taking the T all the time, hanging out in
the city."

"I hadn't even been in Boston before tonight," I said.

"It's pretty much special occasions only," Ben explained. "I guess
last year I went in, like, twice. Beacon Street is pretty cool."

"We've been," my mother said, beaming. I could tell she liked
Ben, and I felt a flutter somewhere in my diaphragm. "Gavin and I,
after we graduated from Oberlin, we lived in Somerville for two
years. They were wonderful years too!"

"That was nineteen thirty-what?" I asked.

"Be nice to your parents," Ben admonished me. "You have no
idea how much cooler they are than mine."

"Thank you!" my father said. "We've been telling him that for
ages, and he doesn't listen."

We'd ordered a large pie with zucchini, garlic, and apple sage
sausage. Apple sage sausage tastes sort of like meat, if you think that
an apple is a type of animal. Otherwise, it's just an imposter, and I

173

hate imposter foods. My parents tried to sell me on a tofu turkey last Thanksgiving. I went hungry that night. Kill the beast, I say.

"Mmm," I said, chomping down my whole wheat crust with a bit of lactose-free cheese and I Can't Believe It's Not Sausage! "Compost."

"What a brat," my mother said. "Isn't he a brat, darling?" she asked my father, who nodded vehemently.

"Yeah, yeah, I'm a terrible son. I know," I said.

"No. Just a brat," my dad said, winking at me.

My parents kept on enthusing over Ben, which would have embarrassed me to pieces if it were me, but Ben didn't seem to mind. He got the self-effacing aspect of their humor, and the gentleness too, and he seemed to like it.

"So what's this Claire Olivia like?" Ben asked my mom, smirking. "I want to know about this girlfriend of Rafe's."

Mom's eyes opened wide, and she glanced over at my dad, who had a pained expression suddenly. It was like, *Act much?* I'd asked them for one tiny little favor, and they appeared to be caving at the first innocent mention of a girl.

"She's . . . artsy, I'd say," my mom said tentatively. "Unique."

"Alternative," my dad added. "They have been inseparable from the time they were about twelve. Sleepovers, you name it."

I knew Dad was goading me. He wasn't a big fan of being told what to do.

"Wow," Ben said. "I was dating this girl Cindy, on and off, for the last couple years, but no early-life sleepovers for us. She's from home. Alton is the town I grew up in. Up north."

"Ah," my mother said, unsure what to do in this role. "That's nice."

"We broke up," Ben added, choking down a piece of crust. "It was just too hard, long distance and all."

"I'm sure that was tough," my mother said.

"How's the distance been for you, Rafe?" my dad asked me.

"Fine," I said. "It's been fine."

"I figured, as close as you two always have been . . ."

"Thanks, Dad," I said. "Can we talk about something else?"

"Touchy," my dad teased, and I wanted to hit him with something large and heavy.

Ben had mentioned Cindy before, so I knew his history. Yet I couldn't help but think: If Ben were gay, and he knew I was gay, would he pick me? The only guy who had ever picked me was Clay, and ever since I'd written about him, I'd been wondering what he even saw in me. *Had* he even picked me? Was I just an easy target for him because he was in the closet and I was openly gay?

For dessert, Mom ordered us carob-chip cookies sweetened with fruit juice, which were about as delectable as that sounds. After we finished eating, we made sure to give the waitress all our food and dirty napkins so they could be composted.

"This is interesting," Ben said.

My mother's eyes lit up. "It's wonderful! In Boulder we are so far ahead of other places in terms of sustainability. I'm thrilled that the rest of the world seems to be catching up."

"That's cool," Ben said. "I'd love to see Boulder."

"Well, you're welcome to come anytime," Mom said, and I felt a strange combination of thrill and panic, imagining Ben in my Boulder world.

We drove through Boston, which is a really cool place. Lots of brick sidewalks and narrow cobblestone one-way streets, beautiful brownstones, and gas-lit streetlamps. It was the kind of place I could imagine living one day, a city that still had an old-fashioned feel to it. Ben asked if we could find a bathroom, and we pulled up to a Ben & Jerry's so he could use the facilities.

He was hardly out of the car for two seconds before they both started in.

"You love him," my mother said, her eyes wide and her smile mischievous.

"No, I don't," I said, blushing. "Stop it. Cease. Desist."

"Sure you do," my dad said, turning around to goose my cheek. I looked around, horrified. "It's as clear as the smile on that goofy face of yours, Rafe."

"Seriously. Stop," I said, wishing I'd gone in with Ben. "Really."

"Oh, I'm so glad. You love a boy," my mom said. "You're still our Rafe, underneath this hideous straight disguise. . . ."

"It's not a disguise," I yelled, surprising even myself. "I know you don't get this, but there's a part of me that this truly is, okay? I know, I'm gay. I'm your gay son. But could you just give me a fucking break for two minutes so I can be just me too? God." I pounded the seat next to me.

It was dead quiet in the car. My parents stared at me, their mouths open. I don't think I'd ever yelled at them. I immediately felt horrible, and I lowered my head.

"Oh, God. I'm sorry," I said. "Please. That was so off-the-charts wrong. I'm sorry. I love you guys. I just, I know you don't get this. But please. Trust me, okay? I know what I'm doing."

Mom put her hand on my arm and rubbed it.

"I'm not sure that you do, Rafe. But, sure, sweetheart, we'll give you space. And I'm sorry. We're sorry, right, Gavin?"

Dad seemed less sure.

"I just don't know," he said. "I'm flabbergasted. I feel like I don't even know who you are anymore, and that makes me feel like curling up in a corner somewhere and crying."

Dad's eyes watered, and I had to look away because I couldn't watch my dad cry without my eyes tearing up too. Then Dad started out-and-out crying, and I was like, *Please don't do this*, but I was choked up and couldn't say it, and I hugged him around the seat and soon he was sobbing.

And of course, that's when Ben came back from the restroom.

"Should be condemned," he said before he saw that something had happened in the car while he was gone. And in classic Ben style, he just took it in. He allowed it to be, and he didn't make a big deal about finding out what was up or why my dad was crying like a baby while he was driving the car. And I have to say, that only made me like Ben more, if that was possible.

Mom and Dad had a meeting with Mr. Scarborough the next day, and I was freaking out, wondering what he was saying and what they were saying too. Ben wasn't around; his parents had driven down for the day, and he was with them. His dad looked kind of like a cowboy — tall and skinny with a pointy, grizzled face and a mustache. It was hard for me to see the resemblance, even though Ben had told me a couple of times that he looked just like his dad, that there were pictures of his dad as a teenager that looked exactly like Ben. Spooky, he'd called it. And it *was* spooky, because I couldn't imagine how Ben could ever metamorphose into *that*.

I liked his folks fine when I met them on Saturday morning. They didn't try to get to know me the way my folks did with Ben, but I think that's the difference between Boulder hippies and repressed New Hampshire farm people. We visited, sitting across Ben's dorm room, talking about how it might snow soon. And that was plenty for me.

While my parents were talking to some of my other teachers in the afternoon, Steve started up a touch football game. I'd played a few times now, and I really liked it. I wasn't the best at catching the ball, but I was fast enough that I could score when I did.

About halfway through the game, the parents started spilling out of Academy Hall. It was like I could feel my mom and dad watching me as I was chasing and catching this kid who'd just caught a long pass, and when I turned around after the play, there they were. My dad had his iPhone in his outstretched left hand, filming me, of course, and my mom was smiling, like real joyfully. She wasn't humoring me; something had made her feel good.

The game ended, and I rushed over to them. Dad was busy re-watching whatever he caught of me on video, and she was enthused about meeting my teachers. Well, some of them, anyway.

"That Scarborough! What a sharp one he is!" she gushed. "He truly gets it, the value of self-expression. I just loved him. Loved him!"

"Yeah, he's pretty cool. What about Mr. Sacks?" I asked, goading her.

"History? Eh," she said, dismissing him. "Just another right-wing zealot, hoping to get you kids hooked on lies. The fifties were a time of great joy and prosperity, my foot. For whom?"

She was getting worked up, and I didn't want the mostly conservative parents all around us to hear, so I took her hand. "Let's go for a walk," I said. "I'll show you around campus."

We went across the quad and down to Dug Pond, where we sat at the only empty picnic table. For my part, I was trying to figure out how to leave things on better terms. I didn't want them hating me, going back home thinking I was this monster who didn't appreciate their love and acceptance and now wanted to be straight.

"I know this is weird to you," I said.

My mother gazed at me, a warm smile on her face, her flower-print blouse flowing with the soft, mid-autumn breeze.

"It is, but I get it too," she said. "I didn't before, but, now . . . I think I do."

"I don't," my father said. "But I'm all ears. Edify us please, Opal."

"Watching you play football there, I saw something I hadn't seen before. You really were enjoying that, weren't you?" my mother said, scratching my back through my sweaty shirt with her fingernails.

"Yeah," I said.

"I hadn't understood that desire in you, the desire to do those sorts of boy things. I don't know how I missed that."

I put my mouth on her shoulder and kissed it. "You missed it because I missed it, Mom," I said. "I would never have said I needed that back home, because I didn't know how much I liked being a part of a group of guys. But I knew I needed something, you know?"

"I do," Mom said.

"Now it just feels like this barrier that was up between me and these other guys is no longer up. And I love that," I said.

My dad put his arm around me. "I just don't understand why you can't be honest and still be friends with a bunch of other boys. Here. Anywhere. What precludes you?"

"I don't know."

"I think that's self-limiting," he said. "Who says there's a barrier? Maybe you put it up."

"I don't think I did, Dad. And I like this. I like it here."

My mother sighed. "This isn't what we'd expected you'd do, sweetheart. We didn't see this phase coming."

"I know," I said.

"But I will absolutely, one hundred percent support you," Mom said. "And I promise. No more jokes about you being in love with Ben. You're not, are you?" she asked.

"No," I said, a little bit too quickly. "He's like . . . there's like this incredibly close bond. I can't explain. I love him, I think, but not like in love, you know?"

"Yes," she said softly. "I understand that."

My dad stood up and paced in front of us just a bit.

"I still think that you're overlooking something," he said. "You say you have this great bond. But how can you, if he doesn't know you?"

"Come on, Dad," I said. "He knows me."

"He does?" he asked.

I could see he didn't understand that knowing a person is about more than knowing whom they fantasize about. That's the small stuff, actually. Not the big stuff. The big stuff is lying next to a guy on the floor and locking eyes and having deep conversations about philosophy. The big stuff is letting a friend know your hopes and your fears and not having to make a joke about it. That's what matters.

Despite him still not quite getting it, I was feeling a million times better as we walked back to the car.

"Is it homophobic here?" my mom asked. "Could you be openly gay?"

"Yeah," I said. "I think so. My roommate? You met Albie. Did you meet Toby?"

"His friend?" Dad asked.

"Yes."

"He's gay."

"We thought so. And you're nice to him?"

"He's, like, one of my best friends here," I said. "Ben likes him too. He's cool. This is cool. I promise."

"Well. That's something, anyway," Dad said.

They kissed me good-bye, and as I watched their rental car drive off, I had the strong sensation that I'd underestimated my parents and their devotion to me. Of course they'd be on my side, whether they understood or not. That was just the kind of parents they were.

Reverse coming out to Claire Olivia was the obvious next step. I didn't anticipate it going real well. I was right.

"So I have something to tell you," I said, as casually as possible, a few days after my parents' visit.

"Is it something scandalous, Shay Shay?" she asked. "I love scandals, especially at all-boys schools!"

"Well, actually, it is a little scandalous," I said.

"Ooh," she said. "Saucy."

I took a deep breath and said, "I'm not gay here, Claire Olivia."

She was silent. Then: "Say again?"

"Not gay. Here. At Natick."

"What does that mean?"

"It means I decided to not be gay. I just wanted to, like, be a normal kid for once. Not the gay kid."

"You went back in the closet?" I could hear the prickliness in her voice, and my heartbeat accelerated.

"No. Not in the closet. To me, the closet is when someone won't admit they're gay at all. I already have. I'm sort of . . . taking a break."

She snorted. "Taking a break?"

"Yeah."

"I'm not getting this. How do you take a break from who you are, Shay Shay?"

I was quiet for a while. I didn't want to get into a fight with her, but something about her tone really pissed me off, like she was so smart that in three seconds she got something that I, having lived with it for months, didn't get.

"You can take a break from a part of yourself," I said. "I mean, you could take a break from being a brunette by, I don't know, dyeing your hair. Right?"

"Oh, come on," she said. "That's completely different than denying part of who you are. This sounds SO crazy, Rafe. Why would you do something like this? You're happy with who you are."

"I am. And I'm happy with who I am here too. Even my mom got it. She saw me, like, playing football. . . ."

She snorted even louder this time. "You? Playing football?"

"Yeah, touch football, Claire Olivia," I said, my voice sharp. "I liked it. I like it."

"I'm sorry, but is this Rafe? Like, my friend Rafe, who is my best friend, whom I've known since I was six? My friend whom I adore, who is GAY, by the way? Not straight, because that would be INSANELY weird?"

"Yeah, this is him," I said, and my voice was shaking. "This is Rafe, and I'm telling you something about me, and you're being mean. How do you think that makes me feel?"

"Oh, I don't know, Rafe. Maybe the same way I feel when I find out that my BEST FRIEND in the world has been lying to me for two months and is now, apparently, a straight guy. Are you, like, a Republican now too?"

"I don't know. Maybe," I said.

"Fantastic," she said. "Go enjoy a football game, drink a beer. Hang with your buddies. Scratch your balls. This one's not interested."

And she hung up on me.

My gut twisted in knots. I had known it wouldn't be good, but I hadn't imagined it would be that bad. My mood dark and my nerves rattled, I went down the hall to Ben's room. He opened the door, glasses on, philosophy book in hand, reading up on Immanuel Kant.

"What happened to you?" he said. "You look like you got hit by a truck."

I walked in and collapsed in the burgundy chair. "Claire Olivia and I just had this huge fight. I think we're . . . done."

"Oh, man," he said, grabbing me an orange drink from the mini-fridge and going for the vodka. "That sucks."

"Yeah," I said. "It sucks."

He handed me the Gatorade and I chugged a third of it down, closing my eyes when brain freeze momentarily attacked me behind the eyes. Then he filled the bottle with vodka, shook, and handed me back the plastic screwdriver.

"It'll cure what ails you," he said, and I laughed, but only a little.

"What happened?" He lay down on his bed.

So I told him an extremely edited version that involved her not getting who I am. The football part I told him verbatim, and he nodded like he understood.

"Cindy used to do that all the time, decide that I had to be exactly the same as I'd always been. It drove me nuts. We're not supposed to ever change, and if we do, and they aren't there to witness it, it's this major affront."

"Yeah," I said. "That's what I mean."

"So is it really over?"

I shrugged and took a deep swig. "She hung up on me, so probably." I kicked off my shoes and put my feet up on his desk.

"Well, you know, the way your parents described her, she really didn't sound like someone I could see you dating."

That made me think about what kind of girl I would date if I really did date girls, and I enjoyed the silence. That was the thing with me and Ben; we shared the best silences.

"Yeah, maybe," I said. "It still sucks."

"I know. That connection. It's hard to replace. I can't tell you how many times last spring I'd hang out all night with Bryce, talking about Cindy. It was like, that friendship, that closeness with Bryce. That was my replacement."

I looked him straight in the eye, not feeling at all ashamed. "Yeah, I feel in a lot of ways closer to you than I ever did to Claire Olivia."

He smiled and his face reddened a little. "Yeah. That's not the kind of thing that people talk about too much, but I get it. It's, like, a bromance."

"Yes!" I shouted. "That's it. A bromance. I love that. I love you, man!"

"I love you too, man," he said, and I went over to the bed and collapsed down next to him as a joke.

Ben laughed, and put his arm around me, also as a joke, and it felt so, so right. I felt like I could almost lose my mind in happiness, being there with his arm around me. I didn't move, and soon he just kept it there, and we lay there, not saying anything.

"Men in India hold hands walking down the street," Ben said, his voice right up against my ear.

"Really?"

"Yeah. It's just part of their culture. They don't, you know, do things sexually. They just hold hands. Here, that would be, like, weird."

"Yeah. We Americans are so uptight," I said. "Why does everyone have to make everything into such a huge deal? Why do we have to label everything?"

We were silent again, except for my pounding heart, and the jitter in my throat, the feeling of waves crashing over my head — waves of some alien feeling that felt ridiculously good. Was this love? Was I in love with Ben? Because whatever I felt was everywhere in my body and it was something I wanted more of, immediately. I so wanted to tell Ben everything about everything, and how I once had an almost boyfriend, but that I would have traded that entire experience for two seconds of this.

But of course I couldn't tell him that. Which sucked. It was hard not to be able to share the entire truth about my past with Ben. Maybe someday I'd be able to.

"Thanks, Ben," I said finally, when I was sure my voice wouldn't crack. "You may be the best friend I've ever had."

After a few unbearable moments, Ben replied: "You too."

A History of Rafe
Part VII

THE THIRD, FOURTH, and fifth times Clay came over, we started with chemistry, and after a while, there was his touch, never going past where it had the time before. And then talking. I learned that Clay was one-eighth Native American and mostly French Canadian, that he had gone to science camp the previous summer, that he liked to play Ping-Pong, and that his favorite food was Brie cheese. Every fact led to follow-up questions, like they were these tender morsels of truth that needed further dissection, and a couple of times, I told him things about me. He didn't ask questions back, and I wasn't sure if he was even listening until the fifth visit, when he referenced the fact that I had gone to Jarrow Montessori School for elementary school. I had mentioned that the previous time.

He's just weird, I realized. It's not that he doesn't listen, or he doesn't care. He just has his own way of expressing himself.

The sixth time, though, things went a little differently.

It started out the same: hovering over my book, me talking about oxidation and reduction, and then isotopes and ions, his finger straying to my thigh, his breath in my ear. Then I asked him a question about the extra outer electron that sodium has, which chlorine could use, and when he didn't answer, I looked up at him.

He was staring into my eyes, and I felt that shivery thing that happens when you look in someone's eyes and you get goose bumps because you're gaining access.

I stopped talking, and I stared back. I wanted to tell him how perfectly eager and scared his eyes were, but I didn't get a chance, because in barely a second his face was mashed into mine.

I couldn't even breathe. His lips pressed into my lips, and even though it was awkward and I didn't want my first kiss to be like that, I let it go because I didn't want to embarrass him, and I knew how hard it must have been to get up the nerve to kiss me. His mouth tasted like stale mint and peanuts.

So I kissed him back, and I grabbed the back of his neck. When I did that, he grabbed the back of mine. We stood at the same time, our faces still mashed together, and the room seemed to spin as we made our way to the bed.

There was a knock on the door. The unlocked door.

"Don't come in!" I yelled, before I could think. Clay looked at me, horrified, and then looked at the door. He started to jump up.

My mother sounded amused when she said, "Sorry to interrupt."

And she walked away. We could hear her steps as she went down the hall, and both of us stood very still. When there was no more sound, I collapsed onto my back on the bed and sighed.

"That was close," Clay said.

I said back, "She probably would have told us we were doing it wrong."

Clay didn't laugh. That line would have killed with Claire Olivia, but he just looked at me like I was some unusual coral formation at the bottom of the ocean, something mildly interesting but beyond his understanding. I realized he really didn't know that much about me, and my family, and my sense of humor.

Still, I jumped up and locked the door.

We went back to kissing, and though my head wasn't in it at first, soon I relaxed and began to enjoy the feel of his mouth against mine. Then we went further.

It was not all I expected it to be.

After, we lay there on my bed, shirtless, side by side, not touching. A bubble of some unpleasant feeling pressed on my rib cage.

"It's my mother's twenty-fifth anniversary of teaching Jazzercise tomorrow," he said, as if that was a normal thing to say after fooling around.

And the thing is, there was no tone at all, nothing sarcastic or ironic or anything in his voice, just a flat statement, and I thought, *What am I doing?*

Here was this guy who had wormed his way into my life, and at first, his non sequitur stories had been cute. But minutes after the first time I had ever kissed a guy, not to mention gone beyond kissing, they were annoying. I mean, he talked and talked about nothing, and he rarely asked me a question, and what kind of guy doesn't ask you about you, ever? Why was I making excuses for bad behavior? I wondered if I should start talking about myself like he had, if I could ever do that to a person: just enter their life and start talking about myself and never ask any questions. I didn't think so.

I didn't respond to his Jazzercise comment, and eventually we dressed and packed up his books and I walked him downstairs. No kiss, but as we got to the door, he reached back and touched my hand, and then grasped it. It caught me off guard, as usual with Clay.

"You're great," he said, and at first I thought maybe he said, "You *were* great," but when I played it back through my mind, I was pretty sure he was making a comment about how he felt about me. Pretty certain, at least.

I lingered in the foyer for a bit after he left, feeling totally different in my skin. I hoped my mom would come down, because I needed to talk to her. I was about to give up when I heard her on the stairs.

"There you are," she said, all smiles. And then she did the most amazing thing. She came over and hugged me, which was exactly what I needed her to do.

"Thanks," I said into her shoulder. I was glad I didn't have to tell her what had just happened. There are some perks to having a mom like mine.

She took me by the hand and led me to the couch, and then we sat there and didn't say much for a while.

"We didn't do that much."

She didn't react. I realized that she hadn't asked.

"It was weird," I said, staring off into space.

"How do you mean?"

"I thought I'd feel, like, very adult after. I don't."

"How do you feel?"

"I don't know. Let down."

She gave me her sympathetic look, and I felt tears welling in my eyes. I didn't want to cry but part of me needed to, and I wasn't exactly sure why.

"His mom teaches Jazzercise."

She looked at me and raised an eyebrow, as if to say, *What am I supposed to do with this information?*

"Thank you!" I said. "Exactly. He tells me random, weird things. We haven't ever had a normal conversation. He never asks me anything."

"Perhaps he's autistic?"

I shrugged.

"It doesn't sound like you have such a great connection."

I knew that she was right, obviously. But part of me didn't want to. I wanted to have someone to call my own so badly that I just couldn't let it go. Clay was a riddle wrapped in another less impressive riddle. Maybe he was a fixer-upper. Maybe with a little work?

"He has his good qualities. He's really sweet. He's just . . . in the closet."

"Well, perhaps you can help him come out."

"I'm pretty sure he's not ready. And I don't think he's my boyfriend. I thought he was, but now I don't even know. Why does this all have to be so hard?"

She laughed, not in a mean way. "Experimentation is the way we learn about who we are and who we want to be with. Before your dad, I tried on quite a few boys in high school and my first year in college."

"Okay, thanks," I said, trying to head off a conversation about my mother's swinging days.

She sighed. "I'm sorry, Rafe. I know you're not comfortable yet with sexuality. Someday you will be. Someday, you'll be glad that your parents are an open book."

"Someday I'll move far, far away," I replied, and she laughed.

Rafe,

I found it interesting that you made the choice to go out of scene and into exposition when the scene got intimate. Good instinct, I think. But why did you decide to leave scene again after the Jazzercize comment? Such a crucial moment, and you chose to stay in your head through it just about until Clay left. What do you gain as a writer by doing that? What do you stand to lose by showing the scene and letting the reader come to his or her own conclusion rather than telling us what to think about Clay and Rafe?

— Mr. Scarborough

As the trees went from fiery yellow and orange to bare, Bryce's desk became my desk, Bryce's bed my bed. Ben and I joked, we talked out the serious stuff, and sometimes we even cried, like when he told me about his uncle's death the year before. Often we'd just sit up at night and talk until three or four in the morning. These were my favorite nights ever, even better than when I'd done the same thing on weekends with Claire Olivia.

"What do you want?" Ben asked me one night, as we lay across the room from each other in our beds.

I cracked up. "General much?" I asked.

He didn't laugh back. "I mean, like, in the future. If you could come up with a perfect scenario for what your life would be, what would it be?"

The question stole my breath. The answer was obvious to me. *You. You and me. Us.*

"You first," I said.

He exhaled. "Maybe a house out in the woods somewhere in Vermont or Maine. You know. Somewhere with fewer people because people aren't my favorite, present company excluded. A black lab who likes to take long walks. A wife — probably not Cindy — who likes to cook lots of unusual meals, someone funny and interesting but also serious, you know? With dark hair and pretty eyes and . . . you know . . . the other stuff too . . . goin' on or whatever."

I laughed. "You're so hip-hop."

"I know," Ben said. "Anyway, probably a couple kids. And at night we don't watch TV, but we sit in the wood-paneled living room as a family and there's a fire in the fireplace, and we read books and we share about what we're reading. Of course, you live nearby with your family."

"Absolutely," I said.

"What about you?" Ben asked.

I paused to think. I'd had so many fantasies about us together in the future, just about every night, and it was hard to pick just one. Would we go to college together and then settle down in the country, somewhere out here in Massachusetts? Or after our college years, would I take him back to Boulder and we'd live in the mountains together? Whatever fantasy I chose, it was off-limits to Ben.

"Pretty much the same."

"It's nice, dreaming about stuff like that, isn't it?" Ben said. "Makes me feel so peaceful."

"Mm-hmm," I replied, feeling a lot less peaceful inside.

"So can I tell you something weird?" he asked, after a long silence.

"Always," I said. I turned and faced him in the darkness. Even with the moonlight I could barely make him out across the room.

"The first time I had sex with Cindy, I cried," Ben said.

194

"Yeah?" I said.

"It was, like, I don't know, there's naked and then there's naked, you know?"

"Not sure I follow?" I said, feeling British as I said it. Sometimes when I say a sentence I feel like I'm trying to be a different person entirely, and this was one of those times.

"I mean, I'd been naked with her before. But this was us totally without any barriers at all. And then to actually be . . . you know . . . in her? That was like . . . You know how the guys talk about sex like it's this game? It wasn't a game to me, Rafe. It was, like, this melding. And I felt responsible for her at that moment, you know? Maybe that's not the right word. But I just felt very open in this incredible way, and I think for me that's the part I liked the most about it. And I would never tell her this, but in the darkness I cried a bit. Or I teared up."

"That's beautiful," I said. *You're beautiful*, I thought, but I didn't say it.

"I'm guessing that didn't happen for you, right?"

"Well," I said, trying to think of what to say. I'd done my best not to lie to Ben, but this didn't feel like a time to be evasive, especially since I'd just evaded his last question. "I guess for me it felt, when it was over, like I was this different person. And I wasn't sure I was ready to be that person? Like something huge had happened and it changed everything, and there was no announcement you could make to the whole world that wouldn't be superweird."

That was all true enough, I realized, after saying it.

"Yeah, but what about the act itself? That's all after stuff. I felt that way too. But, like, when it happened. What did you feel?"

Nothing, I realized, and a lump grew in my throat, thinking about my experience with Clay. By most definitions I was still a virgin, since we'd only fooled around, but still it made me sad to think of how little my first experience had meant to me. But I had to say something, and saying "nothing" was going to lead to a conversation that was going to be really hard for us to have, so I said something else instead. For the first time with Ben, I willingly went deeper into the lie.

"I felt close to her, I guess? Like connected? Spiritually connected. I wasn't the kind of guy who was going to get all high-fiveish about having sex with a girl for the first time, so I guess mostly what I felt was connected on a deeper level with her."

"Sure," Ben said.

And then mostly what I felt was dirty. Lying to a friend sucked. But what choice did I have? Our friendship was amazing and getting better, and that made an occasional small white lie acceptable, right? Not great, but acceptable.

In public, we toned the intensity of our friendship down, knowing that Steve and his posse would not quite get our strange and unusual bond. But in private, we threw away most of our barriers, and that was more than fine with me.

Sex was not on the menu. I hadn't found the line yet where things would be "too much" for Ben, but I had a feeling we were pretty close to it. For all my fantasies about Ben — and I'd had a lot of them — I couldn't really picture any of them coming true. So many nights, after lights out, I snuck off to the bathroom and "took care of business," hoping to God no one would come in and utilize the bathroom in a way that would ruin the mood.

Toby thought it was cute, our bromance. More than once when the four of us were hanging out, he talked about how much he wished he could find what we had, which was funny, since I knew he and Robinson had something going.

One afternoon before dinner, as we did homework in his/our room, Ben got an e-mail from his mom. He groaned, and then read it out loud.

"*Dear Benny,*" he said.

"Oh, I'm definitely calling you that!"

"You are definitely not. *Dear Benny,*" he continued. "*Do you mind if we invite the Tollesons over for Thanksgiving this year? I know Mitch is not your favorite, but it's been five years since we've had them over and I hate to be rude.*"

He pantomimed putting a shotgun in his mouth and pulling the trigger.

"Mitch Tolleson is not exactly your favorite?"

"He's this kid I hung out with when I was six. We parted ways when he shaved his head and got big into hunting. Now he dresses in army fatigues and has a Confederate flag sticker on his pickup truck."

"Delightful. And your parents like him?"

Ben flopped onto his bed and crossed his arms against his chest.

"My parents believe in civility at all costs. Even if your neighbors raise a skinhead, it's better not to make a fuss."

I shook my head. "Our families are not so similar, huh?"

He pursed his lips, like he was already imagining Thanksgiving dinner. Ben was obviously the oddball of the family, into books and ideas. I remembered how uncomfortable his dad looked at Natick, and now it began to make more sense to me. I'd been so caught up in my own stuff that I hadn't even realized that this person, who was superclose to me, felt so alienated from his own family. Suddenly I recognized what I had to do.

"You obviously can't dine with Mitch Tolleson," I said. "He sounds like a Nazi."

He shrugged. "Oh, well," he said.

"Well, you won't be dining with him. What with you being in Boulder and all."

This caught Ben off guard, but then he looked like a kid who had just gotten the best Christmas present ever. He got this goofy smile on his face, like all his cares had lifted. That I could have such an impact on someone as awesome as Ben made me feel amazing.

And then I remembered the obvious: Bringing Ben to Colorado could be total suicide for our relationship. I was going to have to figure out how to "reconcile" with Claire Olivia, for starters, since there was no way I was going to go home and not see her. How the hell was I going to be the same person in Boulder as I was here at Natick?

"You serious?"

"Of course," I said, willing those thoughts away. "It's all done. You're coming with me."

He lowered his head again. I'd forgotten Ben was on scholarship at Natick. My family was well-off enough, but a ticket to Denver wasn't exactly something Ben could call home for.

"My parents bought you a ticket. It was supposed to be a surprise," I said. It wasn't a total lie, because I knew that even if they wouldn't do it, I could. I had a few hundred dollars saved from my summer job at Ripple, this frozen-yogurt place back home. Ben was worth it.

"I can't accept that," he said.

"Yeah, you can," I said. "You're my friend. They want you there. I want you there. Benny."

It took a second, but soon that goofy, slightly uneven smile of his came back, and I knew for sure that I loved Ben. Any fears I had melted away. Ben. In my house. In my room. Yeah, I could make that work.

A History of Rafe
Part VIII

MAYBE IT WAS having a closeted semiboyfriend who wouldn't be seen with me in public, but the little things that used to bug me about being out were making me more and more annoyed.

It was right after Thanksgiving break, and I was in the cafeteria with Claire Olivia, eating Rangeview's version of tacos — reduced-calorie tortillas and ground turkey that tasted like sadness — when the Kaitlins attacked.

Every girl in Boulder who isn't named after a color or a month or a city or a state is named Kaitlin, Brittany, or Ashley, according to Claire Olivia. All the Brittanys wear cool hair bands. The Ashleys are smiley and apolitical and tend to be cheerleaders. The Kaitlins are blond, inquisitive, and prone to be on the yearbook staff or reporters for the *Boulder Tattler*.

Kaitlin One in this case was petite and wearing a peach sweater and dangling turquoise earrings. Kaitlin Two was tall. A volleyball player, I think.

"Hey, Rafe, Claire," Two said. I felt Claire Olivia tense next to me. Call her Claire and you leave yourself open to lotsa bad possibilities, most of them violent. Two didn't wait for any response beyond a nod. "That was so mean, what they did with the church."

I knew she was referring to our history class. Ms. Peavy had taken the subject of church burnings in the South during the civil rights movement and likened it to what had happened locally, four years earlier, at the church where PFLAG met. Someone had spray painted "Die Fagot" on the side of the church, and there was this huge outcry. And of course there should have been. It wasn't a church burning, but it was terrible that someone would vandalize a church, not to mention the spelling issue.

But this being Boulder, the *powers that be* had to organize a vigil. (This was before my mom was involved with PFLAG.) At the vigil, apparently, everyone got to express how they felt, and there was lots of hugging. Then they formed a committee to figure out how to respond to the event. After three months of meetings, the committee started a hotline, which people could use to call in and express their feelings about the hatred shown in the spray-painting act.

Ah, Boulder.

This time, Ms. Peavy hadn't asked me for the official gay opinion on the vandalization. Progress. But now the Kaitlins were. I shrugged.

"It was bad," I said.

"Totally," Kaitlin One said, nodding. "But also too, Mayor Barkley's wife was, like, African-American, so it was like, you know, he understood oppression and he should have organized the vigil."

I nodded, unsure of what she had said, or what that had to do with anything. "Right," I said. "The personal is political, and all of that."

Two nodded this time. "You're so smart. You're going to go to, like, Harvard."

"For spring break," I said, for no apparent reason. I was getting bored with the Kaitlins, and I was afraid that for every minute they stayed there, the likelihood of Claire Olivia starting an international incident was increasing.

Both Kaitlins laughed, and one of them, One or Two, said, "Oh, my God! You're smart like Will and funny like Jack. From *Will & Grace*? Which one are you?"

They didn't wait for a response. "You're Will. Will is so funny."

I stared out the window at some guys playing hacky sack, and sighed. "If that's what makes you comfortable, I guess I can be that," I said.

They walked away. Not two minutes later, Jasmin Price, who is pretty much an Ashley, came up to us.

"Did I see you at Eldora this past weekend?"

I said I was there. She looked surprised and said, "I didn't know gay guys liked skiing."

Claire Olivia looked up from her incessant texting and gave me a moon-eyed look. I ignored it and nodded at Jasmin.

"We really do," I said. "It's a little-known fact. You can tell who is gay by who skis and who snowboards."

And I could actually see the wheels turning. She was thinking, *Wait, doesn't so-and-so ski?* I was about to say, *Just kidding*, but then I got fed up and went to get rid of my tray.

There was Clay, across the room, sitting with his friends. I caught his eye and smiled, and he barely nodded. I envied him then. He could have lunch in peace. Why couldn't I?

And there was Caleb, holding court at another table, surrounded by girls. Everyone was laughing and having a good time. No doubt it was at someone else's expense, but still, they were laughing. That wasn't the kind of guy I was. I mean, I loved the time Claire Olivia and I spent together, but I wasn't flamboyant and always surrounded by girls who wanted to be entertained.

When I got back to Claire Olivia, Jasmin was gone. I rolled my eyes and Claire Olivia rolled hers.

"Hey, did you know I was gay?" I asked.

"Shut up!" she said. "Really? I had no idea, since it's not like the only thing people talk to you about."

"I know, right?" I said. "I am so fucking tired of being seen as 'the gay kid.'"

"Well . . ." She made a face and ran her hand through her hair.

I tensed up. "Well what?"

"I mean, no offense, Shay Shay. But it's not exactly a cosmic mystery how that happened. I mean, it's not like you told the world, and visited other schools to talk about it. It's not like your mom is president of PFLAG Boulder. How rude of people to make a big deal out of you being gay."

I curled my lower lip down to show her my feelings were hurt. Making the face was a joke between us; it was supposed to mean our feelings weren't *really* hurt, but that they would be if we were more sensitive. But the more I think about it, the more I realize that almost every time I did it, my feelings were actually a little hurt. I wonder if that was true for Claire Olivia too.

"Aw," she said, teasing. "Poor Rafe."

"You're always yelling," I said, putting my fingers in my ears.

Rafe,

Okay, here's an assignment for you. It's simple. I want you to take the sentence that begins, "But the more I think about it" from the third-to-last paragraph, and keep writing from there. Do a fastwrite, like the ones we do in class. Notice that you are reflecting now about how you felt then. How does that differ from the (generally well-written) pieces you have given me all semester? Remember Doctorow's quote! Go!

— Mr. Scarborough

For the first round of the soccer play-offs, we played at home against Belmont. We'd beaten them early in the regular season, when we still had Bryce, 4–3. Without him, we knew it wouldn't be easy.

"All right, fellas," Coach Donnelly said in our pregame locker room pep talk. "I want to talk about selflessness. Selflessness involves giving up your self. You become a martyr. Like the Hindu kamikaze warriors. These Japanese Hindus chose to give up their lives, and they were killed if they didn't. Imagine what their families felt. One day you have a father, and next, you're watching him fly a plane into a ship on Pearl Harbor on television. Those kids didn't do anything wrong. They just lived in an evil country. The axis of evil. That sort of evil is beyond anything you or I will experience in our lifetimes. So be glad. Be glad we live in the US of A. Be glad we get to choose, with our freedoms. Now get out there and fight!"

My mind was only half there. I had bigger salmon to sauté, as Claire Olivia would have said. She had called back, and this conversation went a little better.

"I'm really upset," she said. "I'm upset about what you did, and I'm even more upset that I yelled at you and hung up on you. I should not have done that."

"Well, I should have probably told you sooner."

"Yeah. Way sooner."

"I should have just told you last year, when I decided to do this, but I was afraid you'd tell me not to."

"Well, I probably would have, since it's, like, insane," she said.

"Yeah. I know. But I gotta tell you, it feels so right. I am having this bromance like you wouldn't believe. We're really good friends, and that never would have happened if I hadn't done this."

"Bromance? Can gay boys have bromances?" she asked. "Is that why you did this?"

"No! It's just . . . a great perk."

"It's that Ben guy, right?"

"Yup," I said. "You'd adore him. Well, actually, I don't know if you'd adore him. He's really smart and funny, but he's kind of a jock. You might actually hate him."

"Fantastic," she deadpanned.

"Well, there's one way to find out."

"I am NOT coming to Massachusetts to see my best friend, who is straight slash gay. That is so NOT happening."

"I'm coming back for Thanksgiving. With him."

"Wow," she said. "Do your parents know what you're doing? Are they cool with this?"

"Not exactly. But they're trying."

"I don't know. I don't think I'd be very good at playing along."

"Oh, come on," I said. "Think of it as an acting job. Don't you love acting?"

"Ahk-ting . . . is be-ing," she said, in this terrible, stodgy British accent.

"Could you? Please? I wanna hang out with you AND Ben while he's there."

"This is so weird."

"Please? For me?"

"Oh, you know I can't say no to you."

"Tee hee. I thought not."

"You owe me big time."

"I know, I know, I know, I know. Last thing: And, yeah, I owe you for this too. Put it on my tab: You were my girlfriend before you got angry and broke up with me a few weeks ago."

She sighed. "Sounds about right."

Belmont scored a goal forty five seconds into the game, when Robinson let a pretty easy shot slide through his fingertips. A couple of minutes later, he made a nice dive on a shot to his right. Unfortunately, the ball flew by him a second earlier.

Down 2–0, I overkicked Steve by about fifteen feet on a pass. I felt it, in my chest. Failure. This jittery sensation that was like a chill. Steve shot me a look from across the field, and I got the feeling I was going to be hearing about that.

We didn't get another really good chance. In some ways, that made it easier, because when you lose 4–0, one play isn't to blame. But the fact is I didn't have a good game. I stood out. And as we trudged back to the locker room, our season over, I wasn't liking the feeling.

The group was dangerously sullen as we listened to Coach give his final talk of the year, something about a German submarine found off the coast of Carolina "back in the day." I was having trouble paying attention; I just wanted to get showered quickly and slip away to the dorm, where I could hang out with Ben some more. I guess one difference between me and the real jocks was that I didn't care enough to get really passionate about a loss.

Of course, the showers are never a solitary, quick endeavor. The mood, the tone were ugly from the start. I had a feeling I was about to witness what happens when the positive façade of Natick jocks disappears.

"Nice season, Ben, nice season, Zack," Steve said, rinsing off his back. "In fact, most of us had pretty good years. I just wish I knew how you miss a ball that hits you in the hands."

I looked over at Robinson, who was going about his business.

"I'm sorry," he finally said. "I know I sucked."

"Yeah, well, being sorry won't get us to the next round," Steve said. "Maybe if you weren't out getting your cock sucked by Toby twenty-four seven, this wouldn't have happened."

The shower room got real quiet, the sound of rain on tile reverberating through the room.

"Shut up," Robinson said.

Zack took over. "You think people don't notice you guys going into the woods separately, coming back separately? What are we, fucking stupid? You screw that faggot in the ass too?" he asked.

Robinson just stood there and took it. He stood under the water and let it pour over his face and said nothing. I wanted to say: *Stand up for yourself!* But it wasn't for me to say.

Zack continued, "Got a fag goalie who can't stop a fucking shot if it was kicked right at him. . . ."

"Hey," I said, surprising myself. "Cut it out."

"Oh, it's the guy who can't handle making a wide-open pass. Yeah. You should really be talking right now," Zack said.

I stepped toward him. "Shut the fuck up," I said. "You don't talk like that about our teammate. And don't talk like that about my friend Toby." The vibrato in my chest felt like a tremor. It made my head woozy.

"Your friend Toby?" Zack laughed. "He sucking your cock too, Colorado?"

I took another step. Zack took one toward me too. I seized up a bit. I was too skinny for this, but I was also mad, and sometimes when I get mad, I feel bigger than I am.

"If you say another word, I'm gonna blast your head into that wall," Ben said from behind me. Zack froze. I turned around and there was Ben, standing tall. He was big, bigger than anyone on the team, including Steve.

Robinson just went on showering in silence.

"Cut out the homophobic crap," Ben said. "Seriously. Grow up."

Zack skulked back to his showerhead. I tentatively went back to mine, feeling all sorts of conflicting things at once. I was afraid to look at Ben, because my feelings for him were out of control. He was a beautiful, beautiful guy, inside and out.

"He's right," Steve said, ever the leader. "Let's put that stuff away."

I wanted to say, *You started it, asshole.* Everyone in the room should remember that Steve wasn't this perfect guy, but the guy who had started making antigay comments in the shower before someone bigger than him put a stop to it.

But instead, I went back to soaping and rinsing, allowing the hot water to sting the back of my neck, washing away the pain.

The last time I almost got into a fight was back in Boulder.

It was the summer after ninth grade, outside a PFLAG dance in the Methodist church on Spruce Street. Mom was already inside, and I was going to the dance because why not, even though I was not a big "goes to dances" type of guy. And these guys about my age walked by, and one saw the banner for the dance and nudged his friends.

"Fags," he said.

I stopped, turned around, and said, "Gays. We like to be called gays, not fags, just so you know."

And the guy stepped forward and said, "You a fag?"

"No, I'm gay. Like I said. Why?" My heart was pounding in my chest then, and I looked him up and down. He was no bigger than me, but I wasn't sure what I would even do if a fight happened. I'd never punched someone before. Would I kick him too? But here I was, stepping toward him, my chest getting all puffed out like a tough guy's.

"I'll fuckin' waste you," the guy said, and his friends backed off, because they obviously didn't feel the same way he did. Neither did I, really, but I continued forward, and I felt like what I imagine a heart attack feels like. And just as I was about to go after the guy, not knowing whether he would run or if we were gonna throw down, I heard my dad's voice.

"Hey!"

I stopped in my tracks and turned around.

"What's going on here?" Dad hurried out toward us, panic in his eyes. The gay-bashing kid started backing off, and then he turned and ran away.

"He called me a fag," I said, my voice cracking, my head buzzing.

And my dad came and hugged me fiercely. "You're no fag, okay? You don't owe those idiots any explanation about who you are. They'd be lucky to be half the man you are, Rafe. Okay? We love you. Don't fight those idiots. They may never change. You just let them be."

Unspoken in those words was the fact that I probably would have lost that fight. Because I'm not a fighter. And who knows what happens when you're down on the ground, having lost a fight? If my dad hadn't come out, would the kid have killed me?

I lay in Bryce's bed, eyes wide open, the night of the soccer game. Ben slept peacefully on the other side of the room. I thought about the almost-fight with Zack. Something hadn't felt right ever since. Ben and I had hung out and talked, as usual. Nothing had changed with him. But I felt as if a part of me had disappeared in the altercation in the locker room.

Who was I? How could I stand up for gay people while at the same time hiding that part of me?

And I felt so foreign, lying there, the wind howling outside our window. What was I doing here? Who was Rafe, really? Can you just put a part of yourself on hold? And if you do, does it cease to be true?

Straight people have it so much easier. They don't understand. They can't. There's no such thing as openly straight.

Because once, there was something that I was, and it was a difficult thing to be. But at least I was, you know, something. I wasn't just a guy who stood tall in the shower, standing up for someone else, when really, I should have been standing up for myself.

And that was something my best friend Ben couldn't know about me.

Fastwrite: "The More I Think About It . . ."

The more I think about it, the more I realize that almost every time I did it, my feelings were actually a little hurt. I wonder if that was true for Claire Olivia too.

Sometimes my feelings get hurt but I pretend they aren't hurt.

Feelings hurt. I don't like having my feelings hurt. I feel —

Claire Olivia is my friend but sometimes she hurts my feelings and I hurt hers. I feel —

I don't know how I feel, maybe? It's a long time ago. Let me try something more recent:

The more I think about it, the more I realize that when Steve and Zack started making homophobic comments in the shower, I didn't feel angry. I felt hurt because that's how they see me. I hate that they see me as something to make fun of. I hate that I have to hide —

I HATE THIS! AAARRRGGGHHH!

Rafe,

Ha! This may not be the best writing you've done this semester, but it certainly feels the most authentic. And I love the last line! Not because it is fantastic writing, but because it is true. Good try on this. Keep trying. You're a good writer. I want you to think about thinking less, though. You seem pretty set on controlling where your writing goes, and I think the short paragraphs aren't really your friend. I think you think they are, but for this sort of writing, it's very hard to think in short, clipped paragraphs. Just write, Rafe. Don't worry about form. Fast-writing is a really good tool for you. Don't think so much about how it will read to your audience.

— Mr. Scarborough

It was Tuesday night, two days before Thanksgiving. Ben and I were packing and talking about what we were going to do in Colorado the next three days, and there was a knock on the door.

Ben crossed the room and opened it, and I saw his expression before I saw who was there. His mouth opened wide, and then his eyes got wide, and it was like he came to life in a way that I hadn't ever seen.

Standing there at the door was Mr. Donnelly, and by his side, with a sheepish grin on his face, was Bryce.

"B!" Ben said, and the two of them hugged hard. Mr. Donnelly stood smiling at the reunion, and I looked out in the hallway and saw that other kids were milling around.

"How are you?" Ben asked.

Bryce waved the question away, like it didn't matter. Of course it did, but when someone's been depressed, I guess you give them a little leeway.

"You got another roommate?" he asked.

"Unofficially," Ben responded, pointing to me. "Bryce, you remember Rafe?"

"Oh, right. Broken nose guy. What up?"

"Not much," I said, feeling awkward. I went and shook his hand.

"You back to stay?" Ben asked.

"Nah. I'm here to pack up my things. I'm fine, don't worry. Just need to be home for a while."

"Oh. Okay . . ." Ben said, and I couldn't quite read his emotion.

"You guys probably have lots to catch up on," I said.

Ben nodded. "Just for a bit. But I want the three of us to hang out."

Bryce looked at his watch. "My mom's downstairs in the car. I told her an hour."

"See if she'll go for two, okay?"

Bryce texted his mom. She answered right away, and Bryce smiled. "Yeah, I can. She said she'd go get coffee."

"I'm out of here," I said. "Back in?"

"Like an hour," Ben said, and Bryce nodded.

I went and hung out with Albie and Toby in my old room, listening to the police scanner and barely drinking a Red Bull. They talked about EMT training, which Albie was thinking of doing over the summer. He thought maybe he'd take a year off before college and try that. Toby said that if he was going to take a year off from school, it would be to become a Rock Cat. And then he started kicking really high, which was weird.

"What the hell is a Rock Cat?" Albie asked.

"You know. Radio City Music Hall in New York? Every Christmas? The Rock Cats. Duh."

"Did your mom put battery acid in your cereal?" Albie asked. "They're the Rockettes."

"No, they aren't."

"Uh. Yeah. They are."

Toby blushed. "Well, you think that old song is about a 'Hollow Batgirl.'"

"Shut up," Albie said, turning away.

"What's a hollow batgirl?" I asked.

"It's a 'Hollaback Girl' when you have trouble hearing lyrics and all your pop culture references come from *Survival Planet*," Toby said.

I laughed. "Albie. Dude."

"Whatever," Albie said. "I like the image of mine better. A batgirl who is hollow. It's poetic."

"Very. Especially for a song where the singer spells 'bananas' for the audience," Toby said.

"'Help Boy Scouts Blind Kids,'" Albie said in a monotone.

Toby said, "Stop. Shut up."

Albie ignored Toby. "We were at a swap meet in Cochituate last year, and there was this Boy Scout troop with a sign that read, 'Help Boy Scouts, Blind Kids.' Toby saw it, and he grabbed my shirt collar and pulled me away. I asked what was wrong, and with this scared expression on his face, he said, 'That's not right. They need to be stopped.'"

I cracked up. "Oh no," I said.

"When I asked him why helping blind kids and Boy Scouts was bad, Toby's whole face went white. He said, 'Forget it. Let's go.' But I had to know what the hell he was talking about, so I made him walk back over with me. We looked at the sign together, and finally he mumbled, 'I didn't see the comma.'"

I turned to Toby. "You thought the Boy Scouts were collecting money so they could actually blind kids?"

He shrugged. "Well, they're anti-gay, you know. I guess I didn't think it was a huge stretch. Besides, I was mostly joking?"

Albie shook his head. "Yeah. He really wasn't."

"And how were they going to go about blinding kids, in that crazy brain of yours?" I asked.

Toby was making a careful study of the floor below him, like it was really fascinating.

"Slingshot," he finally said.

I couldn't wait for the hour to be up. So at fifty-seven minutes, I knocked on Ben's door.

"Here's the guy," he said, letting me in.

Bryce was sprawled on his bed, which was now stripped of sheets. "Hey. Sorry, but you just lost your sheets and comforter. Gotta bring 'em home."

"I hope it was okay. . . ."

"Oh, yeah, no worries. I'm just glad you're here." Bryce smiled, and I realized why Ben liked him. Bryce was a genuinely nice guy. I saw how Ben's face lit up in his presence.

Ben and I had plastic screwdrivers and Bryce drank the Gatorade straight. He couldn't drink anymore because of his depression medication. We talked and laughed and the time went by like nothing. Bryce really could do amazing impersonations, and he was glad to get caught up on Donnelly's rants, which he joked was the thing he missed most about Natick.

218

I knew Bryce had already told Ben what was going on, but he had no problem telling me too. He was in therapy, like, five times a week. He had to take an antidepressant. His mom was homeschooling him, which was pretty rough, because it meant living with your teacher 24/7.

I couldn't imagine being homeschooled. Especially by my mom. I guarantee I'd become homicidal within a week.

Way too soon, Bryce looked at his watch and said it was time to go.

"I'll text you," he said. "Don't worry, okay?"

"Cool," Ben said. "Just let me know how you're doing, man. Two months without talking to you at all sucked."

"Okay," Bryce said.

"I love you, buddy."

"I know," Bryce said. "Love you too."

He turned to me then. "Thanks for looking out for Ben," he said. "The thing I felt most guilty about the last couple of months was thinking that Ben was all alone here at Natick. He's not, so that's cool."

"Yeah, um, no problem," I said, my face reddening.

When Bryce left, Ben flopped down on his bed. I flopped down on the one that was now really mine. We just hung out there in the calm silence of the moment.

"He's . . . a great guy," I said.

"I know."

"Why do you think he was depressed?" I asked.

Ben thought about it for a minute. "I think being different is really hard, for one."

"Yeah."

"I mean, he was double different, because he's a good, sensitive guy, and he's black. So that's like two lenses."

"Lenses?"

"Yeah," Ben said. "Bryce said it's like lenses that you see the world through. They shift your perspective on everything you see. They create what's real for you, and unlike glasses, you can never take them off and see what normal is to other people, you know? Bryce had two, and he said it was hard to relate to some of the students here, who seem to have none."

"Well, you have one," I said.

"I guess so. You do too."

"Yeah," I said, closing my eyes. I imagined lenses. And then I tried to imagine what Ben's lenses might see. In me. When I opened my eyes, Ben was looking directly at me. I held his gaze and he held mine, and we saw each other. We saw. As clearly as my lenses would allow, I saw who Ben was, and it was good. And I could tell from his expression that he was seeing me too. Really seeing.

We each had another drink and were pretty tired by midnight. Tomorrow would be a long travel day, with the flight from Boston to Denver in the morning. But other than waking up, there wasn't that much we needed to do, so I wasn't too worried. Plus I had a nice buzz on.

"I should go get my sheets and blanket," I said, struggling to stand up. I was a little bleary, but for comic effect I pretended to be worse than I was. I pushed down on the mattress and undulated like I couldn't lift myself, and then I collapsed back onto the bed.

Ben started cracking up. "Don't fall."

I thrashed around for a few more seconds before finally lifting myself to my feet. I swayed exaggeratedly.

220

"You're gonna fall," he said, even though I was joking. "C'mon."

"C'mon what?"

He sat up and patted his bed. "C'mere, you doofus."

I tentatively sat down on the side of the bed. Ben was lying on his back, his eyes closed, his huge arms over his head. He reached out and put his hand on my arm.

"Just sleep here."

"Okay," I said, finding it hard to even breathe.

Silently, he scooted over and pulled up his comforter. He had on his sweatpants and T-shirt. I left mine on too. I settled under the sheets facing away from him, because if I faced him, he would have gotten seriously poked. He turned and put his arm over me.

"I'm so glad I know you, Rafe," he said.

"Me too," I whispered, kind of holding my breath.

He hugged me, and the heat of his torso and stomach against my back made me feel like melting. I could feel and smell his vodka-tinged breath as it blew across my ear and over my cheek. I had to concentrate on my own breathing. I couldn't move. I had never, ever wanted to do something more than I wanted to push back into him, to feel whether he had a hard-on. I wanted to know, needed to. But I just couldn't bring myself to do it.

"Colorado tomorrow," I said.

"I can't wait."

Soon I heard his snores, soft and familiar. The same snores I'd heard and loved from across the room for the past two months. Soon, hard gave way to soft, and I relaxed into Ben. And even though I didn't sleep a wink all night, it was the best night of rest I'd had my whole life.

"This is the longest flight I've ever taken," I said, settling into seat 20E. "By a lot."

Ben was in 20D, and no one was in 20F, the window seat. It was first-come, first-served seating, so Ben told me that to make sure no one else sat in our row, I should scoot over to the window seat during boarding.

"Nobody likes a middle seat, especially between two guys, and especially when one of 'em is me," he said, sitting up straight so his broad shoulders looked even broader.

Then he instructed me to stare menacingly into the eyes of anyone who glanced my way. It was hard to do, because I kept laughing, but Ben seemed pretty intent on following his own rules. And just as he planned, the doors closed and no one sat between us.

The plane took off, and we settled in for the four-hour trip. Neither of us said anything about anything when we woke up that morning (well, when he woke up and when I pretended to), or when we finished packing, or when we got in the cab. It was like it was just our sleeping arrangement. Then I wondered if that was what this was, like a *Brokeback Mountain* thing. We'd sleep in the same bed for a year, and finally we'd do it, but we'd never talk about it, ever, and then Ben would get married and I'd be killed in Texas.

Probably not, but you can never be too careful with these things.

"Do you think Toby and Robinson?" Ben said as we reached cruising altitude and I'd popped my ears so that I could hear.

I looked at him. There was no irony in his voice, nothing that told me he was pretending what happened last night hadn't happened. No *Brokeback* here, I realized. Ben was too good for that.

"I don't know. Hairy butt and all?"

"Perchance," Ben said.

My brain was spinning. Maybe all the guys were doing gay stuff, like if we dug a little bit, we'd find out that Steve and Zack were buddies too. "Do you think it's, like, everyone?"

"Everyone what?"

"Never mind," I said.

We played cards and I ordered spicy tomato juice, which was apparently only available at high altitudes, since I'd never even heard of it before.

"People are really stupid about gay stuff," Ben said while shuffling, after I'd beaten him twice.

"Yeah," I said. "People really are."

The silence was deafening. There were so many things I wanted to ask him, but I was too afraid. How did straight guys do this? Tiptoe toward the line and then maybe cross it, maybe not, without ever discussing the rules? It was exhausting, and I wasn't even sure if there was a line. I mean, nothing had happened, really. Just two guys sleeping together. It happened out in the wild all the time. Of course

Ben had no idea that I was hard as a rock for a good half hour. I was pretty sure he hadn't been, which made me wonder more whether he was simply a nice straight guy with a close guy friend whom he happened to love. Could I be that too, if I tried? Would I want to be?

As we flew over Ohio, and then Indiana — I knew this because the annoying pilot kept telling us where we were — I felt like I needed to say something. It was burning the back of my throat, all the not saying.

"Did you and Bryce ever do that?"

Ben looked up at me. "Ever do what?"

"I dunno. Sleep in the same bed?"

He laughed. "No."

"But we did."

He laughed again, his warm, translucent eyes looking into mine without any fear. "Thanks, Captain Obvious."

"I just wonder . . . what it means, if it means anything, you know?"

He shrugged. "I don't know. I mean, I guess it means we're comfortable with each other and we love each other, I guess."

The old, bald guy in the seat in front of us looked back, saw how big Ben was, and turned forward again. I looked away from Ben too, because I was afraid what my eyes would reveal if I kept looking at him.

"Huh," I said.

"Well, I know what part of it means, and part of it I don't. I guess that's all I can say," Ben said.

I laughed. "Maybe you could just explain that cryptic statement."

Ben lobbed his head from side to side. "Perchance I could."

We looked at each other again, as if we were both asking permission, permission to talk, permission to be open. It seemed crazy to me, given how we talked about everything.

He said, "Part of it means what I said. I love you. You love me. We love each other."

"Right," I said.

He went on, "The Greeks were smarter than us, and they had different words for different kinds of love. There's *storge*, which is family love. That's not us. There's *eros*, which is sexual love. There's *philia*, which is brotherly love. And then there's the highest form. *Agape*." He pronounced it "aga-pay." "That's transcendental love, like when you place the other person above yourself."

"You are so going to get into Harvard."

He laughed. "So, obviously our friendship is to some degree *philia*."

"Like *pedophilia* or *necrophilia*?"

"That's disgusting," he said. "But, yeah, same root, I guess."

I nodded.

"And I don't know about *eros*. I guess that's the part I mean by 'I don't know.' I mean, for me, my *eros* has always been pointed toward girls."

"Girls like that," I said. "Me too."

"I guess I'd like to think of what we have as *agape*. A higher love. Something that transcends. Something not about sex or brotherhood but about two people truly connecting."

That was the thing about Ben. He could get away with saying shit like that. I totally couldn't. I wasn't big or masculine enough. In my mind, anyway. But Ben could get all *agape* on your ass, and you'd just sit there like, huh. *Agape.* Interesting.

"*Agape*," I said. "I like that."

A smile crept across his face. "Me too."

"So we're not . . . aga-gay?"

He laughed. "I knew you were thinking that. I guess I sort of was too. You know what, Rafe? If I was ever gonna be aga-gay with anyone, it would be you."

The guy in the seat in front of us turned and looked at us again. Ben glared at him and he turned back around. I don't know what shade of red I turned or whether Ben even noticed.

"Me too. With you," I said.

Ben reached over and touched my hand, and I opened my fist, and he put his hand in it. It felt warm, slightly damp. I wanted to put my lips on the area between his thumb and forefinger, and keep it there, forever.

"Like in India," I said.

He smiled. "That's right."

Leave it to my dad to wear Birkenstocks and his tan gardening shorts to the Denver airport in late November.

He stood there, on the other side of security, waving ecstatically. I looked over at Ben. "Here goes nothing."

"Oh, please, you've got it good," he said.

"My two favorite guys!" Dad yelled, hugging me tight and kissing me on the cheek. Then he grabbed Ben and hugged him too. Ben seemed to hug him back.

"Good to see you, Mr. G.!" Ben said.

"I like that, *Mr. G.* Go with that. Or just Gavin."

"Okay, Mr. G.," Ben said, and I cracked up.

We got to the outside curb and found it was a sunny, crisp day, not too cold. It felt so good to see the mountains in the distance; this was home. Mom was in the Prius, and when she saw us she moved from the front to the back, giving Ben shotgun. "You're bigger," she said to him, pecking him on the cheek. Then she turned to me and gave me a big, warm, Mom squeeze hello.

I couldn't stop looking out the window at the mountains as we drove west on Route 36. Ben was telling my parents about the last week. I could see my mom and dad exchanging looks through the rearview mirror, wondering everything I was wondering. Here we were, four people in a Prius, wondering.

My mother had been really cool when I called her about inviting Ben. She offered to pay half of Ben's ticket, which I readily agreed to, and then my dad called me later and offered to pay half of the second half.

"Claire Olivia came by earlier this week. She was trying to gauge how much you'd hate a surprise party when you got home," Mom said. "I estimated a lot."

"You estimated correctly." I had explained to Ben that Claire Olivia and I had made up, and now ours was an amicable split.

"Oh, come on, who doesn't like a surprise party?" Dad said.

I raised my hand, and without any coaching from me, Ben raised his too. My parents laughed.

"You two," Mom said. "Way, way too much."

"Who knew that you had a doppelganger from northern New Hampshire?" Dad said. It was always hard to get my dad to give up words like *doppelgangers* and *privileging*. Teaching English overwhelmed his life occasionally. Ben either knew what a doppelganger was or didn't care, since he didn't ask.

When we turned west on Canyon, I was truly happy to see my hometown. We passed the Pearl Street Mall, which, even on a cool November day, was packed with African drummers and street dancers. To our right was the Laughing Goat, and on our left was Bud, Bong and Beyond, where my mom got her medical marijuana —

something she thought I didn't know about. I'm not exactly sure what pain she was in, but from the prescription label I saw in her bedside drawer, I'm guessing she sometimes wasn't in any pain at all.

When we turned the corner and parked in the driveway, all I wanted to say to my parents was "Really? You needed to do this?" Or maybe, "Couldn't you get people to park farther away from the house?" Because the extra cars gave my surprise party away. Then my major exhaling gave away that I had figured it out.

"Humor us," Mom said. "Pretend that you like people, and that you like seeing people who love you. Just for a bit."

"Fine," I said. "Sorry, Ben."

"Hey, no big deal for me," he said. "Always up for a partay."

"Remember? No partay for you," I said, flicking him in the shoulder. He laughed, and I glanced up at my dad and mom, who were sharing this "aren't they precious" look, which thankfully Ben did not see.

We got out of the car, and I was glad at least it was a little late in the year for an outside party, nice day notwithstanding. An indoor party would be smaller and easier to handle. And then I heard the noise, and realized that, no, not for my parents it wasn't. Not for Gavin and Opal Goldberg.

We went around back, and there it was.

"Surprise!" seven people yelled.

"Wow!" I said. "This is, wow! I'm shocked."

There, in winter coats, were Claire Olivia; Claire Olivia's parents; Aunt Ruth and Uncle Sidney; my grandmother Chloe, who has a superhuman resistance to cold, in a yellow sundress; and one other kid I only kind of recognized, wearing braces and an olive-colored peacoat. And I thought: *Mom. Why would you do this to me?*

The kid. He was one of the PFLAG kids.

The backyard was set up with purple streamers hanging from the trees, and a table with drinks and snacks, and then the pièce de résistance: a tofu pig on a spit.

My dad ran across the yard to the table, where he'd set up a boom box, and pressed play. Within seconds, the yard was filled with the sounds of a ukulele and steel guitars, or whatever they use in that mellow Hawaiian music.

> *"Oh, we're going to a hukilau*
> *A huki huki huki huki hukilau. . . ."*

"It's a mountain luau surprise party!" Dad yelled, all cheerful.

Ben started cracking up, and I knew that he'd be fine. It was me I was worried about.

"Of course it is," I said. "Of course it is."

I gave Claire Olivia a big hug, holding her tight. I didn't feel like letting go. She and I were never real huggy people, but I had underestimated how much I'd really missed her.

"God, it's good to see you," I said.

"So we're good?" she asked in an ex-girlfriendish monotone. I almost laughed, because the acting was not up to Claire Olivia par. But I didn't want to press my luck.

"We're fine," I said. "I'm really glad you're my friend."

Which made her smile, and it was a real smile, so I knew I'd struck the right chord between honest and, well, the other thing. We hugged again.

"And I guess this would be Ben," she said, from inside the hug, and I nodded and let go, and they shook hands. Then Claire Olivia excused herself to get some punch.

"Has this happened before?" he asked.

"Not this, exactly. Usually it would be like my parents to do a karaoke rap or something. I think we got off easy."

He laughed. "Your parents are hilarious."

I said hey to my aunt and uncle and Claire Olivia's folks, and then I went over to study the tofu pig. Ben followed. I don't know how they'd made a whole pig out of tofu, but it looked frighteningly real: the burnt pink faux animal appeared to be swallowing and shitting a metal pole at the same time. It had a perfect mauve snout with cashew-shaped nostrils set below two cavernous eye sockets that made it look forever shocked, like it breathed its final, unassuming tofu breath just as the spear appeared.

My grandmother Chloe came over and kissed my ear from behind.

"Don't you just love tofu?" she effused, staring at the beast. "You can do anything with it!"

You can, but should you? That's what I was thinking. And I wouldn't have been surprised if Ben had been thinking the exact same thing.

"Hey, Chloe," I said.

"Good to see you and your special friend!" she said.

I looked at Ben, who seemed, as usual, not particularly shocked.

"Hi," he said.

When Grandma Chloe walked away, I whispered, "I think she thinks we're boyfriends."

"Yeah, I got that," Ben muttered. "Very . . . singular, I guess. Your family and mine are, well, not exactly doppelgangers."

"Nice word usage," I said, and then we went to be social again.

Lavender leis hung from the low branches of the pine trees. Next to the spit, Mom had set up a table with a carved-up biological ham, platters of pineapple, and a mammoth bowl of fruit punch — pink, of course.

"Let's carve this beast up!" my father bellowed. He raised the carving knife and plunged it into the belly of the tofu pig. Grandma Chloe clapped.

Yep. This was my party.

When I had a moment, I walked up behind my mother and put my chin on her shoulder. "Mom, what's with the pink punch and inviting a kid from PFLAG?"

She looked annoyed. "We invited LOTS of people. This is all that we have so far."

"Ouch," I said.

"Oh, sweetie," she said, putting her hand on my shoulder and squeezing. "It's the day before Thanksgiving. I'm sure people wanted to come, but families have plans, you know."

"Of course," I said, still pouting, and I had a new thought that I'd never had before: I was a handful. A second before, I'd been complaining that there was a party. Now, there weren't enough people.

"Would you trade me for Ben?" I asked.

She laughed. "No, sweetie. You're ours for keeps. Of course, the way Ben looks at you, I'm not sure he's not yours for keeps too!"

I looked at her, and we shared a moment, and I could tell she knew that I was in the midst of trying to figure that out, and it made me feel, I don't know, less alone, to know that my struggle wasn't entirely secret.

"I need to tell you stuff. Later," I said.

"You can tell me anything, sweetie," she said, her eyes twinkling like she already knew. "Anything at all. I'm just so glad you're home."

We hugged again. Then she took me over to say hello to Josh, the PFLAG kid. He was a couple of years younger, and I wondered if he felt out of place at this weird party. He didn't seem too worried. I didn't know him at all. Before I left, my mom was always introducing me to kids from the PFLAG group, like, *Hey, Rafe, you're gay. Meet Josh, who also is gay.*

"Congratulations," Josh said, and I turned to him, wondering if he meant having a father who could slay tofu. It took me a few seconds to realize he meant going off to boarding school in Massachusetts.

"Thanks," I said. "So, uh, how have you been?"

"Okay, I guess," he said. "I had to get a root canal." He scrunched up his face.

"That sounds awful."

"It really hurt. They gave me some pills after to make me sleep. I woke up and there was this blood stain on my pillow. The stitches must have like fallen out."

"Wow," I said.

I was aware that this scintillating conversation was suddenly the party's main event, and I searched and searched for a way to keep the dialogue afloat. I had nothing. Thank God for my mother, Boulder's version of Barbara Walters. She started asking all the important questions: which tooth, how was the pain now on a scale of one to ten, who was the dentist. The kid shifted in his shoes as he tried to survive my mom's third degree, no doubt wishing he hadn't said anything at all.

Then it was limbo time. Grandma Chloe insisted on going first. The limbo was apparently invented to break the backs of older people, because the way Grandma was contorting was making me really nervous. Her body started to shake as she approached the bar, so the bar holders raised it a bit, and Grandma exhaled and moved forward, her neck craning back, clearing the new height by centimeters. The strap of her lemon yellow sundress had loosened, and by the time she came up, her right boob was proudly on display. My parents clapped loudly, and everyone else sort of looked at the ground, horrified, as she redressed herself.

I looked over at Ben, who was clearly enjoying the spectacle of my insane family. A part of me was glad he was seeing it. Because even if there was still one major thing he didn't know about me, he was now getting a pretty good sense of where I came from.

"Rafe goes!" my mother yelled, her red hair bobbing as she jumped up and down in her faded overalls. My dad took out his phone and got ready to capture the moment. Claire Olivia pushed me forward. I hid my face. I just wanted to stand still, you know? Most of all, I did not need Ben to see this.

He looked amused, as usual. *What the hell*, I thought. I faced the bar, took a deep breath, and sauntered forward, shaking and shimmying my locked arms. The sound of two parents and a grandma clapping enthusiastically while a bunch of embarrassed kids cringe is pretty singular, and I heard it in my throat. I wondered: *Shouldn't I be smiling?* So as much as I didn't want to, I forced my cheeks into something that resembled a grin, and shimmied my torso exaggeratedly. My mom hooted. Actually hooted. I swayed my hips, and then I bent backward, starting from my knees.

"Go, Rafe!" my dad yelled from behind his iPhone.

I exaggerated the bend farther, until I imagined myself as a pretzel, contorted the way my parents wanted me to be. I was a tabletop, with two legs in the front, bent ninety degrees at the knees. Piece of cake. If they wanted, I'd get lower. If they needed me to be the kind of kid who dances, that's who I'd be. I mean, why stop now? Why sweat the details, like the fact that I don't dance in public because I'm Rafe, not my mom, not my dad, but Rafe, a guy who is more comfortable watching than being watched?

I did more shimmying while passing well under the bar, and I was done. No one else wanted to go, so that was the end of that.

I was standing with Ben and Claire Olivia, purposefully NOT talking about the limboing display they'd just witnessed, when my mom rushed over.

"You were amazing, Rafe!" she shrieked, planting a big wet kiss on my cheek.

"Thanks," I said, looking away from her.

"You should have tried," she said to Ben.

He winced. "I don't think my body goes that way."

She cuffed him in the arm. "Oh, you'd be surprised what your body can do," she said, and Claire Olivia cracked up.

I died a little inside. For the first time, I truly felt like I was playing a joke on Ben. I really wasn't. But the fact that there was this party and everyone other than my grandmother was pretending that something wasn't true about me made me feel slimy, like I needed to take a long shower.

While everyone was talking, I wandered back over to the tofu pig. It looked real, unless you got up really close to it. Then you could see: It was very much not. Up close, you could see how the artist molded the tofu, and the places where there were cracks in the pig-skin. You could even see the finger indentations where he'd tried to massage the tofu flat. It was like when you approach a woman whom you think is beautiful and you see the caked-on blush and mascara, and you realize what you are seeing isn't her; it's her vanity. You're seeing her attempt at beauty, and it's the opposite of beauty that you're looking at.

Ben came up behind me. "Pretty incredible that someone made that," he said. "I just don't want to eat it."

"Yeah, me neither," I said, not turning around.

He put his hand on my shoulder. "You okay?"

I was, and I wasn't. All the people I loved were around me, and I felt like I wasn't even fully there, and for the first time I began to wonder if my decision wasn't catastrophically bad. I mean, why did it all have to feel so dirty, so fake? How did I wind up this far away from the real Rafe, when my only goal had been to find him? And how could I get back to myself without any major damage — not to

Ben, and not to me? Here was the person I was falling in love with, but how did you get from this ugly-feeling, unreal place to a real, romantic relationship with a guy like Ben? I'd never wanted anything more in my life, but it seemed as distant to me as this tofu beast was from a real live pig.

"Yeah," I said, turning around and managing a smile. "I'm okay."

True to form, my dad made a big spastic deal out of sleeping arrangements, confusing himself and everyone else along the way.

"I don't know what the right thing is to do," he said as my mother finished putting individual servings of tofu pig in the freezer after the party. "If Ben was of the opposite sex —"

"Dad," I said, hoping he'd stop.

He just looked baffled. "We'd put him in the guest room, I guess. And since he's a boy, I guess . . . ?"

"Dad," I said. "He's a guest. He'll sleep in the guest room. Duh."

Ben looked over at me like he had a question. I looked away. As much as I craved time with him, I craved sleep even more. So I was okay with Ben in the guest room. It also gave me a chance to degay-ify my room. Not that there was much to be done, but there were a couple of Alex Sanchez novels I wanted to put away.

That night, I slept holding a pillow to my chest, pretending it were Ben. It was a deep sleep, and I woke up Thanksgiving morning feeling like myself again. In a way.

Thanksgiving dinner was, in a word, crazy. Mom busied herself cooking some meatless monstrosity, and also a turkey, which I had pleaded with her to do. My father, in protest, refused to go in the kitchen. Instead of watching the football game, there was a marathon of the show *Intervention* on A&E, and my dad spent several hours watching drunk people and drug addicts do insane things and then agree to get help when their parents yelled at them.

Before dinner, my dad said it was time for gratitudes. In our family, that means going around the table and coming up with things we are truly grateful for, one at a time. The catch: You have only to a count of three to come up with yours, and if you fail, you're out. You also can't repeat any one that had been said. We'd done this every year, and I actually liked the tradition because it made you think about being grateful, like Thanksgiving was supposed to, but it also made you laugh once we got to the end, when everyone started to get silly.

"I'm grateful for my wonderful son," Mom said, smiling at me.

"This trip, my family . . ." Ben said.

"Only one," my dad admonished. "You'll need to keep some for later."

Ben shrugged. "This trip."

"My absurd parents," I said.

Dad smiled. "My snarky son."

It went on from there, and by round fifteen, it was getting a little weak.

"Oreos," Mom said.

"Gerunds," said Ben.

"Lindsay Lohan" was mine.

"Pornog . . ." My dad realized what he'd said, and stopped, and we all laughed, and my mother buzzed him.

"You're not just out, you're cut off," she said. "Okay, ready? Three of us left. Tofu."

Ben: "Soccer."

Me: "Sports cars."

Mom: "Chandeliers."

Ben: "Sex."

Me: ". . ."

Mom: "Zzz. Out. Just me and Ben, I guess. Onions."

Ben: "*Agape*."

Mom: ". . ."

All of us: "Zzz."

And we all applauded Ben, the newcomer, who had come in and beaten us at our own game.

"To *agape*," my dad said, smiling warmly at Ben.

"To *agape*," we all echoed, raising our wineglasses and drinking to higher love.

That night, Ben and I stayed up drinking wine with Mom and Dad. They had always felt that having me drink with them would "normalize" the experience, as Dad said, and make me less prone to drink otherwise. They were half right. We all got a little buzzed, and they started hammering Ben with stories about me as a kid. My mother's favorite was about how I had been horrified by the phrase *hot dog* the first time I heard it, when a vendor offered me one at a fair.

"'Hot. Dog?' he said. 'Hot. Dog?'" Mom laughed. "Rafe was

traumatized, poor thing. We'd hoped it would turn him into a vegetarian, but somehow that didn't happen."

"My dad made me watch him slaughter chickens on the farm," Ben said. "To this day, I can't eat a chicken."

My dad winced at the thought of animals dying, but I could see he was making an effort not to have any big scenes this weekend, and for that I was grateful. Soon it was time to say good night. We both hugged my parents and went upstairs. Ben changed into sweatpants and a T-shirt, and I put on a pair of thin flannel pajama bottoms and a long underwear top. Then he came to my room to hang out.

"So much fun," Ben said as I closed the door.

"It was, wasn't it?"

He laughed. "That was like the most fun I've ever had at Thanksgiving. Seriously. Meanwhile, you guys probably have that much fun every year."

"I wouldn't say that," I said. "A lot of it was the company."

I got in my bed and Ben lingered. I patted the space next to me, and he came and lay down. The bed creaked from his added weight. My heart felt so full, like it could burst. Like I could.

"Would your parents freak out if they walked in?"

I shook my head. "Please. My dad just about married us off already."

"Yeah, what's up with that? I would think any parent would not want their kid to be, you know. And ever since we met, they've treated me like, I don't know. A son-in-law. It's odd."

"Tell me about it," I said. "My mom told me when I was fourteen that she wanted me to be gay."

"Therapy much?" he said, laughing, and I laughed too. I left out the small fact that I'd just told her I *was* gay.

"If I told my parents I was gay, they would probably throw me out of the house," Ben said.

"Wow," I said. I imagined that happening, and how I would be there for him. It would be me and Ben, against the world. The fantasy made me tingle with excitement.

"So we're going skiing tomorrow, eh?" Ben asked.

I nodded.

"Cool. You ever want to get back with Claire Olivia?"

I thought about that. "Nah. I mean, maybe if we go to the same college. Otherwise, what's the point?"

"True," he said. "She's really beautiful. So full of life."

"Yeah," I said. "She really is."

We were quiet for a while, listening to the sounds of neighborhood dogs barking.

"Thanks for bringing me here," Ben said softly. "Your family is so open and accepting. I love them. I wish my family were like them."

"You can take 'em," I said.

"I swear to God, I wish I really was gay. I'd totally marry you."

I had had enough wine to do what I wouldn't have done otherwise. I rolled over onto my side and faced Ben, looking deep into his soulful, kind eyes. "Should we try it?"

Ben took a deep breath and closed his eyes. "I can't figure out any way to get closer to you, and I feel it. Like I want to get closer. It's not sex I want, it's just . . ."

I kissed him then, on the lips, keeping my lips there until he kissed back. And he did, he kissed back, and we opened our lips slightly and then wider, and our mouths were two Os pressing together, and I could taste his tongue because it was so close to mine. Ben breathed into my mouth. It felt like I'd shot to the moon, this pulsing, rushing roller coaster from below that overtook my body, and I shook.

He pulled back. "Wow," he said. "That was, that was different."

I was wet. I could feel it in my pajama bottoms. "Yeah," I said, breathless.

"Did you like it?"

"Did you?" I asked.

"It was — it was okay. Your lips are different than a girl's. It was sort of alien."

"Totally," I said.

"Did you get, you know, hard?" he asked.

"Did you?"

He looked down, so I did too, and he was definitely tenting the front of his sweatpants.

"I guess so," he said.

"Thank God," I said, relieved. "I did more than that."

He looked down at the wet stain forming on my pajama bottoms. Then he looked back up at me, his eyes wide. I felt as if my heart were in my throat.

"That'll happen," Ben said, but his voice was a little shaky, and I knew he was scared. I was too.

"Will it?" I felt so vulnerable. *More naked than naked*, Ben would say.

"I guess *agape* and *eros* are close" was the best he could come up with.

That made me want to hug him tight, because it was so Ben. But I was wet below, and I was pretty sure that hugging was out of the question for the moment.

"Maybe we should . . ." he said, his voice still shaking a bit.

"Sure. Call it a night."

Then he grabbed me by the shoulders and looked into my eyes. "Don't you. Freak out about this. It's okay, all right? It's okay."

But I could hear something different in his voice, like he was looking at me but talking to himself. It was like he was trying to save face with a basically straight buddy who would be feeling all freaked about his first time. And I wasn't that. I felt like that tofu pig, grotesque and in the spotlight and horrible, dishonest in a way that felt so basic that it hurt me behind my eyes to think of it.

"Okay," I said. "We're okay."

He leaned over and softly pecked my cheek, but there was hardly any contact at all.

"Good night, Rafe," he said, the words right but the tone all wrong. "Love you, man. I love who you are inside."

The words rang hollow to my ears.

"Yeah, love you too," I said.

And he left, and I felt like my skin could peel off and there would be this thing underneath, this creature, that would make Ben leave my life. And that scared the hell out of me.

"Just follow my tracks," I said. "Stay forward, and let your skis do the work. Don't force your turns."

Ben lowered his goggles over his eyes and adjusted his gloves. "Yessir," he said, and we were off.

I had gotten us to Eldora as early as I could, because I wanted to be first on the mountain — not just for the day, but for the season. This year, the day after Thanksgiving was their opening day. Skiing the virgin trails first was something I tried to do every year if I could. I loved the sound of my skis carving into the pristine white blankets of each run.

The quiet of the mountain matched the silence of our car trip there, but the one thing that was different was how serene the trails were. Untouched, unbothered. That was hardly the way my dad's Prius had felt as Ben and I wended our way through the mountains.

"Nice morning," Ben had said, sipping his coffee, as we listened to one of my dad's CDs, some lame seventies elevator music thing we were too lazy to change.

245

"Gorgeous," I'd said. "This is perfect."

"Perfect," he'd said, too quickly.

I'd turned up the music, and we'd driven in thick silence to Eldora. On the plane we had gotten around to talking about sleeping in the same bed. This thing that had happened last night felt way harder to deal with.

I took him down Foxtail until it met up with Ho Hum. Two beginner trails — nice and wide, not too steep. The snow was soft and quiet, ideal for some easy runs, and it felt good to be back on familiar terrain, given how unfamiliar everything else in my life felt these days. I made some quick turns, picked up some speed as we reached a short, slightly steeper part of the run, and then slowed at a plateau. I lifted my left ski pole high to let him know I was stopping, then turned to watch him.

He was pretty far up the run still. He made two turns for every one I'd made, traversing the slope before leaning back and swinging his body the opposite way in order to make a quick turn and traverse again. He was controlling his skis, I could tell, yanking them around rather than allowing a weight shift to do the work. When he got to me, his mouth was curled down and he was breathing heavily.

"Show-off," he said, between huffs.

I smiled. "Sorry."

"You're really good."

"I'm from here," I said.

"I just need to get my legs under me. It's been two years. It's not really like riding a bike, I guess."

"Don't worry. We're just here to have fun. How's it feel?"

He adjusted his coat. "Other than petrifying, it's pretty nice. Our mountains aren't quite this tall."

"Your hills," I corrected.

"Whatever," he said. "They're not quite this imposing."

We got a rhythm going. I slowed down and took wider turns, and soon Ben wasn't working so hard to keep up. He wasn't great, but he was skiing, and we were both relaxing into the sport.

On the first chairlift ride all the way to the top, I began to feel more like myself again. I think maybe it's hard to be anxious or unhappy on a ski lift, in the midst of breathtaking beauty. At least for me it is.

"My mom has a saying when we ski," I said. "She always says, 'Lean forward, and head on down the mountain.' I love that. It's true, right? About life?"

Ben swung his right ski back and forth. He rested the left one on the footrest.

"Interesting. What do you think *lean forward* means?"

I wiped my nose. "It means to be unafraid. Lean into the challenges, don't lean back. I don't always do it, but I love it."

"Lean forward and head on down the mountain. I like that," Ben said, and the turned-down edges of his mouth curled up.

I inhaled deeply to get that fresh mountain air into my lungs. It seared my nostrils. This was going to be okay, I realized. We were going to be okay. I felt this great sense of relief.

"I'm glad we did this," I said, looking over at Ben. "I'm glad you came."

"You wish I came," he said.

My face flushed pink, or pinker. The silence felt like it could fill the resort for hours. "Did you just make a sexual joke?" I finally managed to say.

He grinned.

"You're such a dick," I said, laughing.

"Are you trying to make me make another one?"

I smacked him in the goggles, which were resting on his forehead.

The next run was better. I was actually laughing while skiing, thinking of Ben and his stupid joke. My body felt so much lighter than it had before our chair ride, like I could float away if my skis weren't weighing me down. And Ben was getting the hang of it too; I saw he was beginning to make turns just by shifting his weight. As in everything else, Ben had an elegance to him. When he let his legs do the work, he was a pretty skier to watch.

"Thanks for bringing me here. I love seeing where you're from," he said on the next ski lift.

"Thanks," I said. "Maybe you can take me to New Hampshire next."

He placed his skis on the footrest and pretended to slice his own throat.

I laughed. "Are you sure you're not adopted?"

"If it weren't for my uncle, I wouldn't be sure of anything."

We were maybe just a quarter up. That's the great thing about skiing. You get long, gorgeous rests after you fully exert yourself on a long run. The longest one at Eldora is three miles, and I knew Ben had never seen, or skied, anything like it.

"What was he like?" I asked.

Ben looked out at the horizon.

"He was basically the black sheep of the family. Went to college. Traveled the world. Never married. When my parents talked about him, there was always something in their tone. Like he wasn't quite right. When he stayed with us, we'd talk about everything." He lifted his goggles. His eyes were watery, and I didn't know if it was the wind or what he was sharing.

"He was the one person who made me realize that it was possible to do more than, you know. Stay on the farm and work the fields, I guess. Not that there's anything wrong with that, it's just I think that's not really what I'm meant to do. He got that. He got the hell out of Alton. He traveled. Went to China and taught English there. He lived a full life."

"He sounds amazing."

"He was. You know, he didn't care what everyone else thought about his life. I admired that because I can't even . . ."

I didn't ask him to finish the sentence, because I got it. As cool as Ben was, as much as he didn't get caught up in labels, it was pretty clear that they did matter to him too, underneath. There was a big part of Ben that still bought into his parents' way of thinking about life. You work hard, you suffer, you die. It was amazing to me that a person could be as smart as Ben but still feel chained in by what his parents thought. I thought about it. Did I buy everything my parents had raised me to believe? No, or else I'd still be living in Boulder. But while I didn't agree with them on everything, they had taught me that life was an exploration, not a job. That part I definitely liked.

I turned to face him. "Your parents are proud of you," I said.

He didn't react. He looked out into the snowy distance.

"They are. They just don't know how to say it."

He wiped his nose with his glove. For a second I felt very alone, but then I settled into the moment, and we shared one of those perfect silences. I focused on this beautiful, solitary tree on the apex of one of the slopes above. It looked like it was perched there, all alone, waiting to be told what to do.

"So are we okay about last night?" I finally blurted out.

He looked over at me. I took off my sunglasses and we locked eyes.

We just looked at each other for a while. I wondered, as we did, what he saw. What I saw was this incredible person who was exactly who he was. I admired the hell out of that. Maybe he was gay, maybe he wasn't. But he was always Ben.

"Still processing," he said.

I wiped my nose, which was leaking again. "Me too."

Ben turned forward, so I did too. I looked at the empty seats coming toward us, heading back down the mountain. I watched the skiers below, carving into the virgin white powder. Then I felt a weight on my gloved hand. I looked down. His gloved hand was on top of mine. I turned to look at Ben and got a stunning view of his profile — that strong Roman nose of his, pink from the thin, frigid air.

He didn't turn his head, but I could feel him squeezing his hand around mine. So I squeezed back.

We allowed the whistling wind to be our sound track for a full minute. As the zenith approached, it was time to raise the bar. Ben tucked his poles on his lap as he adjusted his hat and goggles, and I grabbed his poles. I motioned and he lifted his skis off the footrest. It was all so easy, communicating with Ben.

The lift reached the plateau, and we raised our ski tips just before they made contact with the crisp snow. Then we stood and let gravity do the work, and we glided down the slope and to the right.

"**What** the hell is Hot Spot Teen Dancing?" I asked as we drove down Broadway. Claire Olivia was in the driver's seat, I was riding shotgun, and big, hulking Ben was pretzeled into the back of Claire Olivia's '89 Cutlass Ciera.

It was about eight o'clock on Saturday, our final night in Colorado, and as we cruised toward Caffè Sole, this cool coffee shop where they sometimes had live music at night, we saw this place that was obviously new, with a glittery sign that read HOT SPOT TEEN DANCING. There was a group of kids outside, skinhead types, mostly.

"Looks really sketchy," Claire Olivia said, looking in the rearview mirror to fix her beehive hairdo. Or hairdon't, depending on how you looked at it. She kept saying she wore it that way special just for me, and I was thinking: *Um, thanks?*

"It looks like the kind of place where a kid would get shot," I said.

"Well, it's a good thing they've created a safe place for teens to congregate minus alcohol," Claire Olivia said, and Ben chuckled from the backseat.

"Do you think preteens try to get into that place like kids are always trying to get into actual, real bars?" he asked, and Claire Olivia shot me a look that said, *Nice, he gets it.*

"Sure," I said. "They probably get fake IDs that say they're thirteen."

"Totally," Claire Olivia answered. "It's a huge industry, the fake teen ID business. They should make Hot Spot Teen Dancing open to preteens."

"Two to twelve," I said, and by this point we were way past it, almost at the coffee shop.

Claire Olivia said, "Fetus to twelve," and then drew a very vivid word picture of pregnant women dirty dancing with twelve-year-olds. It was downright creepy, and I wondered how Ben would react.

"That brings up the very interesting legal argument about whether it's statutory rape if the predator is pregnant," Ben said. "Perchance it could be said that the twelve-year-old and the fetus were, um, comingling."

"Yeah, I don't know if that's an interesting legal argument so much as a prurient one," I said.

Claire Olivia sighed loudly. "Perchance. Comingling. Prurient. Speak English," she said.

We found a parking spot out in front of the café and stepped into the cold night air.

"So what do you think?" I asked no one in particular.

"This is what I think," Claire Olivia said, slamming the driver's side door. "I think anyone who stops at a gas station at night is up to no good. I think that if cops want to stop drunk driving, they should hide out in the bushes at the Taco Bell drive-through. I think if you're a guy and you pull down your pants and the girl you're with starts texting, you have a small penis."

"No fair. That last one was Chelsea Handler," I said.

"Who?" Ben quietly asked me, once Claire Olivia charged ahead of us, anxious for her s'mores cappuccino, which was surely every bit as disgusting as it sounded.

"Don't you worry about it," I said.

"I guess I won't. Why do I feel like an alien?"

"Welcome to my world," I said.

The night before, Ben fell asleep early, exhausted from the day of skiing. I sat in the living room with my mom, and I told her everything that had happened. She seemed overjoyed, which was a bit different from what I was feeling. Other than totally in love, what I was mostly feeling was confused. What we were. What was going to happen. I told my mother this, and she waved off my concern.

"There are so many different kinds of relationships out there, sweetie. The thing that makes one okay and another not is whether it comes from a place of love. Nothing that comes from love could ever be wrong."

It was just such a thing my mother would say. Then she started singing "All You Need Is Love," and I excused myself because there's a certain level of cheese that's too goopy even for me.

Inside, the coffee shop was packed with a mixture of teens and adults. There were some kids from Rangeview — some people Claire Olivia had recently gotten friendly with, I guess, because I didn't remember them. She gave them hugs, and, anxious that they might say something I didn't want Ben to hear, I told him to grab an open table in the corner while I ordered him a coffee.

Once he was gone, Claire Olivia turned to me.

"He is totally gay for you," she said, poking me hard in the shoulder.

I wasn't even sure if I would tell her what happened when we had a chance to really talk. Would she understand?

"I don't know," I said, rubbing my arm. "You think?"

"I know. Also, I'm pretty legendary at figuring out if someone is gay." She scanned the coffee shop. "Shall I?"

"Behave," I said. "Please."

She clasped her hands under her chin. "Angel," she said.

We pushed our way through the crowd to the table where Ben was sitting, facing the wall. I handed him his coffee, sidled into one of the two seats facing the crowd, and put down my bottled water. Claire Olivia sat next to me, which made me feel a little bit like she and I were an interview panel, with Ben as our frightened subject.

"So what's Rafe like at Natick?" Claire Olivia asked him. "I'm dying to know."

Ben glanced at me, a little confused by the question. "He's just Rafe, I guess."

"Whoever that is," she said, and under the table, I kicked her softly.

Ben sipped his coffee and changed the subject. "So this is what you guys would do on a Saturday night in Colorado? I guess I thought we'd go to a hoedown. Or country dancing. Or banjoing. Is that a thing? Banjoing?"

"It could be," I said.

"We're doing all that later," Claire Olivia said, sipping her s'mores. "We'll go eat Rocky Mountain oysters."

Ben shook his head while I took a swig of water. He said, "I have a long-standing agreement with cows that I won't eat their balls if they won't eat mine."

Water spewed from my nose, and then I had to wipe the snot away while Claire Olivia shook her head in mock disgust.

"Drinking problem," Claire Olivia explained to Ben, who nodded.

"I believe he also has a peeing problem," he said, and I cracked up.

We were enjoying our drinks and people watching when a shock of purple hair across the room caught my attention. A kid with big-time acne was standing in front of whoever's hair it was, so all I could see was the spiked hair peering out from above the crowd. I was about to make a joke about "Purple Mountain's Majesty" when the zit-faced kid moved.

The kid with the purple hair was You-Know-Caleb.

And of course, because I was staring at him, he turned and saw us too. His mouth opened wide.

"Whassup, bitches!" he shrieked, sashaying through the crowd over to our table.

"Caleb!" I said, cursing my decision to bring Ben to Caffè Sole on our final night in Boulder. What was I thinking? Way too popular with Rangeview types.

Thank God for Claire Olivia, who jumped up and hugged Caleb. She shouted, "Don't you love my hair?" and while he was busy curling his lip and saying, "No, not really," she led him away from me and Ben.

Most. Awesome. Girl. Ever. She'd tell him what was up.

Ben laughed, sort of awkward. "Interesting friend," he said.

"He's not really my friend," I said, not feeling so bad about it, because it was true. Caleb and I were acquaintances at best. People always tried to group us together, but it just didn't work. I thought Caleb was weird, and he probably thought I was superboring.

Ben and I sat and sipped our coffee and water, and after a while, Claire Olivia came back to the table with You-Know-Caleb, who looked . . . pissed? Annoyed? Bored? All of the above?

"Ben," Claire Olivia said. "This is our friend Caleb. Caleb, Rafe's friend Ben."

Ben stuck out his hand, which Caleb regarded as if it were something on the discount rack at Old Navy. Finally he clasped the hand and curtsied.

"The pleasure is all mine," he said, deadpan.

I looked at Claire Olivia for an explanation, but she was already sending me a message with her eyes. It read something like this: *Don't even think about dissing Caleb as too gay to hang with. I will cut you.*

Caleb sat down next to Ben, and we all looked at one another. It was a weird grouping. Not weird like Albie-Toby-Ben-Rafe weird. More like ominous. I shifted in my seat and looked at my wrist as if I had a watch on it. I didn't.

"So how's life?" I asked Caleb.

"Tragic," he said. "I'm seriously pondering running off to Cali to become a porn star."

"He's kidding," I said to Ben, to which Claire Olivia said, "Duh," while simultaneously Caleb said, "If you say so."

"What's so tragic?" Ben asked.

Caleb shrugged. "I couldn't get a single ticket to the New Kids on the Block reunion tour," he said. I remembered how much I genuinely disliked having conversations with Caleb. A straight answer, no pun intended, was almost impossible to get. "I am so dejected and depressed, I'm thinking about going to some boring-ass East Coast prep school next year."

"Fuck you," I said to Caleb. Then I turned to Ben and said, "What you need to understand is that Caleb is an asshole."

Caleb flipped me off. To Ben, he said, "What you need to understand about Rafe here is that he's your girlfriend."

Everybody got really quiet. Claire Olivia clicked her fingernails. Caleb sipped his fizzy water as if he'd just commented on the weather. I couldn't look at Ben, but I could feel my face heat up like I was standing over a stove.

"Fuck you, Caleb," I said again.

"As if," he said.

Then we all drank our drinks, and watched people walk by, and all the while, my kidneys felt like they were twisting inside me.

In my head, I was computing and translating. Caleb's comment plus no reaction equaled awkward. Caleb's comment plus big reaction equaled more awkward. Caleb's comment plus major reaction plus Rafe was a straight guy and Ben was a straight guy plus the strange sexual escapade two nights ago equaled superconfusing. How to react as Ben's friend? How to react as Claire Olivia's friend? How to react as Rafe?

Too many combinations and permutations. My head spun.

"Wow, there are certainly lots of people here, drinking coffee," Claire Olivia offered.

"Yes," Ben said flatly. "People do drink coffee."

After what seemed like an eternity, Caleb moved away from our table. But the night was ruined. I had no idea how much damage had been done. I couldn't look at Ben, and that wasn't great news.

Against my better judgment, I didn't say a word on the ride home. I knew it wasn't the right way to handle what was basically a stupid comment from a very stupid person. But my gut seized and I turned the CD player up, and we listened to the Yeah Yeah Yeahs, and I watched the jubilant scene along Walnut, my friends around me but a thick wall of despair and music between us.

"So what just happened?" Ben asked me when we got up to my room. He said it patiently, nicely, as if he really wasn't sure of the answer but didn't want to convey how nervous the whole thing made him. Like a mother might ask her son after he'd come home carrying a dead gerbil.

I glanced over at him. I'd gotten us two leftover pieces of my mom's apple pie. We were eating it with vanilla bean gelato. He was on the floor, and I was on the bed.

"I don't know. I sort of wigged out, sorry," I said.

"You told Claire Olivia, didn't you?" he asked, taking a bite of pie. "And she told him."

I shook my head vehemently. "No. I really, really didn't. You have to believe me."

"Huh," Ben said as he scooped some ice cream.

"What's *huh* mean?"

"Well, if you didn't tell her . . ." he said, taking a dramatic pause.

My insides shook. In my mind, I tried to complete the sentence for him. I couldn't come up with an ending for which a major, difficult conversation wouldn't follow. Who is best friends with a girl who wears a beehive? Who prematurely ejaculates when kissing another boy?

A gay boy. Not a kid who is just figuring out that he might be gay, but an actual, real gay boy who has been gay for a long time. That's who.

". . . Maybe it's that gay radar thing?" Ben finished.

I took a deep breath and looked at him. "Huh?"

"Well, I mean," he said, crossing his legs and then uncrossing them. "I mean, maybe he can just tell when two guys, you know?"

"Yeah," I said. "Maybe that's it."

I looked at Ben and could feel myself blushing. I could also feel myself getting a little breathless and excited, and wondered if we were going to kiss again. I could get into that, but didn't want to push him. He was a little red too.

"I've never had feelings like this for a guy. You know?"

"Me neither," I said, which was true.

"I mean, I don't even know if I'm having them. It's you. It's not like toward a guy."

"Thanks."

He laughed. "I mean, you're a guy, obviously. But I can't . . . It's not even like I couldn't handle being gay." He said *gay* softer than the other words, as if my parents would beat us, rather than hug us, if they'd heard him say it. "It's just, it doesn't feel like me, you know?"

I wasn't sure if I believed him. "I hear ya. I hear ya."

He stood then, his plate empty, and placed it on my dresser. I stood too. We faced each other. The door was closed, and I thought I might have a heart attack or at least some sort of bodily malfunction if anything were to happen. The room felt outrageously small, like neither of us could move without bumping into each other.

"Early flight," he said, his eyes averted from mine. "Probably should pack up."

"R-r-r-ight," I stammered.

And then he came over and gave me a hug, and I held him, tentative, and we stood there, our bodies pressed lightly together like they were fragile. And finally, he pulled back and smiled at me, and then he pecked me on the cheek.

"Night, Rafe," he said.

"Night."

And when he left the room, I collapsed on my bed with my arms and legs spread wide, like I was about to do snow angels indoors. I stayed in that exact position and tried to calm my pounding, jittering heart.

Hours later, when the sun began to rise and my eyes were still wide open, I succumbed to the excruciating truth that some things were going to have to get majorly sorted out if I ever wanted to sleep peacefully again.

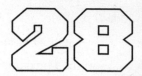

"I want to save the children. I want to celebrate with all the people of the earth. I want to put candles in their hearts."

Toby was standing in the middle of our once-again-disastrous dorm room, swaying, holding a pencil for a microphone and wearing a huge pair of yellow-framed sunglasses that engulfed his face. Albie sat at his desk, his head in his hands, trying to study. I couldn't take my eyes off Toby, who gave new meaning to the phrase *train wreck*.

It was Sunday night after Thanksgiving, I'd just gotten back from Colorado, and Toby was being some weird yellow-framed-sunglasses-wearing version of Michael Jackson. He was holding court in front of a make-believe audience, imploring them to give peace a chance.

"What the fuck is happening?" I asked no one in particular, as Toby began singing a song that neither rhymed nor made sense.

> *"Feed the world.*
> *Give the children Slankets*
> *because Snuggies are too big*
> *and they are hungry."*

"His mom streamed that Michael Jackson movie on Netflix over Thanksgiving," Albie said in a monotone. "Now he thinks he's a pop star and a humanitarian. I'll admit it's one of his more annoying phases."

"And you get a car. And you get a car," Toby was saying, pantomiming handing out small cars to an audience that perhaps only he could see.

Albie went to his refrigerator and took out a Coke. He popped the top and sat down on his bed. "It's been happening off and on since he got back. I don't know how to make it stop."

"How does Oprah Winfrey fit into this?" I asked, watching as Toby seemed to be in deep conversation with one of his audience members. He was showing the person how to steer a car, it appeared.

"I don't know," Albie said, sighing. "Racism?"

"Philanthropy!" Toby yelled, back in his own voice. "I am the great philanthropist with many faces."

Albie and I looked at each other. There was nothing to say, nothing to do but shrug.

"And how was your Thanksgiving?" I asked Albie. I found that as much as I was still bothered by our messy room, I was bothered less than I was at the beginning of the semester. Progress?

Toby sat down on the floor, dropping his character completely. He took a huge swig of Coke. "Thank you for finally asking. God. It was AMAZING. Mom and Jenny disappeared all morning and David — that's my stepdad — took me to a shooting range. He taught me how to shoot a gun! It was so awesome. He is by far my favorite of the dads. He's number three. It was, like, when you aim the gun, you could be like in a movie, and that's what I did. I pretended I was like James Bond."

Toby pantomimed lifting a gun and shooting. He still was wearing the oversize glasses. He was an amazing guy, really. Totally himself. Totally unapologetic about having all these different sides of his personality that didn't quite mesh. He didn't care what people saw, and at that moment, the envy was so powerful, I wanted to punch him in the face.

"How was yours?" Albie asked me.

"We had fun," I said. "Ben liked Colorado, I think."

What I didn't say was that Ben had gotten superweird on the flight back to school. Something had happened between our conversation in my room the previous night and my parents' driving us to the airport this morning. Ben was very polite to them, but really distant with me. On the plane, he told me he should probably get some homework done. Which was fine, because I had to as well. But it felt wrong that we weren't talking at all.

"Did you ski?"

"Yup."

"He meet Claire Olivia?"

"Yup," I said.

"You seem extremely talkative about this," Albie said.

"Did he have a thing for Claire Olivia?" Toby asked. "Did they make out in front of you? Was it like, 'Bromance partner, meet ex-girlfriend'?"

I ignored him and turned to Albie. "Yours?" I asked.

Albie shrugged. "Watched TV a lot," he said. "Are you staying in here again?"

264

It had been a while since I'd slept in my assigned dorm room, but given the fact that Ben had barely mumbled "good-bye" when the shuttle dropped us off at campus, it seemed like yeah, I'd probably be sleeping here.

I was so confused.

"Yep," I said.

"Lovers', oh, I mean, brothers' quarrel?" Toby said.

I stood, walked over to where he was sitting, took the huge yellow glasses off his face, dropped them on the floor, and stomped on them.

Toby looked down at them, and I wondered if he might cry. Instead, he turned philosophical.

"It was bound to happen," he said.

I dreamt that Bryce was back. That he was back and moved in with Ben, and that it had happened while I was in my other room with Albie and Toby. Ben seemed relieved that I wasn't there, and he pretended like I'd never even slept there. Bryce asked him what he did for Thanksgiving, and Ben said he'd had a great time in New Hampshire. I spoke up then, because that was a flat-out lie. But when I opened my mouth to speak, no words came out. My voice was totally gone. I tried to pound on the ground to get their attention, but the sounds were muted, like the ground devoured them, and I broke into a sweat. I wanted to say: *Listen to me! Listen to me!* But I had no volume. And then Toby started walking across a high wire with a pair of huge yellow glasses for shoes, and I woke up, because some things are not worthy of dream time.

Monday was hugely, surreally weird. I saw Ben walking across the quad toward the dorms while I was heading to my calc class, and I felt this huge wave of relief, like a settling in my soul, the return of an old, dear friend from battle or something. I smiled, and I wanted to reach out and hug him, and turn around and head back to East and skip math and hang out with him and just talk again. Because really, there was no reason not to talk; we hadn't had a fight or anything. Maybe it was all in my head that anything was off.

And as we approached I told my feet to slow down but they didn't, and my face contorted and I said, "Hey," but didn't stop or smile, and Ben's face also did some sort of flicker of something and he said, "Hello," but he too didn't stop.

Or maybe it wasn't in my head.

I walked on to math class, feeling like I was trying to pull myself into a boat from a freezing river, but the current was strong, and I couldn't get my balance to hoist myself up. I didn't hear a word all math class, and not in history class after either.

Ben wasn't in his usual carrel in the library — back row, next to the wall — and I looked for him in the cafeteria at dinner. Again, not there. After dinner, I went back to my room to study, but it was impossible. My heart was pounding, and I began to think about how Bryce had gotten depressed and wandered off campus. What if Ben was depressed now? He certainly wasn't himself since we'd gotten back. If something happened to Ben, I wouldn't be able to forgive myself, so I hurried over to his room.

"Hey," he said when he opened the door. He was wearing a red flannel robe over navy blue sweatpants. Such a Ben outfit.

"Hey," I replied.

We just stood there, as if frozen.

"Can I come in?"

"Oh, yeah," he said, stepping aside. "Come on in."

I sat down on Bryce's bed, which had sort of been mine, but now I wasn't sure. It didn't feel right, not the same way it had before we'd gone to Colorado.

"How you doing?" I asked.

"Busy," he said. "Clarkson decided two days after Thanksgiving break would be a good due date for a lab report. The effect of concentration on the rate of a reaction. Snore."

"Sounds scintillating," I said. "How was your day?"

"Good, good," he said. "I mean. Not good. Okay, I guess. You?"

"Fine," I said.

We sat there, straining for words.

"Why are things so weird?" I said.

He exhaled. "I really don't know. I don't feel weird, exactly."

"Yeah, me neither!" I said. "I mean, I'm totally fine. I miss hanging out with you."

"Well, you don't have to miss it. Maybe we can hang out but also, like, I don't know."

"Right," I said, too quickly. "Wait. Like what?"

"I don't know," he said. "Just not, you know. Maybe you should sleep in your room now and we'll just hang out during the day."

"Sure," I said. "That's probably a good idea. That was pretty weird and all. Our *agape* got all *eros*-y."

He laughed. "Right. I guess when the girls are away . . ."

"I guess."

We were quiet again, and Ben finally stood, so I stood too. I wondered if this was his way of saying he wanted me to leave. My heart felt unglued, like it might drop into my stomach if I took another step toward the door and Ben said, "See ya." But I didn't know how to make him not say it.

"I better get back to the lab report," he said. "We'll talk tomorrow?"

"Sure. Definitely."

We didn't make eye contact as I left the room. And when he closed the door, I stood in the hallway, totally hollowed out. Fractured. Stranded.

In the middle of the night, my eyes flashed open. There was evidence in Ben's room. In an ornate wooden box with a red handle. He'd wake up in the middle of the night, spot it, open it, and he'd know everything. He'd never talk to me again. Never.

My heart pounding, I sat up in a hurry. The dark room spun, though I could barely see a foot in front of me. Albie's light snores were the only sound. I focused on my digital clock: 3:49.

I realized I had been dreaming. There was no evidence. It was a dream. But it was like I was naked, terribly naked, this horrendous, vulnerable way I felt. A combination of lust and panic made breathing hard, and the tingles. Someone had set every nerve ending in my body on fire.

The bathroom seemed like a reasonable place to go to release at least some of the pressure. I padded slowly down the hallway, wondering if anyone else was awake.

And when I was about six steps past Ben's door, an amazing thing happened: The door opened. There he was, in his flannel robe, sweatpants, no shirt. He opened the door and the desk lamp was on and our eyes met and nothing had to be said. But Ben said something anyway.

"Those footsteps. I know those footsteps," he whispered. I stopped and went inside.

He closed the door and it was so quick, I couldn't tell you who instigated what. Our foreheads together and then our noses and then our lips entwined and opened slightly, a tip of a tongue probing and I wasn't sure which way, whose was what. He tasted like orange sports drink and vodka and a slight hint of garlic, like Ben. My fingers caressed under his flannel robe, and then it was on the floor and we were on his bed. And Ben, sweet Ben, underneath me, his strong arms around me and then side by side, exploring each other with our lips and fingers.

No words. And thoughts went away for those moments too, and we did what had been in my mind for months.

After, words weren't as hard to come by. It was like something had opened up in Ben, and he could say things that were hard for him to say before.

"I missed you," he said. "I just missed you."

"Me too. Are you drunk?"

"A little. Maybe we're bi?"

"Maybe."

"My uncle was bi."

"Oh!"

"Yeah, and I mean, I know that like with Cindy, I definitely, you know, I like that. With her. But with you too, it's like. That was pretty okay."

"Yeah," I said.

"The same? With you? Like you and Claire Olivia?" He sounded breathless, manic, which wasn't something I was used to hearing from Ben.

"Sort of," I said. "I liked this a ton more."

"Oh," he said, and he was quiet. I felt at peace too. Finally, a step in the right direction. Something approaching true, a pathway fully visible to where I wanted to be. With Ben.

"Maybe," he said. "Maybe you're not even bi?"

"I dunno," I said. "Maybe not."

And we fell asleep, my chest curled into Ben's back, and this time, I was able to close my eyes and drift off. I was finally, totally, home.

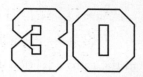

When I woke up, Ben was gone.

The clock said 8:13. That meant I had gotten maybe three hours of sleep in Ben's bed, and that meant he had gotten even less. My eyes felt heavy but at least my head felt lighter. I knew he was probably at his chemistry class, turning in his lab report and trying to stay awake while Clarkson babbled on and on about the periodic table.

I pulled his sheets over my head. His scent was still there, and I inhaled. Ben. My boyfriend. I finally had a boyfriend. I thought back to the way the muscles of his back felt as I touched him. Warm and smooth. The kind of feeling I could get addicted to, and I was pretty sure I didn't care who knew it.

The air felt frosty when I finally pulled his covers off. And then I realized: December 1. I would never, ever forget that date. I looked out the window, and the sky was an odd purple gray that made me want to spend the day hibernating. Waiting for Ben to return. Ben. My Ben.

I took a shower and went to breakfast. Steve and Zack were sitting together, and when they saw me, they called me over to their table.

"Hey," they said, and I put my tray down across from them. I had gotten an omelet with Swiss cheese and tomato and mushrooms. They were eating pancakes.

I dug into my breakfast without much more than a grunt hello. My brain was elsewhere by far, orbiting around something that I knew these guys wouldn't understand.

"Whassup?" Steve said. He was wearing a Red Sox jersey inside out, which I guess was their new thing. I'd noticed some of the guys doing that recently. Like maybe Steve did it the first time by mistake, and suddenly because he had done it, everyone was following.

"*Nada mucho,*" I said.

"You have a good Thanksgiving?" asked Steve.

"Took Ben back to Colorado," I said, sipping orange juice.

"Awesome," Zack said. "You gotta take us next time. Would love to ski out there."

"Sure." I knew that would never in a million years happen.

"You remember that chick Amber, the one you ralphed on?" Steve said.

I laughed. "Kinda sorta."

"Saw her over break. Had a party and some of the kids from Joey Warren drove up," Steve said. I knew he lived in Newton, which was somewhere east of us. "She's still talking about you. Thinks you're cute or something. You wanna hook up with her?"

"Do I wanna hook up with the girl I threw up on?"

Zack laughed. "Colorado's got a way with words."

"Yeah," said Steve.

"Nah, I'm about a thousand percent not interested." I forked a piece of my rubbery omelet up and put it in my mouth.

Steve and Zack looked at each other. "She's pretty hot, you know," Zack said.

"Not my type."

They looked at each other again.

"Oh-kay . . ." Steve said, the same way he'd said it to Bryce before the softball game.

I couldn't have cared less. These guys had about nothing I wanted in a friend. I'd known that for a while now. No personality, not particularly nice, not terribly smart. I looked up at Steve, who was staring at me with what might have been pity in his eyes. This Schroedster just wasn't like the old model, I guessed, and I finally didn't give a shit if anyone knew.

"Hey, Steve," I said. "Your shirt's on inside out. You look like a dork."

And with that, I stood and picked up my tray, brimming with a type of pride I hadn't felt since I'd lived in Colorado.

After English, I went to the library. Ben was there, in his usual carrel, and I snuck up behind him and put my hands over his eyes. He tensed up. I pulled my hands away, and when he turned around, I smiled and whispered, "Surprise!"

He surreptitiously looked both ways. He was wearing his glasses and reading his philosophy textbook. He looked so handsome in his blue cashmere sweater, with those thick, hipster glasses over his owl eyes.

"Hey, what's up?" he said. He stared at me like he was waiting for me to tell him what I was there for, why I'd bothered him in the library.

I opened my mouth to say something funny about how he was acting, but nothing really occurred to me. It wasn't funny. This was the second time, it seemed to me, that he'd gone from hot to cold on me. It sucked.

He saw the hurt in my eyes. I could see it registered in the corner of his eyebrow, which buckled. He took a deep breath, then sighed.

"I just need some time," he whispered. "Some space. Figure this out. Okay?"

I shrugged. "Fine," I said, and I turned and walked away. I heard him say, "Rafe," under his breath, like I was making a big deal out of nothing. I wasn't going to listen to this shit. No way. How come every time I got physical with a guy, they got all weird? Why was it that the simple act of messing around with me automatically led to this, every time, this moment where the guy needed to figure it out, or get away? I would never do that to someone. Never in a million years. I stormed out of the library and sprinted across the quad, the freezing wind biting at my forehead.

I didn't stop running all the way up the stairs to the fourth floor. I hurried down the hall, hoping I'd have the room to myself so that I could scream, or whatever I'd have to do to stop feeling this way.

No such luck. There was Albie, in his usual position at the desk. It was like, *Are you ever NOT in the room?*

"Hey," he said, not looking up as I walked in and slammed the door.

I didn't answer. All I did was throw my book bag on my bed, drop my coat on the floor, storm over, and reach under his bed for a beer.

"You mind?" I said as I pulled one out.

"Help yourself."

I popped the top and chugged. And chugged. And chugged. I just wanted beer in my bloodstream. Something, anything, to knock this pain out of me. I finished the beer, burped, and reached down and felt for another, which I grabbed and took to my bed. I collapsed on my stomach.

"I said, 'Help yourself,' not 'Get insanely drunk,'" Albie said.

I wanted to say *fuck you* so bad. But I didn't want to have a fight with Albie.

"Sorry," I said.

"Apologize to your liver."

I looked up at him. He had turned his chair away from his desk and was facing me. I wasn't much up for conversation.

"I thought you slept here last night?" he said.

"I started here," I said, rubbing my head and then taking another sip of beer. It tasted awful, like warm, carbonated piss.

"Ah," he said, as if that made sense, as if people often split their nights between two beds. I looked over at Albie, unassuming, nerdy Albie. Who was funny. Who was my friend. Who didn't judge. And I felt the overwhelming urge to tell him what was going on.

He went to the refrigerator and took out a Coke. "Scanner pong?" he said.

I nodded. I didn't care whether the scanner was on or not, and

Albie knew enough to turn the scanner on but not ask me what my word was.

"I'm in love," I said.

He nodded.

"Like, seriously in love. And it hurts."

"Claire Olivia," he said.

"No."

"Someone else?"

I nodded. I tried to think about how to explain this all to Albie.

"So Ben is or isn't in love back?" he asked.

I looked out the window. Snow was beginning to fall in big clumps, the kind of snow that was too wet to do anything but evaporate when it hit the ground. Thirty-three-degrees snow.

"Hard to tell," I said. "You knew?"

"You took him home with you for break. You sleep in the same room. Who gives a shit?"

"Does Toby know?"

He shrugged. "It's not something we really talk about. Gee, what is it about me that attracts all the gays? I'm like Lady Gaga or something."

"That's it. That's exactly who you're like. We're drawn to your persona and your frequent outfit changes. Albie Gaga."

He nodded. "How about, for your word, we use *gay*?"

I scrunched up my face like, what? And then I realized he meant scanner pong, and that made me laugh.

"And yours is *apocalypse*," I said, and we drank to that.

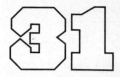

Ben's "figuring it out" period lasted the full week, during which time I got comfortable back in my own room, generally avoided the object of my *eros/agape*, and spent most of my time with Albie and Toby. Albie, to his credit, didn't tell Toby anything, and I decided that it might be a good idea not to tell him at all. You never knew with Toby when he'd say something unexpected, and I didn't want my secret to be that something. I had enough problems.

Albie, Toby, and I were walking across the quad to lunch on Saturday afternoon when we saw Steve and Zack walking the other way. I felt that familiar rumble in my belly, wondering if they were going to say something, and wondering what I'd say back. Ever since that day I'd had breakfast with them, I'd been pretty much cut out of that world of popular jocks. I didn't care, really. I was happier talking to people who actually had brains. And Toby.

So Steve and Zack approached, and I held Steve's eye contact. We stared at each other as we passed, and then he looked away, like he was dismissing me, like he was too good to be wasting his time on me. I was like, *Good*. If that's how he felt, I was fine with it, so long as he left me and my friends alone.

After lunch, Toby told us he had something to show us. He led us halfway across the quad, and then we turned left. There was a small path between two pine trees, and he led us onto it, knocking away branches and holding them so they wouldn't snap in our faces.

Finally we reached a clearing, maybe fifteen feet of damp grass and dirt, and clumps of icy snow not yet melted after a snowstorm earlier that week, surrounded by woods. Behind us, I could see a glimpse of frozen Dug Pond.

"This is where we come," he said.

Albie and I looked at each other. "We?"

"Me and, you know."

Albie's eyes got wide. "I really don't think I want to know about this," he said.

I surprised myself. "I do," I said. I guess I was tired of having to withhold the truth from Toby. Other than Ben, he and Albie were easily my best friends at Natick.

Toby looked a little surprised, like he'd just assumed we wouldn't want to hear the details.

"You do?"

"Yeah."

He looked around to make sure we were alone. We definitely were. No one else came back here to my knowledge. Also it was cold. Like twenty degrees. Only three idiots would be in the woods in the winter, it seemed to me.

"Robinson," he said.

"Gorilla Butt," I said, nodding. "I know."

"You know?"

"Yup."

Toby crossed his arms and then deflated into a fake pout. "You're stealing my scene, bitch. Scene stealer."

"Sorry," I said. "So you and Gorilla Butt. Wow."

He flipped me off. "He hates that," Toby said. "But, yeah. It's hairy."

"Oh, look, almost anything else in the universe," Albie said, heading back to campus and leaving us in the clearing.

"He's such a prude," Toby said, rolling his eyes. "I kind of figured you would be too."

I shivered. My gloved hands were cold even though I'd stuck them in my jacket pockets, and the tip of my nose felt icy. But inside I felt a warmth that felt good. I realized it was because of Toby. Letting me in on a secret. That felt good. And it occurred to me that there was more of that warm feeling if I wanted it. It was really up to me.

"Not so much," I said. I took a deep breath. "I'm gay, Toby."

He pushed me, and my feet slipped against the wet leaves. I barely avoided falling on my butt. "Leave the room."

"I'd love to, if by *room* you mean the woods. It's freezing."

He crossed his skinny arms in front of him. "But you said you weren't."

I sighed. "I said a lot of things. I guess I lied. Sorry."

He pursed his lips at me. "Bad boy."

"Tell me about it. I have all sorts of shit to tell you. Up for trading war stories?"

He laughed. "Hells yeah."

He plopped right down on his butt, as if the ground weren't freezing and wet. I started to say something snarky, but then I realized if I didn't also sit, I'd be standing and looking down at him. He didn't seem to think getting a frozen ass was such a major big deal, so I sat down too.

Cold. Like icicles climbing up my spine cold.

"Me and Ben," I said, my teeth nearly chattering.

His eyes lit up. "Are you cercal?"

"Totally. Totally cereal."

"That's great!" he said.

I grimaced. "Well, not so great, actually."

"He hits you?"

I did a double take. With Toby, it was hard to tell when he was serious.

"No. He's scared."

"Ah. The scared thing."

"Yeah."

"Well, I've been there. You just have to, like, wait it out. And sometimes they're fine, and sometimes they run off and you never see them again."

My stomach turned. The idea that I'd never see Ben again hurt like a stabbing. Like a stabbing and then a twisting of the knife. I touched my belly through my down jacket.

"Well, it's even worse than that," I said.

He waited for me to tell him, and I tried to think of all the reasons not to tell my whole story, and other than the fact I didn't come off well in it, I couldn't really think of any. It was better to let it all go.

So I told him. Toby listened with his mouth open.

"That's . . . wow," he said. "You need to tell him."

"I guess," I said. "I just don't want anything more to come between us. I mean, he's already freaked out. I can't drop this on him. Can I?"

He didn't have an answer for that.

We talked more, and Toby told me all about Robinson, who was deep in the closet and scared to death that people would find out. Robinson kept saying he couldn't wait for college — maybe the University of Michigan? — where he could start over and be himself, and avoid assholes who wouldn't respect him.

I pictured Robinson. He was about as nonstereotypical a gay person as you could get. His face was strong but covered in that acne. His body strong but covered in fur. There had always been a part of me that thought guys like that were the luckiest because they could pass as straight. But now I realized just the opposite was true; being able to pass for something you're not is a kind of curse. Especially if you try it.

"My butt may never thaw," I said, attempting to stand. I needed to use my arms, because my legs felt brittle, frozen through. But I also felt thankful that I was friends with Toby, who was a truly cool person, other than the parts of him that were entirely uncool. Which actually made him cooler, in my book.

"Another gay friend. Yay!" Toby said, singsongy. "Are you going to tell people?"

I cringed at the thought. Another coming out? Why was it all so hard?

"Eventually," I said. "Yeah."

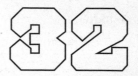

I chose Sunday morning to talk to Ben. Maybe it was a church thing, like my way of doing the right thing when most folks were out doing their version of the right thing.

I knocked on his door and he answered it in a black T-shirt and his blue sweatpants. He looked at me and a smile crossed his face, and a strong feeling of relief surged through my temples. I wanted to say, *I love you, I'm in love with you, let's stay in love no matter what after this conversation.* But that isn't how it works, maybe. I guessed I was about to find out.

He let me in and closed the door, and I sat down on Bryce's/my old bed. It felt cold, unslept in. Not much mine anymore. He sat down on his bed, and tapped the space next to him.

"C'mon," he said. "We need to talk. Come over here."

My heartbeat accelerated as I crossed the room and sat down next to him, picking up his usual garlicky, sweaty scent. We were inches from each other. I glanced up at his eyes and was surprised to find them looking soft, kind. Red.

"I miss you so bad," he said, and the first tear fell. "This week hasn't been right. It's been all wrong. I just . . . I miss you so bad, but this is hard."

"I know," I said, putting my hand on his leg and rubbing.

He settled into the touch, breathed into it, relaxed.

"You see, I do love you, Rafe. But. And I know you love me. I know that. But. I just can't bear the thought of you being mad at me, and this is fucking tearing me apart."

The tears were streaming pretty good now, and I let myself cry too. Here we were, two jocks, crying together.

"Please don't hate me. It's just, I know I love you. But the thing is, I lied to you."

I couldn't swallow.

"I lied to you when I said I was perfectly okay with being gay or straight. I'm not. I mean, for other people, I am. But for me, I'm not. I have to be straight."

My stomach dropped. "I understand," I said.

"Here's the thing, Rafe. I've been thinking a lot about this, so please just hear me out before you say anything or walk away.

"I love you. I really do. You're the best friend I've ever had, you're the person I'm closest to in the whole world."

And the tears again, but he didn't wipe them away and he didn't stop talking.

"The thing is, I'm pretty sure you're gay. I just know it. You never talk about Claire Olivia unless I bring her up. I think you're gonna figure out over time that you're gay, and I'm totally okay with that. But the thing is, this, us, is something that's just not gonna happen, because it can't."

I didn't say anything. I didn't know what to say.

"So even if you tell me you aren't gay, I think you probably are. And I'm pretty sure I'm not. Because I can't be. My family just isn't like yours, and . . . I'm not ready to give them up. They're all I have, Rafe. Other than you. So we need to not do that. Okay? Can you still love me as your friend even if we don't go there?"

As noisy as my head was, it took me a few moments until I was actually able to speak.

"Well, you're right, Ben. I am gay."

"Yeah, I know," he said, breathing a sigh of relief. "And it's so good that you know too."

I wanted to stand up. I wanted to stand and pace. I wanted to pull my hand off Ben's leg and pace around the room. But I felt glued down.

"Well, there's more. There's more that I have to say. But promise me if I tell you what I have to tell you, you'll let me tell the whole thing, and not let this come between us? Not just walk out or walk away?"

Ben's expression was pained then, and I felt like my head could explode because of the pressure in there.

"I promise, Rafe. Just tell me. You're scaring me."

The entire explanation took a little over ten minutes. I told him the truth about what my life had been like in Boulder, and how I wanted things to be different at Natick. I told him that I didn't mean to fall in love, and that by the time I had it was too late to say anything without risking the friendship. Ben sat quietly for a moment, not looking at me exactly, not really looking anywhere. His eyes, his liquid, beautiful blue eyes, were painfully unfocused, and I just wanted to go envelop him, and tell him again and again how sorry I was for not telling him everything, and especially for not telling him sooner.

When I finished talking, the room was dead quiet. Ben and me, sitting together. My hand still on his leg, but now awkward, wrong. I took it off.

And then Ben stood up, walked across the room, grabbed his shoes and coat, and walked out the door.

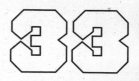

I found him in the library. Sundays aren't a big library day at Natick, at least not in the morning, and he was alone in the carrels, reading. He looked up and saw me, and turned away.

"Can't you just leave me alone?" he said.

"No," I said. "I can't. We need to talk this out. This isn't the end, Ben. I mean, it doesn't have to be. If you can just let me explain . . ."

"Really, no," Ben said, raising his voice a bit, even though we were in public. "This isn't a friendship anymore. Do you have any idea what you put me through? I can't believe I thought I fucking loved you."

"I did love you. I do," I said.

"Yeah, well, *I* didn't have all the facts," Ben said, lowering his voice again. "I thought we were going through the same thing."

"What does that mean?"

"Like experimenting," Ben said. "Two guys figuring stuff out together."

"But that's exactly what it was. What we are."

He shook his head. "Apparently you were way ahead of me. You just didn't tell me."

"So you wouldn't have loved me if you knew I was gay?" I asked him.

He said, "I guess we'll never know."

I sat on the floor at the foot of his carrel and said, "You know, I get that I screwed up. And I'm so sorry. But what I don't get is why me not telling you everything about my inner thoughts is worse than you not telling me about yours."

He closed his eyes and shook his head. "Whatever," he said.

That pissed me off. "Because it's not like you shared everything with me. Fuck *agape*. That was *sex*, Ben. And I'm a guy. And don't even tell me that you never thought about that before, because obviously you did." I was surprising myself with how bold I was being.

"It's totally different," he said. "It's normal not to share every inner thought with someone. It's not normal to actually BE openly gay and not share that little fact."

Now I shook my head. "This is about the label, isn't it? If it's two straight guys playing around, experimenting, that's cool. But if one of the guys is gay, it's not okay. Perfect."

Ben took a deep breath. "You can make this about whatever you want to make this about. But the fact is, you made up an entire person who was my best friend. Who I had *sex* with," he said, lowering his voice again. "How do you expect me to feel?"

"Everything else was really me," I said. "Just the one thing that wasn't."

He cringed. "What does that even mean? How can you turn off such an important part of yourself and expect everything else to stay the same? You lied to me, Rafe. That's who you are. Not gay, not straight. Someone who lied to me and who I can't trust."

"You don't get it. I didn't want to lie. It was just, this barrier. There was this barrier between me and so many guys. I couldn't take it anymore. You have to understand. I was so tired of feeling different. I just wanted to feel like one of the guys for once."

He bit his lip so hard I worried it was going to bleed. "So it's okay you lied because you wanted to feel like, what? One of the guys? What does that even mean? You lied, Rafe. That's the only thing that matters here. Not why. Just that you lied."

"I'm sorry," I said, hiding my face with my hands. "Really I am. Just try to understand. I need you to understand because if you don't, I won't have anything or anyone."

Ben stood up. He said, "The barrier isn't straight versus gay; it's real versus bullshit. I thought you were real and honest and now I think that was nothing but a load of crap. I'll never forgive you for that."

"It just snowballed. It's kind of hard to tell somebody something when you don't tell them up front," I said.

"That's why you shouldn't do that," Ben said. "So that a few months later, your once closest friend doesn't feel like killing you."

I could not have imagined he could get that angry over a simple omission. "What about Robinson? I'm not the only guy who's ever not told people about being gay."

"No," Ben said, gathering his books. "But you're the only one who ever did it to me."

290

That one stung. I didn't know what to say. Ben shook his head, and once again he walked away. Ben leaving a room. That was something I was getting used to. But before he walked off, he said one last thing.

"I should have gone with what I thought of you that first day. I knew what you were." His eyes were cold, dead to me.

"Gay?" I asked.

"No," he said, exasperated. "Fundamentally dishonest."

"You were quiet all period," Mr. Scarborough said, when I visited him in his office after class on Monday. "Not a fan of A. M. Homes's?"

"She's fine. Mostly just not a fan of Rafe's today." I flopped down in the chair across the desk from him.

"Uh-oh," he said. "What happened?"

I put my head in my hands. "My lives have officially collided," I said. "Huge crash. Major casualties."

"Ah," he said. "So what now?"

I hadn't told him about Ben. When I stopped by, we mostly talked about books and writing. "I have absolutely no idea," I said.

"Write about it."

"But what about *A History of Rafe*?"

"What about it? Seems like your history caught up to your present. Write about the present. Write about how your attempt to divorce yourself from your past is working today. From what I can see, I'd say it's not going so well."

"It's not. My best friend . . ."

He waved his hands. "Don't tell me about it. Write it down. I'm pretty sure at this point you're well past the part where you start with nothing. Just go from where you are. Okay?"

"Okay."

The Current State of Rafe

I am fully aware that I'm not an orphan in Somalia,
or an impoverished ten-year-old working in a Chinese
factory, or growing up in the slums of New Orleans.
I mean it. I really get that I'm far from one of the
world's unfortunates. But that only makes this
harder to say, in some ways.

I feel like I'm cursed.

I dropped my pen and groaned. "This is bullshit," I said. "I'm doing it again."

I looked around the empty room. It was Tuesday morning and Albie was at class. I was skipping math, because this felt more important.

"And now I'm talking to myself. Great. This is an excellent sign."

Why did it always feel like I was on stage in my writing? Who said shit like "I am fully aware that I'm not an orphan in Somalia?" It was just more bullshit, wasn't it? That's what Mr. Scarborough had been saying all this time, but that's how I was used to writing.

"Okay, Rafe," I said to myself. "Try again. Stop writing shit."

I don't think being gay is a curse. Definitely not. But we all know that being open about it comes with a lot of things that make life harder. Even if you have great parents and a school where you're treated well, it adds stuff to your life. The worst to me is how everybody looks at you differently. I got so tired of being looked at.

Cut to my life in Boulder. I'd take the trash out, down the alley on the side of our house, and there I'd see my neighbor Mr. Meyers. I'd wave and smile, and he'd wave back, but the smile was so forced. Every time. It was like I could read his mind. I could see him looking at me and thinking that I like boys, not girls. The same way I could see it in the guy tearing tickets at the Lady Gaga concert in Denver, or in the eyes of my soccer teammates. That damn camera, on me all the time. And just because I am gay.

I got up from the desk and went and got a soda from Albie's refrigerator. I'd owe him one. I sat back down at the desk and tried to concentrate. Why was I writing about Lady Gaga and cameras? What the hell did this have to do with what I was feeling?

But that's what a fastwrite is about, another part of me argued. I re-read the page. The line "I got so tired of being looked at," stared me in the face.

The words blended together. Looked at. Lookedat. Igotsotired. What did it all mean? I picked up my pen and took a deep breath. *Write until something happens,* I told myself. *Just go.*

So maybe being openly gay isn't a curse, but it's fucking exhausting. Always wondering what people are seeing, and feeling separated from so much of the world, that's hard. It would have been one thing if I could at least get a boyfriend, but that wasn't happening. Clay was the wrong guy, and he wasn't close to ready. After the time when things got physical, he texted me once and asked if I wanted to hang out. I wrote back and said: "Laughing Goat?"

"Your house?" he asked back.

I wrote, "Let's talk. Do something in public."

His reply: "I just wanna hang out."

I didn't respond to that. That's not what I was looking for.

I got tired of feeling isolated, okay? So I decided to tear down that barrier. I came to Natick, and I made a different choice. Not like gay is a choice, but being out definitely is one.

And you know what? That barrier did come down. I arrived here, and for the first time maybe ever, that barrier between me and so-called straight guys disappeared. I felt like I was truly seen. Ben. He saw me. He saw who I was inside, and he liked it, and I liked it. I liked who he saw. Me but not the label. I know you don't know what I'm talking about, but that's okay. I'm exploring something here.

I wanted that. I needed it.

I didn't tell him I was gay because I didn't want anything to come between us.

I picked up the paper and re-read what I'd just written.

"I didn't tell him I was gay because I didn't want anything to come between us," I said out loud.

I chewed on the edge of my pen and let those words and their meaning seep into my brain. And I was like, *Wow. Did I just write that? I didn't want who I am to come between us? How could I not have seen that?*

I ran my pen over my top teeth like a percussion stick across a xylophone. I didn't want anything to come between us, so I withheld a part of me? How hadn't I realized that doesn't make sense? How was I expecting to get closer to someone by not being truly me?

I felt drunk, wobbly. I looked at the Coke can to make sure I wasn't drinking beer without knowing it. How had I not seen that before?

I had to keep going. See what other crazy shit was occupying my brain.

Obviously that's a crazy idea, and I just realized that. Not brilliant to try to get closer to someone by hiding the truth from them.

I guess I decided the gay thing was an accessory, not an actual internal part of me. Like a sweater I could take off.

And I can't, can I? It's as simple as that. It's inside me. And I've never really stopped to think about how I feel about that. Maybe I skipped over that part of the process. Because my parents were so cool with me being gay, I guess in some ways I decided I was too.

How do I really feel about being gay? I always thought I was okay with it. Am I, though? I mean, I stopped being open about it, so maybe I wasn't okay? I need to get better, because it's not a part of me I can remove.

As soon as I tried to remove the label, a lie formed. In the end, that lie created a barrier way worse than the original one. How crazy is that? Ironic, I mean. I created a barrier getting rid of a barrier.

At the beginning of class, when you said the "You start from nothing and learn as you go" quote, I have to admit I wasn't listening to you. What I was really doing was plotting out how I could tell you what I already know in a way that would be pleasing to you, the reader. I see that now. Even as I wrote, I was playing to the camera in a way, wasn't I? I don't know if that makes sense, but it's new. That's why I'm writing here. Because it's new and it's unrehearsed. Here I am complaining about always being watched, but in reality I just spent a semester writing stuff to you that was really just me on stage. But this is really me, Mr. Scarborough, and I don't know what the hell I've learned but I know that I don't know everything. So I guess that's something, right?

I spent all morning writing. Once I finished, I lay down in my bed and called my mother to tell her what was going on. I knew she wouldn't say she told me so. That's just not the kind of mom she is.

"Oh, sweetie," she said. "Feel my arms around you from across the country."

"I could really use that," I said.

"What are you going to do?"

I closed my eyes and let the room spin. My brain was tired from all the writing and thinking. "I dunno. I don't want anything I say to hurt Ben. But I think I probably need to tell people the truth."

"How do you think that will go?"

"I don't care," I said. "I'm not ashamed of being gay."

"I never thought you were. You always seemed to be fine with it."

"I was. I am. And then I went and screwed it all up. My whole life."

She laughed. "You screwed a few months of your life up. Not all of it. You can make it better anytime you want to."

I knew she was right, but it pissed me off a little too. Because why do I always have to do the right thing? Around the globe, people do the wrong thing all the time and the world doesn't end. Then I go and avoid being totally honest for once in my life, and it blows up in my face.

"Why can't I just be bad?" I asked, figuring my mom would have no idea what I was talking about.

"Well, that's easy, sweetie. You can be anything you want, but when you go against who you are inside, it doesn't feel good."

I let that sink in a little. Yeah. Simple. Funny that I'd never thought of that before. There was no law against not being openly gay. It only hurt me inside. A lot. Because gay *was* inside me. And when outside didn't match inside . . .

"Earth to Rafe."

"I'm here," I said. "It's just . . . Thank you."

"You're welcome."

"And one other thing."

"What?"

"Thanks for the coming-out dinner at Hamburger Mary's."

My mother laughed. "That was years ago. Why are you saying that now?"

"Just because. I'm pretty sure I didn't say it back then. Thanks."

"You are very welcome. Dad and I love you exactly as you are, and we want you to be happy. That's all."

"I know. Thanks, Mom. So can you up my allowance?"

"No," she said, laughing.

"I thought it was worth a try."

I had lunch with Albie and Toby, which was reasonably fun, although Toby's game of Vacation, Move to, Bomb (someone yells out three

300

places, and you have to decide which place you'd like to vacation, where you'd move to, and where you'd bomb) wore thin after about three rounds. Then I went to my afternoon classes, feeling a little better. I didn't want to see Ben, but I also didn't want to flunk out of Natick.

As soon as class was done for the day, I called Claire Olivia, even though I knew it was two hours earlier in Colorado, so she'd still be in school. She answered anyway.

"So how's Boulder?" I asked, curling up under my blanket, still in my clothes.

"It misses you. Are you okay?"

"Not really," I said. "Guess what happened?"

She sighed, weary. "You repressed your sexuality in the name of boredom, and now you're sad?"

"I told Ben. Everything."

"Uh-oh."

"Huge blowup," I said, chewing my fingernail. "Very not good here."

"Sorry, Rafe. I really am. I know I gave you shit, but I am sorry. I know you really liked him."

"Loved him," I said. It was the first time I'd admitted that to her. I wondered if she knew how much losing him had hurt me.

"Loved him," she repeated. "What are you gonna do?"

"I have absolutely no idea," I said. "Am I a terrible person?"

"Yes."

"Come on."

"Well, don't ask questions when you know the answer already!"

"Okay. So why do I feel like a terrible person? Like you were mad at me for lying, and now Ben is furious at me. If I'm not a terrible person, why have my two closest friends both called me a liar?"

"Well, it's pretty simple, really," Claire Olivia said, and in the background I could hear the noises of Rangeview — lockers shutting, people shouting. "We called you a liar because you were lying. You're a great person who was lying. Obviously you felt like you had to lie, or else you wouldn't have, because, as I said, you're this incredibly great person. And great people don't just go and lie about things unless they really feel like they need to."

The line went silent, but my brain was filled with thoughts. What she'd said reminded me of one of the things my mom always said: "Guilt is about something you do. Shame is about who you are." Guilt, she'd explained, was useful because a person could learn from it and do the right thing next time. Shame, on the other hand, was useless, she'd always said. What is to be gained from thinking you're a bad person? I wasn't bad.

So I was guilty. Not shameful, but guilty. Guilty of what? Lying. I knew that. But like Claire Olivia had said, I had felt like I needed to lie.

I pictured Ben, and how hurt he'd looked when I'd told him everything. My heart lurched into my stomach. I realized this was simple, really. I had done something wrong, and it didn't matter why. And it didn't make me a terrible person, just a person who had lied to someone he loved and needed to make it right.

"You still there?"

"Yeah," I said. "Just . . . pondering. What you said."

"Good," she said. "But there's something else I want to say."

"Say anything. I'm listening."

"Good, because for a while there, these last few months, I wasn't sure if you were."

"I know. I'm sorry."

"Well, that's the thing I wanted to say. Because maybe I wasn't exactly the best friend I could have been, because I totally didn't pay attention when you were telling me about all this stuff last year. I didn't get it, and maybe if I did, you wouldn't have gone across the country to get away. So who's the terrible person now?"

"Not a terrible person. Just someone who maybe could have . . . I don't know," I said. "Anyway, you're a great friend. Always were. My best."

"I just wish I had let you talk about it for once, and not been such a bitch."

"Not a bitch. Never."

"Well, sometimes."

"Yeah, true. Sometimes. But thanks, I needed that," I said.

"Anytime, Shay Shay," she said.

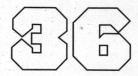

When the door swung open, six hopeful faces turned and looked to see who it could be. Toby smiled right away, and I smiled back. Mr. Scarborough also gave me a nod, which I returned.

"Boys, it appears we have a new member!" Mr. Scarborough said. "I'm sure you all know Rafe Goldberg."

The other four members of the GSA were people I didn't know very well. I mean, I'd seen them around. Natick School isn't so huge that there are too many kids whom I'd absolutely never seen. But they weren't in my circle. Whatever that was.

"Hey," I said, and everyone welcomed me in and Mr. Scarborough pointed to one of the empty chairs in the circle. There were twelve — *I guess you'd call that wishful thinking?* — and I took the empty one next to Toby, who reached out and squeezed my arm.

I felt super-self-conscious. These kids could become a big part of my future at Natick, and I wondered if they'd like me. My eyes darted around to the different members, knowing that they were all sizing me up. Was I a good addition, in their minds? I hoped so.

One of the kids I recognized as a sophomore from the cross-country team. He was blond, with big eyes and smooth, pale skin, and he always wore this black overcoat and a green-and-blue scarf. His name was Jeff and I had maybe said two words to him, but I'd definitely had him on my cute list when I arrived. I nodded at Jeff and he nodded back.

Toby leaned over and nudged me.

"You're drooling," he whispered. "Is Jeff the next Ben?"

I looked at him, horrified.

"Too soon?" he asked.

"Too soon," I said, knowing that Toby couldn't possibly know how much the loss of Ben was still twisting me up inside. I liked Toby a lot, but that wasn't something I was planning on sharing with him. I tried to put it out of my mind.

Everyone got settled and the sharing started. Basically, it was like a feather circle back home, only without the feather. (Feather circles may be only a Boulder thing, come to think of it.) This one kid named Ned talked about whether he could come out to his roommate. It was kind of interesting, emphasis on *kind of*, because he punctuated every sentence with the phrase *or so*, which made sense about 6 percent of the time.

"So I think I might tell him before the break or so. Maybe it'll be good to give him a chance to think it over while he's at home with his family or so."

I drifted off as he went on, looking around the circle. Across from me was this freshman I'd seen on campus several times, Carlton. It was hard to miss him. His features were so feminine — his mouth framed by pouty lips, his eyebrows arched up like he'd plucked them, which perhaps he had. He was wearing black skinny jeans and a formfitting black blazer that looked like it had been cut for a woman, and his hair was impeccably styled — perfectly tousled like Justin Bieber's.

Here was someone who could pass for a girl if he tried. I had never wanted to be a girl; that one time as a rocker chick had been plenty for me, thanks. I imagined me wearing his outfit and thought: *Oh my God, how would Steve and Zack react if I walked across campus like that?* And then I imagined what it would be like to spend so much time in front of a mirror to look that perfect, and did anyone at Natick really care or compliment him? What did he do it for? Could it ever work for me?

And those eyes, so hazel. Hazel, was that right? They were looking right at me, and that's when I realized Carlton was watching me watch him. I looked away. Then I glanced back, and even though he didn't look offended, I wanted to say to him, *Don't worry, I wasn't really judging you. I was thinking about myself.*

Oh.

Wow.

I was thinking about myself!

It was like the world opened up to me at that moment, and my thoughts tripped over one another. I was staring at this effeminate kid, and judging my own masculinity, or lack thereof. And was I so different from everyone else? Who was to say what Mr. Meyers in Boulder was thinking about when he looked at me? How come I was assuming his staring at me had anything to do with me? It was probably all about him. Same with everyone.

And as I thought these things, I realized that I wasn't listening either. Here Ned was talking, presumably about something that mattered a lot to him. He'd probably spent a lot of time choosing his words and thinking about how it would all sound. And here I was, thinking about myself yet again. Was everyone this way? And if so, did that mean that maybe I was off the hook a little? Maybe I could spend a little less time worrying about what people thought about me, since they probably *weren't* thinking about me at all. They were probably thinking about themselves instead.

"Rafe?" Mr. Scarborough said.

The room was quiet. Everyone was looking at me.

Oh, shit. My turn. I'd spaced out at the end of Ned's sharing completely.

"Just wanted a dramatic pause," I said, cursing myself. I really needed to learn how to listen. I looked at Mr. Scarborough and it was as if he could read my mind, because I could see that he knew I was thinking that. It was unnerving.

So I talked about coming out for the first time and being out, and then deciding I wanted the label to go away. I explained a bit about my time at Natick, leaving out the bromance, since it would be pretty obvious to anyone who had eyes who I was talking about if I mentioned those details. I focused mostly on why I'd come there and why I hadn't been out.

"I just wanted to be me for a bit. Without my sexuality being on display, you know?"

Blank stares from Ned and Carlton and the other kid I didn't know too well, Mickey.

"I get that," Jeff said. He had a deep voice that I liked. "Go under the radar a little. I'm like that sometimes too. Like, why do we have to march in parades and all that stuff?"

"But if we don't march in parades, people don't see us," Mickey said. He was wearing a paisley shirt and his hair was pulled back into a ponytail.

"What do you mean?" Jeff said. "People aren't going to stop seeing gays because they don't march in some stupid parade. Straight people don't march in a parade."

"Well, they don't have to," Mickey said. "What do you call it when a straight person comes out?"

"What?" Jeff asked.

"A conversation," Mickey said. "Straight people don't have to think, every time they talk, about whether they are coming out. We do. That might be hard, but that's also why we have to come out. If we don't, it's pretty much impossible to have a conversation about anything beyond the weather without lying. We really have no choice, do we?"

Jeff crossed and uncrossed his legs. "Except that's not true," he said. "Gay is just one thing I am. It doesn't define me."

"Maybe not," said Mickey. "But if you don't embrace that one part of you, forget it. Rafe just said it. How did that go for you, Rafe? Leaving part of yourself behind?"

I realized two things right then: One, I didn't like this Mickey guy. Two, he was totally onto something.

"You're right," I said. "When I put away the label, things were great for a bit because the burden of it all went away. But then it was like I went away too, and that part sucked."

Finally Carlton said, "I hate labels. I'm just me."

And this started a really cool conversation about what it meant to be yourself that Jeff got into, and then Toby disagreed and sided with Mickey and Carlton, and Ned wasn't sure where he stood on it. We laughed about the time Toby did march in the parade in Boston, with a youth group. Toby was wearing a camouflage T-shirt and torn jeans, and this superqueeny kid from the group came up to him as they walked together and said, "Oh, Toby. I'd like to take you home, undress you, and redress you." There was something so natural about the give and take of the conversation, and we were all involved, and it kept on like that.

And that's when I noticed it. For the first time in a long time, I had lost myself. The camera. Gone. I had forgotten that the other kids might be looking at me, and I had stopped trying to come across in a particular way. And I almost laughed, because it was so simple.

No one had really been looking at me all the time. Other than me.

That felt like a huge thing to realize, and I wanted to figure out how to spend the rest of my life turning that camera off, or pointing it outward so I could see other people as they were. Not, like, to judge, but just to see. Because here were a bunch of people I didn't know that well yet, and if I was lucky, I could get to know them.

And maybe they could even get to know me a little too.

For the rest of the meeting, I stopped worrying about how I looked to anyone else or what they were thinking. I was smiling and not worried if I had food stuck in my teeth. I was laughing and not wondering what it sounded like. Along with my times with Ben, and some of the time I spent with Albie and Toby, this was the happiest

I'd been since coming to Natick. I realized I wanted more of that. And the cool thing was, with these guys, all possible new friends, maybe I could have that.

As I walked out of the GSA meeting with my new buddies, Steve happened to be coming down the hallway toward us. He scanned the group of guys I was walking with, and he gave me an odd look. I realized I should probably just tell him now. He'd know sooner or later, and even if I no longer liked him and his posse, we were still going to be teammates. I told the GSA guys I'd meet up with them at dinner, and I ran after Steve.

"So you're probably wondering what that was all about," I said as I caught up to him in the stairwell.

He shrugged and didn't stop descending. "Not really."

"Well, so it's said: I'm gay. I wanted to let you know so you didn't hear it from someone else," I said, stopping walking as we came to the landing.

He stopped too, but I could tell he didn't want to. "Oh-kay . . ."

We looked at each other, and at least for me, it was like seeing him for the first time. He was just this guy. Well built and handsome, sure. But whatever power he once had over me, as if he was this icon of what a male person ought to be, was gone.

"So I just wanted you to know," I repeated.

He shrugged. "I don't give a shit who you have sex with. So long as it isn't me."

I had to laugh. *Problem solved, Steve. No need to worry.* As good-looking as he was, he was about last on my list. And I remembered his comments in the shower, so I knew there was at least a part of him that gave a shit.

"So if I had come out before the soccer season, would you have been as nice to me?"

"Sure," he said, crossing his arms in front of his chest.

"Oh-kay . . ." I said, imitating him.

"I mean, we would have had to figure out some other shower arrangement, because, you know."

I wanted to say: *No, I don't know. Not every gay guy wants to go to bed with you, you asshole.* But I didn't say that.

"Well, have a good holiday," I said instead, and he said, "You too," and kept walking, and I realized I wasn't going to miss the soccer posse all that much during the off-season. What had I ever seen in them in the first place?

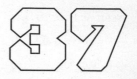

"Hey," I said, when Ben opened his door. It was the night before our first finals, and I had finally decided I couldn't put my apology off any longer. It was seriously getting in the way of my studying.

His face showed no emotion. His eyes were blank.

"Can I come in for a second? I know you don't want to talk to me, but I really need to say something to you. Please?"

He pursed his lips slightly, but otherwise his expression didn't change. He stepped aside and let me in.

I stood in the middle of his room, the room where I'd slept so many nights across from him, the room where he and I had been so close at one time.

"I'm here to apologize," I said. "I lied to you, and I'm sorry. I don't think I realized what I was doing to you all that time. I didn't mean to, if that matters. It probably doesn't. I just wanted you to know that I truly get it now."

"Fantastic timing," he said, no inflection in his voice.

I felt myself getting a little red in the face. "Come on," I said. "Is that all I'm going to get?"

He shook his head. "You still don't get it, do you? You walk in here like I'm sitting around twiddling my thumbs. I'm studying, Rafe. I don't know about you, but getting into a good college is pretty much my only goal, so coming here twelve hours before my history final pretty much sucks. Isn't the apology supposed to be for my sake?"

As much as I didn't want to, I realized he was right, and that it wasn't just a small way in which he was right. I had been out of tune with how important I was to him, and how much lying to him would injure him, and now I was so involved in my own things that I hadn't even thought about whether the night before finals might be a bad time for an apology.

I couldn't find any words, and I think Ben saw that, because his tone changed. He sat down on his bed. "I loved you, Rafe. And more than that, I liked you. You were my one true friend left. My uncle is dead. Bryce is gone. You were all I had, and then you broke my heart."

I sat down on the floor, facing him, and looked up at him. "Well, I broke my heart too, if that helps."

He laughed and shook his head. "How would that help?"

"Well, so at least it wasn't an aggressive act? I don't know. Help me out here. I'm trying to make things better."

He rubbed his eyes and ran his hand through his disheveled hair. It really looked as if he hadn't slept in a while.

"I think it'll just take a little time, Rafe. Okay?"

"Okay," I said. And I did understand. The hole in my heart, I can't even begin to describe. It's hard when you open your heart and let someone in and then suddenly they're not in it anymore. It doesn't matter whose fault it is; that empty spot stings so bad that you want to find any kind of relief, or wrap yourself up so tight you can't feel it anymore. I knew it might be there a little while. Or maybe even a long while. For both of us.

He stood up and looked out the window, facing away from me. I stood up too. It was definitely like a barrier was up, and I knew that, for a while, he wasn't going to be inviting anybody in. That's just the way Ben was. Hard to gain entrance, but real valuable once you did.

"Well, I'll leave you alone now," I said. "I'm sorry to barge in here the night before finals and all. Anyway, I hope they go well and I hope your holiday break is good. Merry early Christmas from the Jewish kid."

"Right back at ya," he said, not turning to look at me. "From a nonpracticing Christian guy."

"Yup," I said. There was a silence. "Please say something more interesting, so my final word of the semester to you isn't 'yup.'"

Now he turned. "Well, I can't say I'm glad I met you exactly. I mean, I was glad for your friendship this year. Other than being fucking crazy, there are some good things about you."

"Thanks, I guess. Well, I, for one, am glad I met you. Even with the pain. Which I'm sorry for, again."

He nodded.

"I wish we could be friends again," I said.

Ben looked at me and cocked his head. "Who knows? No promises."

I wasn't sure if he really meant it, or if he was just saying it. I smiled as best I could. "Well, maybe in the new year we'll take a walk or something. Catch up. Have a plastic screwdriver."

"I'm done with drinking," he said. "A little too much like a problem." He looked away.

"Cool," I said. "Probably not a bad idea for me either."

"Right," he said, but I got the feeling we were just delaying the inevitable, which was saying good-bye for now.

I leaned in a little, for one last time, and said, "You know, I really wasn't trying to fool you into bed with me. You have to believe me. I would never, ever do that. I fell in love with you. I wasn't out to hurt you."

Ben smiled. "You know what's crazy? I believe you, Rafe. I believe you didn't mean it. Doesn't mean it didn't hurt. But I believe you, if that makes you feel any better."

"I wish it did," I said.

As the first semester ended, I found that I was openly gay again, for the first time at Natick, and the second time in my life. I knew a little bit about what to expect this time, so it was a little easier. I let the rumor mill do a lot of the work for me in telling people. Hanging out with Carlton and Mickey and Toby (Jeff wouldn't be seen in public with us yet) certainly seemed to help. I also got involved with the literary magazine, which was cool. Lots of new possible friends, and not all based on my sexual preference.

On the last day before holiday break, I was walking back to the dorms after a nearly edible pizza lunch with Toby and Carlton. We were talking and laughing and generally having a good time when I noticed a kid who sometimes hung out with the jocks. He was walking toward us, and he was staring at me with a funny expression on his face, like he was about to laugh.

I immediately did what I used to do, which was to look away and pretend I didn't notice, and then I realized — the hell with that. I wasn't okay with people giving me nasty looks just because I was part of a group of openly gay kids walking across the quad. I didn't care if he was seeing us as a mirror for himself or whatever. I was over it.

As soon as we got close, I said, "Hey. What's your problem?"

The kid looked surprised. He pointed to himself. "Me?"

"Yeah, you. You never see three gay dudes walking together before?"

"I didn't . . ." he stammered.

"Is that so fucking hilarious that you can't keep it to yourself?" I snarled.

"Dude," he said. "You have tomato sauce all over your chin."

I reached down, and there it was, a wet saucy spot right on the center of my chin. I wiped it off, then wiped my hand on a tissue I had in my jacket pocket.

"Never mind," I mumbled. "My bad."

The kid passed by, and we walked on in silence for a moment.

"Wow, you told him," Toby said. "Maybe next time you can walk around with a booger in your nose and then call anyone who looks your way an anti-Semite!"

"Stop talking," I said. "Seriously. Just stop talking."

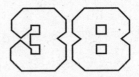

December 28 was one of those sixty-degree days that sometimes happen in Colorado winters, when you can walk around with the lightest of jackets and the sun shines so bright that you're sure it's April. I made a mental note to write the meteorologist jocks back at school about the weather. I knew they would find it fascinating.

Claire Olivia and I went for coffee at the Pearl Street Mall. I had so much making up to do with her before heading back to school that it wasn't even remotely funny. How many times could I piss her off, and she'd still be there for me? I was a lucky guy to have such a loyal, real friend.

We walked past the Boulder *Daily Camera* building, and I felt so glad to be back in my life that I did a little jumping jack. I was going to jump and spin, but at the last second I decided against the second part.

"Oh, my, you're a jumper now," Claire Olivia said. "This is an odd development."

"You ever feel like people are looking at you and you want them to stop?" I asked.

She thought about this, and she did a twirl. She was wearing a tie-dye skirt with some brown and orange and a streak of blue in it. It suited her, and the way the colors spun together as she twirled was beautiful.

"No, I wish *more* people would look at me," she said, and then she screamed: "Look at me!"

But passersby barely looked, because she was hardly the oddest sight on our little patch of the street. Claire Olivia hadn't noticed she was competing with a little person who was juggling knives, two bald twin sisters who were crooning a folk tune while strumming identical guitars, and four white guys with dreadlocks — we called them trustafarians in Boulder — smoking up on a bench.

"Whenever the rest of the world won't, I'll be happy to look at you," I said. "Anytime."

"Well, thank you, kind sir," she said, and she grabbed my hand and started skipping down the street. So I joined her. We saw the nuns on Segways at the same time.

"Hey! Segway nuns!" Claire Olivia called, and she went running toward the group of them. I followed. The nuns seemed perfectly okay with being called Segway nuns, and they smiled when they saw us. I guessed they remembered the time last summer when we took pictures with them.

"Did you have a nice Christmas?" one of them asked Claire Olivia.

"Hella cool," she said, and they nodded, like those words made sense to them. "Did you do anything fun?"

I laughed. What did nuns do for fun, anyway? Besides Segway riding?

"We had a delightful time at the soup kitchen," another nun said. "Have you volunteered there? Would you like to, sometime?"

Claire Olivia looked at me. Helping others was never really our mode, though I'd been thinking about it as part of this idea about getting outside of myself. My mom had told me about this place called Carriage House, a local organization that serves homeless people and especially gay teens, and I wanted to do something there. Having a mom who is president of PFLAG Boulder has its perks.

"Sure," Claire Olivia said now. "Sign us up. Rafe here will come with me, because he owes me, like, SO big time."

"Is this your boyfriend?" the first nun asked.

Claire Olivia looked me up and down. "No. This is my gay friend who decided he was straight and single-handedly wreaked havoc at an all-boys school in Massachusetts this fall. He's gay again and home for Christmas, so, yay!"

"That's nice," the second nun said, smiling, and I knew, for a fact, that we must be in Boulder.

We walked a little farther as the sun went down, watching first the little person juggle his not-so-little knives, and then a performance by a group of African drummers. The beat rippled through the crowd, and after a while Claire Olivia began to dance along. Soon, others joined in. Black, white, brown, homeless, wealthy-looking, young, old, stoned, totally sober — soon there was a whole throng of dancers, and I watched them jump and twist to the thumping beat.

I felt a certain desire to jump and twist too, like my father would, like Toby might. All those people who weren't constricted in their movements the way I was by my brain. And just as I was about to say the hell with it and join in the fun, I stopped. My hands half in the air over my head, half protecting my face as if someone were about to hurl a dodgeball at me, I stopped. I put my arms down and smiled to myself. I knew I could have danced if I wanted to, really. But I didn't, so I didn't have to. The world needs people who are more comfortable standing still. We keep the earth on its axis when everyone else is bouncing around.

So I quietly tapped my foot to the beat, like I did anytime I went to a concert at Red Rocks and wanted to move a little. And I watched my best friend as she got her groove on, and she loved it, and I loved her.

We were dancers and drummers and standers and jugglers, and there was nothing anyone needed to accept or tolerate. We celebrated.

ACKNOWLEDGMENTS

All the schools in this novel are fictitious institutions set in real towns. I have tried to remain as true as possible to the actual geography of Natick, Massachusetts, and Boulder, Colorado, two towns with which I am familiar from my own travels.

I'm extremely grateful to my family and friends, who stuck with me through everything. I'm also eternally grateful to Cheryl Klein and the wonderful folks at Arthur A. Levine Books, who believed in this book and helped me improve my own vision.

Special thanks to:

Chuck Cahoy, my life, perhaps the only person who would put up with me when I'm in creative mode; my mother, Shelley Doctors, for always being my best cheerleader; my father, Bob Konigsberg, for his love, support, and (occasionally painful) wit; my sister, Pam, for her love and kindness; my boss/brother, Dan, for being my friend, employer, and Boulder liaison; my excellent agent, Linda Epstein of the Jennifer De Chiara Literary Agency, who may actually be me; Debbie Schenk, my Montana savior; Melissa Druckman, for taking the time to talk to me about PFLAG Boulder; Rose Lupinacci at Fairview High School for helping me understand the Boulder high school scene; Kriste Peoples, for responding to Rafe's weird emails;

Lisa McMann, for telling me to stop talking and start writing; Jim Blasingame, for being Jim Blasingame; Chuck Wright, for his wisdom and friendship; Phyllis Hodge, for her wisdom and friendship; ditto Steve Feinberg; Jim Wink, for making me smile and also for coming up with the best ever fake marijuana dispensary name; Craig Neddle, for Mwah!; Bob Nogueira, for putting up with me at my most selfish and loving me anyway; my wonderfully talented writer friends Liz Weld and Beth Staples for their friendship, feedback, and impromptu therapy sessions; Greg Watson, for all his questions; Terry Buffington, for his intricate orders at restaurants throughout the Phoenix area; Mabel, for her constant ear licks; and never least, my fans, who have helped sustain me when it felt like this was all too hard. I love you and appreciate you always.

ABOUT THE AUTHOR

Bill Konigsberg's many identities include (*not* in order of importance): full-time writer, part-time candy-maker, former sports journalist, pretty decent softball player, injury-prone racquetballer, exasperated Labradoodle-wrangler, adequate karaoke performer, and occasionally cloying husband. He is the author of *Out of the Pocket*, which won the Lambda Literary Award for young adult fiction, and *The Porcupine of Truth*. Bill lives in Chandler, Arizona, with his husband, Chuck, and their dogs, Mabel and Buford. Please visit his website at www.billkonigsberg.com or follow him at @billkonigsberg.

START AT THE HOT GIRL.

TURN RIGHT AT THE MISSING GRANDPA.

PROCEED FOR 1,293 MILES.

YOU HAVE ARRIVED AT

"Bill Konigsberg's *The Porcupine of Truth* is at once heartwarming and heartbreaking, a funny and thought-provoking road trip with remarkable friends Carson and Aisha, who share tough lessons about mending fractures, forging bonds, and discovering grace. Undeniably human and unforgettably wise, this book is a gift for us all."
— **Andrew Smith**, author of *Grasshopper Jungle* and
100 Sideways Miles

Two Guys. Two Books. One Incredible Story.

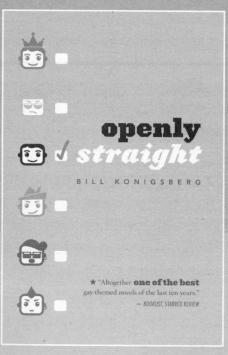

Tired of being known as "the gay guy," Rafe decides to be "openly straight" at his new school. But he doesn't count on falling in love . . .

Ben Carver always succeeds, and he's getting a scholarship to prove it. But after the thing with Rafe last semester, suddenly he's not sure what success really means. What will it take to be honestly Ben?

Winner of the Sid Fleischman Award for Humor

ARTHUR A. LEVINE BOOKS

thisisteen.com

BKONIG

Rafe and Ben's story continues in *Honestly Ben*— read on for a sneak peek!

When the announcement came over the loudspeaker that I needed to go to the headmaster's office, I thought: *Maybe they're putting me on academic probation?*

It was the first morning of classes after winter break, and as I hurried across the empty quad to the administration building, all bundled up in my brown hooded jacket, part of me realized how crazy that was—one C plus wasn't exactly probation-worthy. Another part of me couldn't stop my heart from pounding because I was sure I'd done something bad.

I'd never been to Headmaster Taylor's office. Swank. I sat in the waiting room, which was all wood paneling and high ceilings and sculptures. It even smelled manly, like the aftershave lotion my old roommate, Bryce, used to put on before parties.

The secretary told me the headmaster would see me, and I stood up and slowly walked toward his door, trying to get my heart to stop pounding in my ears. I opened the door.

"Benjamin Carver," Headmaster Taylor said, a little too buoyantly. "My man."

"Hello, sir," I said back.

It was rumored that Headmaster Zachary Taylor was a descendent of the twelfth president of the United States, which was why they had the same name. I had always meant to research that to find out if it was true. Taylor was the kind of guy who would shake your hand real strong, and flash you a perfect-toothed smile, and call you "my man," and tell you that his door was always open.

His door was generally never open.

"Sit down, sit down," he said. "How are Richard and Marlene?"

My parents. "Um, they're fine. They—"

"Right, right," he said, and my throat got tight. I realized this was going to be bad news. You don't greet a kid so kindly unless it's something bad. "So I called you here with some news."

I could barely move my neck to nod.

"Tell me, what do you know about Peter Pappas?"

My mouth dropped open and my arms went numb. Peter Pappas was a Natick student in the 1960s. He was an all-around great guy, a student athlete who had enlisted in the Vietnam War voluntarily after his junior year. He was killed in service, and now a major scholarship award was named after him. Each year, it was given to a junior who was also considered an all-around great guy. Last year, Kyle Guidry had won it, and he'd given a speech in front of the whole school.

"Um," I said. "I know quite a bit, actually." I could barely breathe. No way.

He laughed. "That doesn't surprise me in the least. Your teachers say you're studious to a fault, that you take an interest in just about everything."

"Thank you, sir," I said, but I was thinking: *But what about my bad math grade last semester?*

"Congratulations, Ben. You're this year's recipient of the award!"

"Me?" I said.

"Yes, you, good sir! Congratulations!"

I stared at his desk. It was like I was waiting to wake up from a dream or something. I'd never won an award before. And this one, this was a big deal. Huge. It came with a scholarship for college. Oh my God. A college scholarship!

I felt a wave of some foreign feeling sweep through my chest. "Thanks!" I said. "Thanks. Thank you."

Taylor gave me a tight-lipped smile and ran his hands through his graying hair. "You are very welcome, sir. We don't take this lightly around here. Your teachers and your coach all had glowing things to say about you, and it simply can't be denied, Ben. Everyone likes you. You're a gifted young man, and you have a very bright future. The foundation was quite pleased when they heard us talk about you."

You can't cry in moments like these, but it felt like a definite possibility. I felt dizzy and light and giddy, like my body didn't know how to react.

"Thanks," I said again. "Thanks."

"Now, it's provisional. The foundation has certain requirements that must be met throughout your time at Natick. For that reason, we will alert a runner-up. I don't anticipate a problem, but I want to make sure you're aware. You must abide by the code of conduct and remain among the top ten percent of the class in terms of GPA." He looked down at some papers in front of him. "Now, I saw that last semester, you took a dip in calculus."

"Yes, sir. But I'll do better this semester. I promise."

"Good. I think you'll want to stay above a three-point-seven to stay in the acceptable range."

I nodded and nodded, and in that moment, I promised myself I wouldn't take on anything new that could get in the way of focusing on my studies. Nothing could be more important than that.

"Also, the foundation was really impressed with your activities.

As long as you keep playing baseball and doing Model Congress, I think you'll be fine there."

"Yes, sir."

He smiled at me again. "The assembly will be the Friday before spring break. You'll give a speech, and then you'll receive the Pappas Foundation's four-year scholarship. Now, it's a partial scholarship, and I know you may well need more aid, but you wouldn't be the first Natick student to pair it with another scholarship or grant. You'll focus on that next year with your advisor."

"Thanks," I said again. "This is amazing."

"Your speech should pay homage to Pappas. You should also share a little bit about your life plans and goals. Kyle did such a nice job last year."

I nodded. I remembered the speech. It had been very good.

"Good man. We'd love it if you invited your family down from New Hampshire. And a large wooden plaque with your name and your picture will be placed in the hallway of the main building, next to all the other winners."

Me. A plaque with my name and face. I felt full. That's what I felt. Full and deeply grateful. I didn't want to get weird, so I just said, again, "Thanks. Thank you. Thanks."

He gave me a hearty handshake, and after I left the office, I nearly sprinted across the quad, feeling ticklish, like parts of my body I'd never felt before were all now very awake and alive.

The Pappas Award recipient. Me.

Back in my room, I called my parents.

"Mom," I said. "I won the Peter Pappas Award."

"Oh. What's that?" she asked.

"It's a scholarship. Well, it comes with one, for college. Partial, but still. It goes with an all-around student award they named after this guy who died. It's a . . . kind of a big deal."

"Oh! Well! Isn't that nice, Benny!"

"Yeah," I said, laughing. "Imagine that! I never won an award before."

"That's terrific, Benny. Let me tell your father."

My throat got tight. I knew she'd tell him, obviously, but I wasn't sure if I could take it right now, him telling me to not get a big head.

My mother said, "Richard! Ben won a big award!"

I braced for the letdown.

"You don't say?" I heard him say. "Let me talk to him." He took the phone. "What's this, Benny?"

"I, um, won this award. It's not, like, a huge deal, but . . . it'll pay for some of my college. I mean, there's a scholarship. It's called the Peter Pappas Award. Named after a guy who volunteered to fight in Vietnam and died there. He was a great all-around kid, very popular, good athlete, good student. Good guy. They'll put up a plaque with my name and face on it, I guess."

I heard a noise that I hadn't heard too much in my life: my dad chuckling. "Well, I'll be," he said. "Ben Carver, award winner. I am so damn proud of you, Benny!"

I couldn't help it. I gasped, and then I turned it into a cough, as if the gasp had been me clearing my lungs. I just couldn't remember my dad ever saying that before. But I sucked my feelings down and said, "Thanks. Thanks. I guess they want you to come for the ceremony. It's the Friday before spring break? If you can, I mean."

"Well, I'm sure we can get some help here on the farm and get on down there, sure," he said.

"Maybe you can stay over? Stay in a hotel?" I surprised myself. I never suggested anything that would cost my dad money, because I knew he'd tell me that he wasn't made of money. But for once I wasn't in control of my mouth.

"Well, then. Maybe," he said. "Maybe we'll do just that."

I got off the phone with this full feeling I wasn't used to in my chest. I imagined my dad, at the store, telling the Stevensons, maybe, or the Majkowskis. *Yeah, we're heading down to Massachu-setts tomorrow. Gonna close the store, even. My boy Benny's getting an award. I'm so proud of him!*

I shivered. *Careful*, I told myself. *You don't want to set yourself up for a fall. Be happy. Just not too happy.*

A pounding on my door woke me from a deep, upright sleep.

"What?" I groaned, rolling my neck to fix a kink in it. It was my first Monday night back at Natick, and after finishing up homework, I'd fallen asleep in the burgundy desk chair Bryce left me when he withdrew from school last semester. I wiped the sleep from my eyes and looked at my phone: 1:44 A.M. On the windowsill outside, several inches of snow had piled high, and I remembered I'd fallen asleep watching the snowstorm.

"Blizzard Bowl, baby!" the voice yelled, and I managed a sleepy smile. It was definitely Steve Nickelson's voice, and this was a great Natick tradition. Once a year, we celebrated the end of the season's first blizzard with a pickup football game at whatever hour the snow stopped. My freshman year, the blizzard ended during class, and we'd simply walked out, no explanation necessary. Headmaster Taylor even played with us. Last year it was a night game, and I liked that one better; there was something delicious about moonlit snowflakes, the way you could see actual grains of snow if you stood under one of the streetlamps lining the path.

"I'll be right down!" I yelled, and I could hear Steve stomp off and bang on the next door. I jumped up, suddenly wide-awake, and bundled myself up in layers. The other kids might have the newest in boot technology and snow pants, but somehow I was never the first one to whine about the cold. *Sometimes old and ratty gets the job done best,* I thought, looking at the olive-green work gloves I'd gotten as hand-me-downs from my dad in ninth grade.

Outside, the snow was knee-deep, and as I stepped into a

virgin pile, I felt the sweet chill curl into my calves. After last year's game, Bryce had lent me an extra blanket and we'd drunk hot chocolate in the dark. It still was a few hours before I thawed out. That was how I was built; it took a while for the cold to seep in there, but once it got to my bones, it would stay.

"Yo, Ben!" this kid named Standish called over. He had stringy blond hair, and the probability that he would move to Southern California and be a surf instructor in his twenties was 100 percent. "What up, Blood?"

I tromped through the snow toward the others. "Hey," I said. Each step was work, as I had to dig my already sopping boots out of the pack, then break through the crust of an untouched snow blanket.

"Congrats on the Pappas," Standish said, and I mumbled, "Thanks." Word had gotten out about the award sometime before lunch, and people had started to congratulate me. I wasn't used to the kudos, and truthfully I was looking forward to that part being over.

"Yeah, congrats, dude," this senior named Tommy Mendenhall said. Tommy was shortstop on the baseball team, and last year I'd played varsity third base. Other than some monosyllabic orders on the baseball field, he'd never uttered a word to me before.

"Thanks, thanks," I said, picking imaginary lint off my jacket.

"You ready for some serious baseball?" he asked. "Big year for us."

I smiled. "Absolutely. Can't wait."

I'd been looking forward to the first practice for a month, and now it was about twelve hours away. If you wanted to play baseball here, you couldn't play basketball, because practice began in

January, three months before actual games. The reason was the spring break tournament. Each year, Natick was one of the very few northern schools to participate in a weeklong tournament in Fort Lauderdale. The varsity players got to stay at a nice hotel, eat in cool restaurants, and even go to the beach while they were down there. It was one of the reasons our basketball team sucked rocks.

I'd been one of four sophomores to play varsity last year—Steve was one of the others. But when it had come time for the tournament, I couldn't go for financial reasons. It kind of stunk, because when the guys came back, they had all bonded and I felt like an outsider. This year, Coach Donnelly said he hoped to find some funds for me.

"Where'd you go over break?" asked Zack, our left fielder. He was short and looked nearly orange from tanning on whatever rich people's island his folks had taken him to for Christmas.

"Home," I said. "New Hampshire."

"Your family didn't do anything special?"

I stared at Zack. To me, being home with my family is special.

"All right. Good talk," Zack said, turning away from me. The guys were used to me not saying much, and I was used to them giving me a little shit about it.

Steve gave Zack a chest-bump, and the guys started talking about the Boston Bruins. I stretched out my still sleepy legs.

"Carver." Steve came up behind me and hit my back with his forearms.

"Yo," I said.

"We gonna kill it this year?"

"Yes. It's going to be dead," I said, and he laughed. A lot of the guys were dolts—Steve included—but they were my dolts.

Perhaps because it was two in the morning, only the true Blizzard Bowl fanatics had shown up. I was teamed with Steve, Zack, and Mendenhall. We got the ball first. Mendenhall called quarterback.

"Flag, twenty yards," Mendenhall barked my way, and I nodded. Flag meant go straight and then angle out toward the sideline and end zone.

Mendenhall called hike, and that's when we all remembered: The idea of Blizzard Bowl was always better than the game itself. I attempted to run through the knee-high drifts, but it was impossible. We started laughing as the sense memory kicked in. Zack tried to make it look like he was running by exaggeratedly swinging his down jacket–enclosed arms, but really he was walking too. And there was the slight issue of sight, since the brown leather ball could barely be seen except when under one of the streetlamps.

Mendenhall rifled the ball toward Steve, who had run-walked toward one of the lights and yelled, "Throw it here." The ball slipped straight through Steve's hands and landed fifteen feet behind him. It drilled the snow like a diagonal missile and disappeared, and a search and rescue mission commenced, with a guy from the other team finally coming up with the ball plus a face full of snow.

Both teams began to realize that the only way to complete passes was to throw short and toward the sideline where the lights were, and after a while the game degenerated into a game of catch and trash talk about local Natick townie girls.

"You gonna tap that ass?"

"Who? Allie? That trick? Fuck that bitch, yo."

Things tended to get a little hip-hop when all the guys got together, which made no sense, as we were all white and, other than me, exceedingly wealthy. I wondered if we could get a transcript of one of these conversations, and perchance have a social anthropologist sound off on it, or post it on the school website for prospective students, so they could all decide whether they could hang, yo.

That would have been helpful for me, for instance. Because while I can hang, yo, the reason is a little weird.

I'm big.

When you're a big guy, people just assume you fit in. They assume you run things, that you're in control, that you know what to do. I've noticed that if I don't say anything, people will continue to assume these things about me. Because I am athletic, because I have broad shoulders—farm work, by the way, not the gym—other guys salute me wherever I go. I get reverential nods.

I appreciate that it makes my life easier. But it also means that people don't really get me. They don't know what's up in my brain. I think, maybe, when you're a big guy, it's assumed your intellect is not as important as whether you can throw a ball.

We soon tired of digging for lost footballs and gave up on the game. I was walking with the others toward the dorm when some familiar laughter grabbed my attention. I could barely see, as the lights were now well behind us all, but I could hear it, about twenty feet to my right. It was the inimitable, melodic, high-pitched giggle of Toby Rylander, matched with the thundering chortle of Albie Harris. I stopped.

"You coming, Carver?" Mendenhall yelled.

"Go on without me," I said, bending down, pretending to tie my boots, which were well under the snowpack. They kept walking.

My sort-of friendship with Toby and Albie was part of the brain-dead Rafe haze I'd been in the previous semester. Toby and Albie were such a weird duo; it was as if they spoke an alien language. And while they could be amusing, they were also annoying. The first time I drove somewhere with them, I distinctly remember this one time, as we were pulling out of the school parking lot, when Toby, wearing a fake mustache, announced he was a crime reporter. In the end there were way more fun moments than weird ones. But that friendship was in the past, with the rest of the Rafe wreckage. It belonged there.

Yet I moved toward them as if on autopilot, and soon I could make their shapes out in the moonlight. I could barely see what they were doing, but it appeared they were clearing a circle, building a huge wall of snow all around them. Then I saw an indentation in the snow, on the opposite side of their snow wall, and I realized that of course there weren't just two of them. There were three.

My pulse went rogue on me. Wild, crazy, strange, nonsyncopated beats. I felt my heart soar, and then plunge, and then soar again. I hadn't been pulled toward Toby and Albie; subconsciously it was Rafe I'd wanted to see, and that was just crazy.

I slowed my pace but continued walking, and sure enough, there was Rafe, illuminated by the moonlight and the light of the snow, all bundled up, about six inches below the powder surface. He was making a snow angel.

He was wearing the same bright red jacket and black hat he'd worn when we'd gone skiing in Colorado over Thanksgiving. I flashed on Rafe skiing in front of me, his legs moving from side to side like a pendulum while his upper body stayed totally still.

On the long chairlift rides, his visible breath dissipated into the cold mountain air, while everything around us felt crisp and clear and right.

It had been one of the happiest days of my life.

But that was then. Now my insides were all messed up about it, and I knew if I let myself feel even a little bit of that it would be a lot, and I didn't have room for a lot anymore. It might break me in two, and I was a big guy, and big guys who play baseball don't break in two. I wished I could just disappear.

"Snow angels have no place in an igloo community," Toby said.

Rafe kept making his arm and leg motions. I could hear them scraping the snow. "Maybe igloos have no place in a snow angel community," Rafe yelled.

"Snow angel community. There are no communities of snow angels. There are flocks. Everyone knows that." This was Albie, who was currently carving a pile of heavy snow into bricks.

I shifted my frigid legs, and it made a sound, and I silently cursed my stupid, thick body. Toby looked over, and it took a moment for him to see me, but then he gave a tiny, tentative wave, the kind of wave you give someone you're not sure if you're friends with anymore. We hadn't spoken since Thanksgiving, when everything blew up.

"I think there could be communities of snow angels that have yet to be discovered," Rafe said, hoisting himself up from his angel shell with his arms. That's when he saw me standing there, maybe fifteen feet away.

Rafe smiled, a questioning smile, like, *Can we be okay, please?* No. Yes. No. I didn't know.

Part of me wanted him to burn for putting me through everything I'd felt since then. The sleepless nights; the need to talk to someone when there was absolutely no one, *no one* who would understand. And another part of me? No way no how did I want Rafe to think I hated him. I wasn't sure what I wanted, but my mouth naturally curves down into a frown, and I didn't want to frown at Rafe. So I flickered my mouth just a bit, and Rafe's face lit up into a tentative smile, but then I adjusted back into what I figured was a neutral expression, and his face unlit.

"Hey, Ben. Congrats on the award," Albie said, and I nodded. "We need builders," he added, looking at me, and I realized that Rafe must not have told them about what had happened between us. A part of me wanted to reach out and hug him for protecting me, but the bigger part of me, the thick part that sinks in water, stayed totally still.

"So cold," I said. "I'm gonna . . ."

"Sure," Rafe said, his voice soft, and I had to turn away because I couldn't stand anyone looking at me when I felt the way that voice made me feel. All mixed up inside and not in control and not like a Pappas Award winner, not in the least.